(cw)

KT-196-018

Tunbridge We...
Tel 01892 522352
Fax 01892 514657
tunbridgewellslibrary@kent.gov.uk

Paddock Wood Library
Tel 01892 832006
Fax 01892 832065
paddockwoodlibrary@kent.gov.uk

low

05. MAY 07
01. SEP 07
16. NOV 07
01. MAR AR
21. APR 08.

02. JUL 08.

- 3 JUL 2009

Books should be returned or renewed by the
last date stamped above

Young, Francis Brett
Cold Harbour

CHARTER MARK
CUSTOMER SERVICE EXCELLENCE

Libraries & Archives

Kent
County
Council

05 MAY 07

C152866333

COLD HARBOUR

COLD HARBOUR

by

Francis Brett Young

Dales Large Print Books
Long Preston, North Yorkshire,
BD23 4ND, England.

British Library Cataloguing in Publication Data.

Brett Young, Francis   CI 52866333
    Cold harbour.

    A catalogue record of this book is
    available from the British Library

    ISBN   1-84262-374-5 pbk

KENT
ARTS & LIBRARIES

Copyright © The University of Birmingham

Cover illustration by arrangement with House of Stratus

The moral right of the author has been asserted

Published in Large Print 2005 by arrangement with
House of Stratus

All Rights reserved. No part of this publication may be
reproduced, stored in a retrieval system, or transmitted in any
form or by any means, electronic, mechanical, photocopying,
recording or otherwise without the prior permission of the
Copyright owner.

Dales Large Print is an imprint of Library Magna Books Ltd.

Printed and bound in Great Britain by
T.J. (International) Ltd., Cornwall, PL28 8RW

This is a fictional work and all characters
are drawn from the author's imagination.
Any resemblances or similarities to
persons either living or dead
are entirely coincidental.

Contents

Prelude

On the evening of the Wakes' arrival we all stayed out smoking on the terrace after dinner. We sat there silent; for Ronald Wake and his wife, who was a stranger to me, had hardly recovered from the violence with which they had been whirled out of autumnal London into this blander air, and the fourth member of the party, Harley, the island's new chaplain, lay under the weight of diffidence which constrains a parson in the company of the obviously unorthodox and a stranger present at the meeting of old friends. I couldn't help liking Harley in spite of his awkwardness. A long-limbed, ruddy, simple-minded fellow, who'd roughed it through the Salonika Campaign and been invalided to this thankless charge with a malarial heart. I felt rather sorry for him, too. It wasn't his fault that his first visit had happened on this particular night. Even at the expense of the older and more familiar guest, I felt it my duty to put him at his ease, if only to persuade him that we literary people weren't quite as extravagant as the old ladies in the *pensione* had told him; and for this persuasion no evidence could have been stronger than the presence of Ronald and his wife.

Ronald particularly: as yet I could not guess what Evelyn was made of; but he, the best and oldest of my student friends, was as near the perfect type of medical devotion, humanity, and level-mindedness as one could imagine. There are very few doctors, even the worst of them, whose souls the practice of medicine has not in some degree ennobled; its very seriousness imposes a discipline and invites sacrifices which they are often at pains to conceal, being as shy of their virtues as most of us, and having more virtues than most to be shy of; and Ronald Wake, more than any man I know, carried his character on his face. It was good to see him again in the first relaxation of this Italian holiday for which he had been waiting ever since the end of the war. No one but a doctor or a doctor's wife can realize exactly what such a holiday meant. I knew it, for I had been a doctor myself; I knew how the early stages of such a freedom must be haunted by the tinkle of a phantasmal night-bell; I knew the luxury of waking in a room where such irritations don't exist, and it did me good to see the contentment that gradually settled over his face as he lay back in his chair, a fat Havana between his teeth, and, at his elbow, a glass of the Sindaco's wine in the garnet perfection of its fourth year.

We sat, as I have said, most quietly. When old friends meet after many years, there is surprisingly little need for speech. The moon came sailing over Solaro, revealing the mountain's huge and kindly curves, imprisoning the silhouette of a solitary stone pine, etched as with Indian ink; its light trembled down over the olives in ripples of tarnished silver, waking them as it passed, and gradually the outstretched arm of the land revealed itself like the paw of a sleeping lion laid upon the somnolent sea. No other light; no other sound. One of those mysterious moments of beauty and of silence in which familiar things and people become doubtful, questionable, and one asks oneself, suddenly, what it is all about. No doubt Mr Harley could have explained.

But I did not ask him. For the present I was happy to dwell on the memories that the vision of Wake, so familiar from the thinning hair on his temples to his supple surgical fingers, renewed. Once our lines had lain in the same groove; we had talked the same language, read the same books, moved to the same enthusiasms; but the war had separated us, and, more than the war, the peace. Now all my life was different from his. In our converse, even in our unspoken thoughts, there must be reservations, suppressions of individual experience that delicacy withheld.

And now, of course, he was married.

There, in the long chair beside him, lay the woman who had absorbed him, the shadowy Evelyn, who had bloomed and faded in his infrequent letters, suddenly made manifest in the flesh. How many times had marriage been the solvent of such friendships as ours? As I gazed at this slim, dark creature, lost in the woolly whiteness of her cloak, I wondered what she really was, and if her heart were as free from grudging as my own. That she was beautiful in a shy, dark, fragile way I must admit. That she was passionately devoted to Ronald I could guess; for in the darkness her hand had stolen to find his. But her eyes had only met mine once, and that for the merest moment, and it had seemed to me that they were frightened, not necessarily of me, but of some danger, present or barely past, of which Ronald's were wholly innocent. I wondered...

Harley cleared his throat. It was lucky, in a way, I reflected, that a fourth person should be present at this encounter. The reflection was ungenerous but justified by the situation's delicacy.

'The evenings,' he said, 'are growing decidedly more chilly. Last night the thermometer fell to sixty.'

'But that,' said Mrs Wake slowly, 'is an English summer temperature. When we left London it was freezing. I feel as if this moonlight actually warmed me. The air's so still here.'

'Yes,' Wake murmured deeply. 'And the whole place so intensely peaceful and kindly. There's something old and settled about it, in spite of your neighbour the volcano. Something clear-cut and stable that makes for healthiness. I should imagine that your islanders aren't overtroubled by their imaginations like us Northerners.' And he glanced tenderly at his wife. 'The silence too,' he went on. 'There's only one sound I can hear. Down in the olives there. Like a dove crooning, only hollower and louder. Perhaps the quietness of everything else magnifies the sound. Sometimes it stops for five minutes together.'

'Ah, that's the *gufo*,' I told him.

'The *gufo*?'

'A kind of owl that lives in the caves on Solaro and comes down to hunt at night.'

'*Strix Bubo*,' the parson put in dolefully. 'We used to hear the brutes in the Struma Valley. They're not such big birds as you'd imagine from their voices.'

'I think I prefer them to our owls,' said Mrs Wake dreamily. 'The brown owls at home are rather eerie with their little ghostly whimperings and soundless wings. Ronald and I–'

'It's a thousand miles away, my child,' said Wake quickly. 'Don't think of it.'

'All primitive people are frightened of

15

owls,' said Harley. 'The villagers here are scared to death of the *gufo*. Birds of ill omen. If they see one they think they'll die. But they never do. See one, I mean, of course,' he added with a little laugh.

'The devil is very much in evidence in this island, Padre,' I said. 'I expect you've realized that?'

'In that sense, yes,' he answered earnestly. 'And in another as well. I don't take these things lightly. In my own opinion, and in the opinion of many men more competent to judge, one of the great evils of modern thought is the decay of belief in the powers of evil.'

'Such a belief,' I agreed, 'is certainly a great asset to all mystical religions. But after all ... the powers of evil: I wonder if such a thing as positive evil exists?'

'To people who do not believe in positive good,' he answered quietly, 'that is not surprising. Naturally *I* do. And the existence of the one surely implies the other.'

'That's just what we said, isn't it?' Evelyn Wake whispered.

Ronald nodded assent as he touched her hand.

'For myself,' said Harley, 'I believe in the devil as I believe in God.'

He rose from his chair as though such a confession compelled him to depart.

'Don't go, Padre,' I begged him.

He hesitated. Evidently, he didn't really want to go.

'I merely felt,' he said, 'that a theological discussion might seem out of place. I don't think it's part of my job, you know, to talk shop whenever I make a call. And people here are rather touchy on serious subjects.'

'Not at all,' I said; 'you must have been unfortunate in your experience. I think we're all interested. Mrs Wake, at any rate, was intriguingly mysterious just now. It sounded as if you and Ronald had something very definite in your minds,' I rallied her.

Ronald laughed quietly. 'Well, perhaps we have, old fellow. The longer one lives the more mysterious life seems. Don't you find that yourself?'

'Hardly in that way. But I'm a very ordinary person. And so, I should have said, are you.'

'He is,' Evelyn assented eagerly. 'But this wasn't an ordinary experience.'

'Psychical experiences aren't, if that's what you mean.'

'I don't know whether you call it that,' she said. 'In any case, it was so real that we very nearly didn't come here.'

'I'm glad it wasn't any more real than that. Can't you tell us about it?'

For a moment they looked at one another in silence.

'It's a long story,' Wake said at last, 'and awkward to tell. There's a certain lack of coherence in it. Part is mine, and part is Evelyn's, and neither of us can tell the other's; which means that you'll have to piece the two narratives together. Then there's another difficulty. Up to the present we don't exactly know the end of it.'

'And the possibilities of the end frighten us.' Mrs Wake shivered.

'Suppose we go indoors?' I suggested.

'No, no,' she answered quickly. 'You'll think me silly, and yet I feel as if this sweet house might be ... how can one put it? ... contaminated by a story like this. Under the open sky it's different: safer, somehow. Don't you feel that, Ronald?'

'I know what you mean,' said Wake. 'Yes, I think you're right.'

'Then we'll stay here,' I said. 'I'll fetch out some rugs.'

'If I'm not intruding...' Harley began modestly.

'Of course you aren't. We'll all be delighted.'

'I should like him to stay,' said Mrs Wake, as we disappeared.

So we fetched out our rugs and wrapped them round us as we sat on in the moonlight, in the placid, pure loveliness of that amphitheatre of sea and mountain. We sat there, without a word, while Ronald Wake filled his pipe and the *gufo* hooted among the olives beneath us. A match-head spat and flared in the red cup of his fingers; the bowl of the lighted pipe glowed, the only real thing in out phantasmal group of four. Then, with the sound of Wake's voice, we returned to the plane of ordinary life.

Chapter One

The Fox

'It was only a fortnight ago,' he began. 'Looking backward I find that difficult to believe. We seem to have lived a lifetime since it happened; but, after all, we crammed a good deal of experience into that twenty-four hours. And then the journey through France and Italy: a change of that kind makes a big break when you aren't used to it.' He paused. 'You'll have to forgive me if I take some time to get going,' he went on, 'I don't want to miss anything. One of the first things we said to one another when it was over was: "There's a story for our novelist!" Possibly you won't agree. You novelists are very capricious about your material. It wouldn't be the first yarn of mine that you've politely turned down. But that can't be helped: we still feel the weight of it, both of us, and, in any case, I've got to get it off my chest. Confession is good for the soul, eh, Padre?'

Harley nodded half-heartedly. 'The question of auricular confession...' he began, and then subsided.

20

'A fortnight ago,' Wake continued. 'Of course, this trip had been settled by then, so Eve and I decided to snatch a short weekend in the Marches: Clun, Radnor Forest, the Stiperstones, and that sort of thing. The grayling were just coming on nicely in the Teme with the fall of the leaf, and I'd had no fishing all summer. So we bundled a few things together and set off in the old Darracq. A splendid time we had, the car running like an angel and the country showing up for all it was worth: a regular Indian summer: still skies, positively flagrant colour on the woods, and all the dear places looking their very best and most wistful. After two days of it, we felt years younger. I'll say no more of that; you can picture it for yourself much better than I can tell you.

'Very well. On the third day we left Pen–y-bont and knew that it was all over, not only our trip, but the celestial weather. All the way up the Long Mynd it threatened, and when we crossed the bridge at Shrewsbury and got on to Watling Street we knew we were in for it. These new tarmac roads have an extraordinary sullen look in stormy weather; they don't blend with the land-scape like the roads we used to walk on. Every main road in England nowadays is just like another, and motoring's ceased to be a pleasure with a fool on his wrong side round every corner. But that didn't matter

21

to us, as it happened. We knew what we were in for, and only wanted to make speed in front of the dirty weather that was coming up out of the west.

'We just went plugging on all out, and all the time the Welsh hills behind us grew clearer and blacker, just as if they were racing after us. At Wroxeter, by the wall of Uriconium, the wind gave us a great hit in the back, and the rain came so thick that we couldn't even see the Wrekin in front of us; so we resigned ourselves and made what speed we could. Wet macadam, ragged hedgerows, blurred, empty villages; the tyres hissing and skidding over potholes, and the engine full of strange noises as if it knew it was being overdriven and hated it. The Severn at Ironbridge was like a dirty ditch. We crossed it; we'd planned to put in the last night at Far Forest or Mamble, one of those villages near Clow's Top, but when we saw the rain dripping off black thatches the idea of a strange cottage somehow lost its appeal. The only thing that could put us right was a bath in a civilised hotel, so we went through Bewdley by the main road to North Bromwich, thinking of you in Italy, you lucky devil! By this time, of course, it was getting late.

'Then the poor old car struck. First a puncture. We tried to persuade ourselves it was only a Worcestershire road, but that regular *bump-bump* wouldn't be denied, so I had to crawl out and change a wheel that covered me with red Radnor mud. Eve was behaving like a saint. The change took me ten minutes, but we hadn't gone another mile before the engine started misfiring so badly that I had to grind up every rise on low gear, and even then couldn't be sure that she'd reach the top. So I crawled out into the road again and swore and stared at the steaming bonnet. First, I took out the plugs one by one. Of course, they were all right. Then I cleaned up the magneto distributor; nothing much wrong there either. Then I took down the petrol filters and cleared out a fair amount of the alluvium that they sell you in these road pumps, but not enough to account for all the trouble; and last of all I ran the mischief to earth in the float-chamber of the carburettor. Water, of course. That cost us half an hour, and it was growing dark earlier than usual with that black sky.

'Off we went again, the engine willing as a horse when you've taken a stone out of its frog; and we regretted all the names we'd called it. Three miles of good going, and then *bump-bump-bump* again. Another puncture, and only one spare wheel! By this time we were too far gone to curse; we felt more like crying. You see, we were still ten miles or more from that civilised bathroom, every jolt of the wheel was making waste rubber of a new cover and tube, and the rain was still coming down in bucketfuls.

'We huddled up in a blank of consternation as we climbed the brow of the hill on which the puncture had caught us. To the right lay a big expanse of parkland, whose name you probably know, and over beyond it two conical hills, each with smooth slopes and a fleece of firs on top. To the left we could see nothing for trees until we reached the summit and pulled up at a crossroad by a squat turnpike house. And as we stood there a curious thing happened: a kind of window opened in the rain, just as if the cloud had been hitched aside like a curtain, and in the space between we saw a landscape that took our breath away. The high ground along which the road ran fell away through a black woody belt, and beyond it, for more miles than you can imagine, lay the whole basin of the Black Country, clear, amazingly clear, with innumerable smokestacks rising out of it like the merchant shipping of the world laid up in an estuary at low tide, each chimney flying a great pennant of smoke that blew away eastward on the wind, and the whole scene bleared by the light of a sulphurous sunset. No one need ever tell me again that the Black Country isn't beautiful. In all Shropshire and Radnor we'd seen nothing to touch it for vastness and savagery. And then this apocalyptic light! It was like a landscape of the end of the world, and, curiously enough, though men had built the chimneys and fired the furnaces that bred the smoke, you felt that the magnificence of the scene owed nothing to them. Its beauty was singularly inhuman and its terror – for it was terrible, you know – elemental. It made me wonder why you people who were born and bred there ever write about anything else.

'For the moment it knocked us so much that we forgot our puncture. We sat staring at it without a word to say for ourselves. And then, suddenly, Eve nudged my arm and pointed to the signpost at the crossroads. To "Fox Inn and Cold Harbour", it said. It didn't tell us how far off the Fox Inn or Cold Harbour might be, but an inn was an inn, however cold its harbourage might be, and, frankly, we'd had enough of it. "Well, shall we give it a trial?" I said. And Eve, like the sportsman she is, said, "Yes." So far, we'd generally been pretty lucky in our choice of English inns, and any port in a storm.

'So we turned quietly out of the main road and down the lane, a reddish sandstone lane that seemed unusually human after so many miles of blue macadam. At first the surface felt reasonably decent, but after fifty yards or so of straight running, the road changed its mind and made a series of turns on itself as though it had taken fright, degenerating at the same time into a green drive, with turfy ruts on either side, and, overhead, a roof of hazels that made a tunnel of it.

'At first we thought we must have been mistaken and missed another branch at the first turn; the drive looked as if it must end in a farmyard. But, in any case, it was quite impossible to turn, for the brambles and hazels swept the wings of the car as we went lumbering down, and when we'd passed a muddy water-splash, the lane recovered its dignity, pulling us up a sharp, stony rise into the open, with a deep green fosse on either side of it.

'We hadn't been exploring Uriconium and Caerwent for nothing. If ever a road were Roman this one was. And a confirmation suddenly jumped to my mind. I remembered reading somewhere that all the Cold Harbours in England, and there are lots of them, are associated with Roman remains. Cold Harbour, the books say, is a corruption of *Colonia Arborum*. It sounds as far-fetched as many archeological etymologies; but there, in this case, were the raised road and the double ditch to prove it, and we were just debating how the road had ever got there when all of a sudden we ran up another rise and slap in the face of the Fox Inn itself.' Wake turned to me. 'I expect you know it?'

'Yes, I know it quite well,' I told him. 'I remember being driven there as a child to a meet of the Stourton Hounds, though I don't think I've ever seen it since.'

'Nothing very unusual about the Fox,' he went on; 'an ordinary country inn; two stories of red brick, half timbered, beneath a hipped roof of curled tiles. You'd have taken it for a farmhouse rather than an inn, because of the barns and sheds at the back of it, if it hadn't been for the sign over the door. Once, I suppose, the Fox had been there as large as life, but when his colour faded with sun and rain they'd decided it would be cheaper to replace his image by his superscription in black paint. Underneath this you could read the name of the licensee, Hannah Higgins; but the Higgins was many years older than the Hannah, and the letters of Hannah were so cramped that one could guess how some years since Mrs Higgins had lost her man and couldn't afford to have her signboard repainted, poor soul! From the desolation of the whole place, we couldn't expect more than a melancholy comfort; but in such cases, of course, you never know.

'And, as it happened, we were quite wrong. When we pulled up in front of the inn door and knocked, it was opened by a buxom woman of anything between thirty and forty with a sanguine, youthful face,

27

and remarkably fine grey eyes. She welcomed us with a smile, and when we asked for rooms and shelter for the car she ran out into the mud, in slippers whose heels were far too high for the job, and pushed open the gate of the farmyard for me to drive in. There were two wide doors at the end of the barn and a huge empty space inside, warm and smelling of old hay. She shooed a score of broody hens out of the darkness to make way for me. "They come in here to *rust*," she said. "I'd best clear them all out first, or they'll be making a mess of the car." She came back flushed, almost pretty, with a bundle of musty sacks to spread over the radiator, running on with her chatter all the time, as though it were a relief for her to open her mouth. Sometimes she'd give her hair an embarrassed poke. I suppose she wasn't sure that she was looking her best.

'I thanked her for the sacking. "You seem used to this sort of thing," I said. "I shouldn't have thought that you'd get many people here, right off the main road."

'She laughed. "No, that we don't," she said. "Not as many as I'd like myself. Mother's getting up in years, and it makes no odds to her. It's not the trade one misses, so much as the company. But then, we can't complain; they might easily have taken the license away, and we do have people, on and off, who take a fancy to stay the night. Some

28

come to look at the old Roman road, and they used to come to visit Mr Furnival at Cold Harbour."'

Wake paused and looked at me. 'Mr Furnival at Cold Harbour,' he repeated. 'Does that mean anything to you?'

'It means a deuce of a lot,' I said, 'if your Mr Furnival is mine. But I didn't know he lived at Cold Harbour; and in any case I'm not going to interrupt you. Let's get on with Miss Higgins, if that's what she was.'

'Very well, I'll continue. "The road ends at Cold Harbour," she said, "so consequently there's no through traffic as you might call it. Well, that's all right! So now, if you'll excuse me, I'll just pop in and tell mother and get your room ready. You'd like a fire in it, wouldn't you? And a drop of hot water? Reely, you must be perished, ma'am."

'So off she went. The rain had stopped, and that curious yellow light had gone, leaving nothing but a white mist hanging in the hedges. We tramped in, carrying our sodden overcoats, and heard, as we passed through the hall, the voice of Alma (that was her name, by the way) discussing us in rapid whispers with the old woman. She was far too deeply engrossed to hear us coming, so we pushed through the door on the left, into a long room with one low window looking out on to the green in front, and smiled at each other with the curious restraint that

29

comes over one in entering a strange house. By this time it was too dark to see what the room was like, but it smelt warm and inhabited; it held subdued lights of polished wood and glass and copper; and when Alma came in, a moment later, carrying a lighted lamp, we felt comfortable at once. These things are difficult to describe. I have to fall back on that lame word atmosphere and say that this was friendly.

'There was hot water in the bedroom, Alma told us. Beautifully clean, too, the whole place, with a ripe smell of autumn. I believe they'd been storing apples on the floor. We came downstairs in an odour of frying bacon. That, and eggs, had been our staple food for the last three days, so, having got into the habit, we'd ordered it again. As we entered the room it positively welcomed us, and we began to thank our stars that we hadn't finished up, as we had hoped, in one of the North Bromwich hotels. There was a bright fire burning, and as we settled down to eat Alma stood at the foot of the table, just outside our circle of light, as diffident as you can imagine, and yet unmistakably reluctant to leave us as long as there was any chance of gossip.

'You couldn't blame her. There she was, a fine girl in her way, wasting the best part of her life in a place where she had no chance of any society but that of a handful of farm labourers in the bar, or an odd visitor to Cold Harbour. The last evidently provided her with more entertainment. Whatever we talked about – and we just went on in the lazy discursive way that comes natural at the end of a day in open air – the conversation always seemed to swing back to that house, and particularly its owner, the Mr Furnival whose name had cropped up in the very first sentences of our acquaintance.

'The signpost that had brought us to the Fox: Mr Furnival had had it put up. The shocking road: Mr Furnival had defied the County Council to touch it; of course, it was all on his property. The car: Mr Furnival was fed up with cars. (So, for the moment, were we.) The admirable beer: only yesterday Mr Furnival had remarked that it was in prime condition, and, as mother said, if it satisfied *him* it must be all right. All through our gossip she kept us so firmly anchored to Mr Furnival that, whenever we drifted away from him, his influence pulled up the conversation with a tug.

'It became ludicrous, but since Alma was evidently anxious to talk, and to talk on no other subject, we gave her the chance she wanted with a direct question: "Who *is* this Mr Furnival?"

'And that, apparently, embarrassed her. Surely everybody knew Mr Furnival! He was the owner of Cold Harbour, the big house by the church. There was no village to speak of, just a number of small farms scattered round and the ruins of the vicarage which had been burnt ten years ago. Rich? Well, of course he must be a wealthy gentleman to live there. Old? She could hardly say. Certainly he was "getting on"; but then, he wasn't the sort of man whose age you ever thought about: she couldn't even guess how old he was, now she came to think of it. Old enough, at any rate, to have three grown-up children, or was it four?

"'I suppose he's a widower?" Eve asked quietly. The girl threw back her head and laughed. A widower? Mr Furnival? What an idea! But Mrs Furnival, it seemed, was an invalid, and always had been since she could remember. By all accounts – what the servants said – she was a very nice lady, quiet, you know, and considerate; never made a fuss about anything. "But to tell you the honest truth," she said, "I've never spoken to her nor even set eyes on her since I was a child except through the garden hedge. You see," she explained in a lowered voice, "she doesn't even go out to church. Funny, isn't it? Particularly with Mr Furnival being such a religious man. But I think something went wrong there. The fact is, she turned Roman Catholic. I'm sure that was a great grief to Mr Furnival, poor man! I don't think she likes the house either, from what he lets slip, and I must say I don't blame her. But, of course, *he's* mad on it."

'That, I suggested, was natural enough. I supposed it had been in his family for generations. She shook her head. From what her mother had told her, it seemed that Cold Harbour had been a dower house of the Pomfrets, the family that once owned Mawne Hall, where Mr Willis the ironmaster now lived. The Pomfrets, in a manner of speaking, had died out, and mother had told her that before Mr Furnival came there fifteen years ago and spent a fortune on it, Cold Harbour had been empty for years on end. They did say, of course, that the place was haunted; but folk always made up stories of that kind when a place was left empty for long, and Mr Furnival often made his joke about it. "Still, I shouldn't like to live there myself," she volunteered.

'"Why not?" I asked. Again she threw back her head and laughed. Her throat was magnificent. She couldn't say why not, there was something extra quiet about it; those crazy, bricked-up windows. And then it was built right over against the graveyard; you'd feel that something was always watching you, taking note of what you did. Of course, it was just silly to get fancies like that into your head. Mr Furnival laughed at her; he said that *he'd* never seen anything, and he'd lived there long enough; but once you did

33

get a fancy about a place it wasn't easy to shift it. And so many stories...

'What sort of stories? I tried to fix her, but she only laughed nervously. Only the story that the place was haunted: she supposed it was those old Romans or Normans or whatever they were. Mr Furnival was always explaining; but what was the use of improving one's mind if they were going to end their days in a place like the Fox? She let him talk; that's what she did. It was a pity if a man hadn't some one to talk to.

'The front door scraped open. We heard heavy steps on the flags of the passage and a drone of rustic speech. Alma turned to listen and we hastened to suggest that she need not stay with us.

'"Oh, that's all right," she answered a little scornfully, "it's only two of Moseley's men dropped in for their pint. Mother'll tend to them. It isn't as often as that that I get the chance of a chat when the winter sets in. We used to have the meets of the foxhounds here. Foxes are something cruel, too. There's one labouring man that had more than twenty fowl savaged last week, poor chap! But Mr Furnival's had some sort of ructions with the Master, and now they don't come here any more. It's a pity, isn't it? It was fine to see the red coats on a winter morning. Mr Furnival explained to me what it was, and I'm sure he was right too; but I just forget what happened. I always tell him he's a quarrelsome nature. He doesn't mind. He just turns it off with a laugh. When you come to understand him, you know, it's – it's–"

'She broke off suddenly; or rather the thread of the sentence that her mind had framed seemed to dwindle, then snap. We both of us looked up quickly. There she was, standing at the foot of the table, lost to the world. If you'll forgive me being medical, I should say it was like the state of suspension you find in a sufferer from *petit mal*, minor epilepsy, you know. Then, before she had really come to herself again, we saw a flush of colour sweeping over that fine white throat of hers into her cheeks, and her hands suddenly clenched. The door of the passage grated open again. Light steps echoed in the hall. A man breathed heavily and hung up a flapping mackintosh. "What is it? Are you ill?" Eve asked quickly. "No, no, it's nothing," she answered in a whisper. "Will you excuse me, please?" And she went off; so flustered that she forgot to close the door behind her.

'We stared at each other for a moment. "Poor thing," said Eve, "she's in love with the man." "Afraid of him," I whispered. "Why not both?" she said. "In any case, it's rather dreadful," we agreed. But why? Why? Why should we be sitting there whispering guiltily like children in a schoolroom, listening, glancing anxiously at the open door? The sensation of eavesdropping made me ashamed. I rose quietly to shut it. "Don't do that," Eve implored me. "It isn't that I want to listen," she explained. "I feel so sorry, so frightened for her."

'And so, for that matter, did I. Of course it was ridiculous. I doubt if either of us alone would have felt anything of the sort, but the curious atmosphere of our arrival in this unreal place – I can't define its unreality or explain it except by the light of that apocalyptic sunset – had made us jointly sensitive. It was just as if those two abrupt turnings, at the place where the Roman road lost itself, had switched us into another plane, dimension, whatever you like to call it, of existence, in which the support of ordinary earthly reason were denied. It wouldn't do, for a moment, to admit it, to give way to this emotional panic. It was our duty as rational human beings to fight against it. I determined to permit no nonsense with either of us, so I got up again and shut the door firmly in spite of Eve's protests.

'"There's no reason why we should behave like two children," I said. "There's no need to imagine anything extraordinary about the case. Here is this girl, Alma, a strong, handsome creature of uncertain age, old enough, at least, to have been happily married many years since, tied by the leg to an old woman in this remote house on a road that leads nowhere. Too much beauty and self-respect to yield to the persuasions of Mr Moseley's farm labourers: no chance of setting eyes on an eligible man except when some Roman-British enthusiast wanders along here to have a look at the road, or the remains, whatever they are, at Cold Harbour. Not a man in the neighbourhood except this Mr Furnival, a fellow who's quarrelled with everybody, including the local MFH. And Furnival, by all accounts, is equally lonely. His wife has been an invalid for years; his children are all grown up. He has no more outlet than the unfortunate Alma, and so, naturally enough, they find some outlet, of a sort, in each other. The poor chap's so bored that he takes the trouble to walk down here on a wet October night. He hangs up his mackintosh in the hall as if he belonged here, and spends the evening with Alma and the old lady. Perfectly properly, as far as we know. Why, he even tries to improve her education, talking to her about those old Romans or Normans or whatever they were. But what's the use of improving one's mind if they're going to end their days in a place like the Fox? The position's pathetic, if you like, but nothing else. And certainly it's no business of ours."

'I thought I'd summed up the case pretty

37

reasonably, but Eve wouldn't have it. As a matter of fact, I'm bound to give her credit for an extraordinarily acute instinct in the matter of human relationships: part of the female savage's protective armament, I suppose. "All that may be true enough," she said, "but I'm positive that we were both of us right in our first impressions. I said she was in love with him, and you said she was afraid of him: she's unhappy and she's frightened, and she thinks about nothing else. That's why she stayed talking to us, like a child that wants a hand to hold in the dark. All the time that she was here she couldn't utter a sentence without mentioning his name. She's haunted by him: that's the real truth. She knew that he was coming before anyone could hear his step, and as soon as he came in she lost possession of herself; simply gave up the ghost. You're a fine sort of doctor if you couldn't realize that! Why, I can see her standing there now, with the words drying up in her mouth and the will fading out of her. I've never seen anything so pitiable in my life. There must be something wrong with the man, there simply must. I don't think I've ever felt so sorry for anyone. It's our absolute duty to stand by her. That's why I wish you hadn't shut the door."

'She was so intense about it that I had to tease her. "How much pity and how much curiosity? Don't I know you?" I said.

'We seemed to be taking the thing so seriously that I felt forced to lighten it in some way. After all, I told her, we had no right to consider ourselves sent by heaven to censor the morality of Miss Alma Higgins; but the thing had so got on her nerves that she couldn't take my joke, which simply means that she was the more sensitive of the two, as she is, bless her! "It's not the body of Alma Higgins I'm worrying about," she said, "it's her soul." "Well, well, if it comes to that," I said, "I really do disclaim all responsibility." "We can't," she said, "we *can't!*" Looking at her now you couldn't possibly believe her capable of such intensity, her eyes blazing, and one cheek so flushed that I began to wonder if the drenching we'd got had landed her into an attack of pneumonia. "Look here, young woman," I said, "I'm going to take your temperature." It almost made the poor child cry. "Oh, don't be stupid, dearest," she said, "I'm as well as ever I was; it's only *that.*" All the same I couldn't be satisfied till I'd counted her pulse. No doctor should ever be allowed to treat his wife. It was as quiet and regular as my own. "Now I hope you're satisfied," she said.

'I was, in that particular direction, but not in the other. Evelyn isn't in the ordinary way a nervous or fanciful person, but something in the nature of this place, this encounter, this complex of circumstances, had so unsettled her that I was anxious to get her away from their influence. If you were married you'd appreciate the infinite shades of feeling by which a man knows when his wife isn't herself; and when a conviction of that kind comes suddenly, mysteriously, without any reasons of the kind to which he's susceptible, it's an alarming experience. It's my business, of course, to deal with states of health and disease; and this state, whatever else it might be, was certainly unhealthy. Terror, you know, like most spiritual diseases, is infectious. The obvious treatment, in this case, was to remove the patient from the infected area. We couldn't, as you'll agree, turn out again and leave the Fox without an explanation, but we could make sure of an early start next morning by getting to work at once on the wretched puncture that had landed us there.

'Naturally, I wanted to do this un-dramatically and without frightening her, so I got up casually and invited her to come and keep me company in the barn. "Put on your coat," I said, "and then you'll be quite cosy."

'She answered me without a second's hesitation. "I can't," she said. "I'm sorry, but I feel I want to stay." "I know you're tired," I told her, "but I'm sure it'll do you good. I don't want to leave you alone like this." "Like what?" she said, "haven't I told you there's nothing the matter with me? There's no reason why you shouldn't go alone if you want to." I tried to persuade her, but she was as stubborn as a horse in a burning stable, and I saw the moment coming when she'd become definitely upset; so, at last, I went out alone with no comfort except the faith I always have in the rightness of her instincts. Even so, I confess that I felt horribly uneasy. "Please don't shut the door," she whispered as I went out...'

Chapter Two

The Visitor

'…Leaving me alone,' the voice of Mrs Wake continued.

All the way through her husband's recital we had hardly been aware of her white presence. Even when he repeated her own words we had been thinking not of her, the living present woman, but of another figure of his creation sitting in the lamplight of the parlour at the Fox with clasped hands and one burning cheek. Her sudden entrance into the story came with the effect of an apparition, intensifying rather than breaking the effect with its ghostly confirmation; but, when the first shock of it had subsided, we felt that the tale had not suffered in continuity; the vision of the lamp-lit table and the woman sitting at it returned, and seemed, indeed, to become more actual as she continued in her low, level voice:

'It wasn't only,' she said, 'that I didn't want to go out with Ronald to the car: I actually wished him to go and leave me alone. I had a feeling stronger and more positive than anything reasonable, that something which mattered most awfully was going to happen or be said. I felt that I had to see it or hear it, and that he, poor dear, was somehow in the way. We have to be shockingly candid about each other in a story of this kind: it's so important to us, saving your presence, that we should stick to the absolute truth, so you won't be shocked, will you, if we seem a little inconsiderate for each other's feelings? It doesn't mean that we don't... But I'm sure you understand.

'Well, there I was, sitting at the table with the lamp in front of me looking into the darkness of the passage through the open door, waiting for something, whatever it was, to happen, quite happy and contented about it, too, and not in the least, as Ronald suggested, frightened. Not in the least. I suppose I sat there for five minutes, after which I began to feel that I'd made rather a fool of myself by being so intense and sending him out into that miserable barn alone. I'd almost decided to put on my fur coat and follow him and confess how silly I'd been, when somebody – I couldn't see who it was – hurried along the passage into the taproom and left the door of the little private bar behind it open so that I could hear quite clearly everything that was being said. Then curiosity – I suppose it was curiosity – got the better of me, and I sat still and listened. Ronald, with his exaggerated sense of honour, would probably have shut the door. So you see I was right: he *would* have been in the way.

'Two voices were talking together in the private bar. One, I made sure, was Alma's, and the other, I supposed, was Mr Furnival's. It was his that did most of the talking. In my own funny little way, Ronald would tell you, I'm rather good at voices. I mean that I can guess much better, for my own satisfaction, what a person is like by hearing his voice than by listening to what he says. Some people go by eyes, and some by mouths; but for me the voice is much more important. And this voice of Mr Furnival's was something of a puzzle. It was rather light, but low in pitch: what you'd call a musical voice. His speech was educated and refined, but somehow the voice itself wasn't. That's a queer paradox, and I'm afraid I can't explain it more definitely; but there was just one thing more: he had the trick of ending each sentence with a shrill cackle of a laugh. You'll say that it was unfair to judge a man's character by what may have been nothing but a nervous habit, but in this laugh there seemed to be something un-natural, strange, uncontrolled – there's only one word for it – mad. Whatever impression of culture or kindliness his words might give one, each time he came to the end of his sentence that laugh destroyed it. It seemed to explain the mixture of fascination and fear that poor Alma had shown us. And, of course, when once you got over that, it was awfully interesting.

'At first they seemed to be talking on the subject that was naturally uppermost in Alma's mind: ourselves. That was the point at which Ronald's scruples would have begun to trouble him; mine didn't trouble me a bit, and Alma, poor innocent, had nothing but good to say of us. At any rate, it was amusing to hear her description of my old clothes. Evidently she was impressed. She had the idea that we must be "very high-up people".

'Then, to my astonishment, they – or rather he – began to talk about books. It seemed that Mr Furnival was in the habit of lending books to Alma and even of reading poetry aloud to her. This must have been the "improvement" of which the poor girl had spoken to us so pathetically. It made me feel sorry for her, and sorry, in spite of his laugh, for Mr Furnival. It betrayed such a tremendous desolation in the life of this man, full of enthusiasm for good writing, to find him thrusting it into Alma's unresponsive mind; for if he were half as keen as he seemed to be, he must surely have realized that it was a waste of time.

'Still, there he was, quoting Chaucer to her. Quite incredibly, unless one explained it by imagining that he knew, as well as I did, that she couldn't tell the difference between Chaucer and Ella Wheeler Wilcox, and merely provided a hypnotised listener into whose ears he could let his enthusiasm flow with a sense of companionship: something more responsive than four blank walls. But then, hadn't Alma mentioned an invalid wife? And, in any case, the man must have hypnotised himself to be unaware of Alma's lack of receptivity, sensibility, understanding of any kind. Unless it were all a cruel and fantastic joke, as the inhuman cackle at the end of his quotations might have suggested?

'As for the reason, I soon gave it up; but that, of course, didn't make the phenomenon less fascinating; it made no difference, either, to the interest of this one-sided conversation. Apart from his cackle, Mr Furnival was a very good talker. All through the time that I listened to him, he never said a thing that wasn't individual, peculiar to himself; just as if he looked at everything from an angle out of the reach of you and me and other ordinary people. He went on in his easy, mocking way, saying the most brilliant things. I don't suppose Alma, poor darling, enjoyed them; not in the way that they were intended; but I did, every word. So much that I quite forgot poor Ronald grunting away in the barn with a spotlight and tyre levers.

'It never struck me then, as we've both realized since, that dear Mr Furnival was not talking for Alma at all, and that all this brilliant stuff that he was scattering over the pot-house floor was just – how shall I put it? – ground-bait for *me*. If that were so, he must have been even cleverer than we gave him credit for; his intelligence must have been able to project itself through the length of the passage and guess exactly the kind of bait that I was likely to be taking. Ronald and I have talked it over many times since; but between us we've never been able to decide by what stroke of divination, after all these exciting feelers, he managed to hit on my own pet, particular, fatal literary weakness: Martock.

'George Martock, as Ronald will tell you, is my King Charles' head, my private literary infatuation. His poems seldom get into anthologies, and the two volumes have never been reprinted since he died about forty years ago. I suppose you know the usual things about him. He was a schoolmaster in one of the villages on the top of Mendip, in Somerset: an awfully lonely life among curious people. My father was his doctor, so I know his history. He began by writing poems in dialect, rather like Barnes. Then, during the year before he died of pneumonia, his whole style changed. The last third of the second volume is full of things that make me want to howl like a child because they express all the nostalgia that we

Mendip folk feel when we're anywhere else in the world. Lots of people can't see anything in them; Ronald himself is an awful heretic; I dare say they aren't really as good as I imagine, but for me they express everything I've ever felt about that precious country. There's one poem in particular, just a landscape of an October morning: mist, dewy gossamer, black crows rising all together from an empty field, that always stabs me to the heart; and that, the very choicest of my favourites, was what the voice of Mr Furnival, without the least warning, began to recite.

'When I heard the first line of it, something possessed me. I can't tell you even now what it was. I got up from the table, my heart jumping out of my body, and went on tiptoe down the passage till I reached the door of the private bar. I stood there, breathless with excitement, until he had finished. The door was half closed. I couldn't see Mr Furnival himself, only the fire burning with a gentle crackle, and Alma sitting opposite him in a rocking-chair with her eyes wide open, fixed on him, and the firelight playing on her white throat. She looked so placid, so subdued, so awfully insensitive, that I didn't know whether to be sorry for her or angry. When he'd finished, she stayed in exactly the same position, fixed, lifeless, just as she had stood at the end of our table. There was a second of silence, and then the sound of Mr Furnival's cackle that was just as if some devil had slashed the canvas of that exquisite picture with a knife.

'"Well, Alma," he said, "what do you think of that?" Of the poem, of course, you'd imagine; but somehow, although I still couldn't see him, I felt that his words had a double meaning, that his eyes were turned to the door behind which I stood hidden, that the sentence was really addressed, not to Alma, but to me, and that his "that" referred not to the lines which he had just finished reciting, but to the triumphant ease with which he had decoyed me out of my room and along the passage.

'I felt so certain that he knew I was there that I was ashamed to conceal myself any longer. I'd acted with the impetuosity of a schoolgirl and supposed I must make the best of it. I felt that he was now waiting for me to enter, so in I came. Alma, suddenly aware of my presence, jumped up from the rocking-chair with a start. "Oh!" she cried. "Oh, ma'am, you *did* give me a start." She seemed shocked, and at the same time relieved, as though my coming had broken some spell and set her free. "I *am* a one!" she said. "Of course, you're waiting for me to clear the table. I'd clean forgot it!" She smoothed down her apron and hurried out with hot cheeks.

'Mr Furnival and I faced one another. Of course, you'll expect me to tell you what he was like, but I shall leave that to Ronald, not only because he'll be more anatomically exact, but because, at the end of this meeting I simply couldn't have told you. That sounds ridiculous; but I assure you it's literally true. During all the next half-hour through which I stayed and talked with him, I can honestly say that I had nothing but the mistiest idea of his appearance. Of course, there was no light except that of the fire; but to me he was just a voice and a personality. No, there I'm wrong; two voices, two personalities. The voice that had evoked all the wistful loveliness of Martock's poem, and the mad, devilish cackle that had destroyed it.

'It was with the first voice that he spoke to me. "Good evening," he said. "Won't you sit down?" He pointed to the rocking-chair that Alma had just left. I couldn't ... not there. It would have been like delivering myself over to the insinuating comfort of those plushy horrors in a dentist's surgery. No sooner are you in them than he tilts you backward with a ratchet, and there you are at his mercy. No, thank you! I sat down, as frightened as a mouse, on a stiff-backed chair just inside the door where the firelight mercifully didn't reach me.

'"Excuse me," I said, by way of explanation, though he, I'm sure, didn't need one,

"I thought I heard you reciting one of George Martock's poems."

""'October?' Yes," he said. "That's very clever of you. Very few people have heard of them. Educated people, I mean."

"'That's just what I thought," I said. "That's why I asked you."

"'Do you know 'Viaticum'?" he asked quietly. Really this part of his voice was very beautiful. "Yes, I do," I said; "but don't you think that's rather too terrible?" "'Viaticum'," he repeated quietly: "terrible! Ah!" And then he went off into that dreadful laugh that was made – I can't express it – for the destruction of beauty, and seemed to exult in it. Oh, how I hated him!

"'That poem," he went on soberly, "was written in the early part of his last illness; just four days before he died. Poor chap, he went up in a flare like a spent candle."

"'I know," I said. "My father lived at Axcombe and attended him till the end. You speak as if you'd known him. Did you?"

"'Didn't I!" he answered. "What's more, my dear lady, I paid for the publication of his second volume."

"'But you aren't a Mendip man," I said. "Your name–"

"'My name?" he laughed. "So Alma's been chattering? No, you're quite right. I happened to meet George Martock by accident in the course of my business."

'He didn't specify what the business was, and indeed it was difficult to guess what it might have been unless it were that of a school inspector, which isn't the kind of calling one associates with a country gentleman. Matthew Arnold? Still, it was no affair of mine. As a matter of fact, I'd already shown myself a little too interested by admitting that I knew his name; so I decided to say no more. There was no need for more, as it happened, for when once he'd got over his little flare-up he began talking about Martock of his own accord. I sat in the dark and listened. To me it was all very thrilling, for my father, who was just a plain-sailing general practitioner, had only regarded Martock as a club patient, and by the time that I began to be interested in him had very nearly forgotten all about him.

'Mr Furnival was a beautiful talker. He really was; I can't be too emphatic on that point. A conscious artist, if ever there was one, full of understanding and love for his subject. Sometimes, as he spoke, he affected a kind of slangy brutality, as if he were trying deliberately to disfigure the beauty of his theme, and sometimes that awful laugh of his would rip the whole of his picture into shreds, but in spite of all this I sat there enthralled, transported by what he said. He made George Martock live with something like the poignancy of his own poems. Tears came into my eyes. I couldn't stop them, and the worst of it was that I felt he knew how deeply he had affected me. Of course he knew. When he had come to an end, he proved it by asking if I could stand any more.

'I had to pull myself together before I answered, pretending that I'd taken it all in cold blood. I did so with a great effort of which I'm still proud.

'"Please go on," I said. "There's nothing that you can tell me about George Martock that won't interest me. The people who admire him are a very small band, but we're very faithful. And, of course, with you the interest's quite extraordinary. You must have been practically the only person who understood him. He'd been dead ten years when I picked up the first volume in my father's surgery, and by that time he was almost forgotten. There's an actuality about meeting you that I haven't felt before."

'He chuckled. "I can give you something more actual than that" he said, "if you'll come over and see me at Cold Harbour. It's only ten minutes' walk from here. I have the manuscript of the second volume complete, and any number of his notebooks in which he used to scribble his first ideas. How does that appeal to you?"

'"It's very kind of you to give me the chance," I said; "I must speak to my husband about it."

"'Naturally,' he said, with a mocking inclination of his head. "I'm afraid you have the advantage of me in knowing my name."

"'Ours is Wake," I told him. "My husband is a surgeon. We came here quite by chance on our way from Shropshire to London. Our time, unfortunately, isn't our own: tomorrow we have to be back in town."

"'Yes, that's unfortunate," he nodded. "I myself am not an idle man, and it just happens that all tomorrow morning I shall be engaged; but in the afternoon—"

'That, I told him, would almost certainly be too late.

"'Even to see George Martock's manuscripts?" he scoffed. "Well, that's a pity. I guess that your husband isn't equally enthusiastic." He put a shade of scorn into the sentence that made me angry. What right had a stranger to pass reflections on Ronald? But before I'd time to express my indignation he knew that he had ruffled me, and threw in a little sop of flattery. "Of course I know his name," he said; "his genius expresses itself in other directions. But quite apart from Martock it would be a pity to miss Cold Harbour. The shell of the house is relatively modern, but the interior is full of good things: quite a lot of it pre-Reformation. It was the site, you know, of a Roman villa, the only one for miles. The road you came in on is Roman, and during recent excavations we've found a number of things that are unique, including a pavement that hasn't yet been described. Though I say it, it'll be a thousand pities if you miss the opportunity, for your own sakes as well as for mine. Then there's another inducement: the house is said to be haunted. Does that attract you?"'

Evelyn Wake paused for a moment.

'Now comes a curious thing,' she said. 'During all the time that he'd been talking of Martock's life and death, and, after that, of the pride that he took in Cold Harbour, I'd felt entirely at ease with him. I'd experienced nothing, I mean, of the indefinitely frightening atmosphere that he brought into the house with him; he had seemed just an ordinary, cultured, sensitive person talking quite naturally of his enthusiasms. I suppose I had yielded myself unconsciously to the extraordinary beauty of his voice and my own greedy interest in what he was saying. But when he came to his mention of the house's evil reputation, the quality of his voice suddenly changed, and when he reached the end, it seemed as if he could contain himself no longer and burst into that awful cackle that had made me shiver when I listened to him from a distance.

'With that cackle, all my feeling of friendliness and normality disappeared. I

55

couldn't accept him on those terms any longer. I felt that I'd been weak to surrender myself to his story. I felt... To tell the honest truth, I felt that I hated him. My mind and body grew tense with apprehensiveness. In a state of that kind, reason has no chance against instinct; if I'd reasoned I should have held my tongue; but literally before I had time to think I heard myself asking him what had made him recite Martock's "October" to Alma. "You knew I was in the next room, listening," I said, "and you knew that I was interested. You laid a trap for me. Why did you do that?"

'He rose and faced me, as if he felt I had an advantage over him in standing. I was trembling from head to foot. The fire had died down so that I was still unable to see his face. For a moment he said nothing. Then, once again, he laughed. He didn't attempt to deny my suggestion; it seemed as if it pleased him. "Yes. Curious, isn't it?" he said. Then, in that bitter, half-jocular tone, "It's time I went home and put my old woman to bed, Mrs Wake, so I'll wish you good-night. *Au revoir;* not goodbye. I look forward to seeing you both tomorrow afternoon."

'He pushed back a chair and walked straight past me standing there stiff as a statue. "Alma!" he called. "Where the devil's the girl got to?" She ran into the passage to meet him. I heard them whispering together, and then the sound of another laugh and a cheerful goodnight.

'I knew that he'd gone, and still I couldn't move. Alma came into the room, as flushed and fluttered as if she'd just been kissed. She spoke with a little breathless laugh. "What a long talk you and Mr Furnival have had, ma'am! He'll go on for hours like that. He's a funny gentleman, isn't he? I don't understand a tenth part of what he says; but one has to sit and listen just the same, haven't they? I'm sure you're very kind to put up with him!" She went on with a busy nervousness, scraping back into position the chair that he'd displaced. "I'm very grateful to you, I'm sure. He's such a hindrance. Gave me a chance of putting your room ready. I'm sure I don't know what he comes here for. As I sometimes say to mother..."

'And all this time she was longing for me to speak. I couldn't do it. I suppose she'd have listened to us if she'd dared, and as she hadn't dared, she was anxious to know what had passed between us. Not out of sheer curiosity, but out of jealousy: that was why she made such a point of treating me and herself as equal sufferers, disclaiming any enjoyment in Mr Furnival's company. At last, with a sigh, she gave it up. "There's a lovely fire burnt up in the parlour," she said. "If I was you, ma'am, I think I'd go and sit by it. The gentleman can't be very much longer, surely."

'I had to force myself to speak, she was looking at me so hard and so slyly. "Yes, he ought to have finished by now," I said. I crossed the passage to the parlour. The fire, as Alma had said, was now flaring brightly behind the lamplight, and yet I couldn't stay there. I wanted most awfully to hear Ronald's voice, to put my arm in his. I wasn't frightened; I wasn't lonely; merely unhappy, detached, disorientated. It made me ashamed to admit it, but the feeling was so real that as soon as I'd sat down I could stick it no longer, and just when Alma imagined that she'd got me settled for the evening, I jumped up in a hurry, threw on my cloak, and went out to find Ronald in the barn.

'The rain had stopped. It was a soft autumnal night, half lit by moonlight that the mist spread over the whole countryside. It seemed to me so quiet and homely and natural that I felt more ashamed of myself than ever, and very nearly turned back. Halfway across the farmyard I saw Ronald coming to meet me, awfully pleased with himself; and whistling the forging song from *Siegfried*. He was so engrossed in it that he nearly ran into me. "Hallo, Eve!" he said. "What on earth are you doing here? You look like a ghost in that white cloak." I suppose I did. It was the thing I'm wearing now. "Do I?" I said – I felt quite happy again all of a sudden as he took my arm – "I'd begun to think that you were never coming." "The tyre was a beast," he said. "It hadn't been off before, so I had to wrestle with it like a dwarf in a cave. The glass is going up again: I can feel it in my wound. We shall have a fine day tomorrow and get off early."

'Shall we? I thought. I knew we shouldn't, but I didn't say a word. We walked out of the yard arm in arm, and stood for a moment on the green platform in front of the Fox listening to the little owls that whimpered in the mist. That moonlight was just as different from this as it could be; you couldn't see a thing ten yards away from you. Ronald had stopped his whistling and grown sentimental. "I wonder," he said, "how many times the Romans saw it like this, standing to take breath on the top of the hill. I suppose it was all thick forest then. *Colonia Arborum.* But they wouldn't be able to see the trees for the mist. I wonder if this site has ever been excavated. I'm pretty well up in those things, but I don't seem to remember having seen it mentioned. What fun it would be to settle down here at the Fox for a month and get permission to dig!"

'"It has been excavated," I told him, "but nothing's been published."

'"Really?" He was quite excited. "Who

59

told you that? The distracted Alma?"

'"No," said I, "Mr Furnival. I've been talking to him. He's invited us to go and see his treasures at Cold Harbour tomorrow afternoon."

'"What luck! But afternoon makes it difficult. That means cutting it a bit fine."

'"I know that, I told him." I couldn't keep it back any longer: "He's got all George Martock's manuscripts too."

'"Well, I dare say we could manage it at a pinch," said Ronald. He knew how near anything of Martock's was to my heart. "What do you feel about it yourself? Would you like to risk it and stay?"

'I couldn't answer him. For the moment my mind was curiously divided. My first and most honest thought was an overwhelming "No"; but the chance of seeing and handling Martock's manuscripts, the only opportunity, as I told myself, that I should ever get, made me hesitate; and Ronald, who's used to quick decisions on my part, grew anxious at once. "If there's any doubt about it," he said, "we won't give it another thought. As a matter of fact, it seems to me that this place has been getting on your nerves; I felt that from the very first, so we'll push off early tomorrow morning for the good of our consciences. How's that?"

'But by this time the balance of my

thoughts had tilted over; I'd told myself that it was just childish to be frightened of Mr Furnival or his house; I wanted, more than I could possibly express, to stay, and invented all sorts of specious arguments for staying.

'"I'm not really nervous," I told him, "and, after all, it would be a pity to miss the chance of seeing things that appeal to both of us. I should never forgive myself if you didn't examine that pavement, and if we leave about five we can surely get home by bedtime; it's only a four hours' run."

'"Barring accidents," he agreed.

'"And the law of averages," I said, "is against us having another."

'He laughed. "You can't spoof me with your law of averages," he said. "What you really mean is that you want to stay, and I'm not at all sure that it's good for you. We'll discuss it over the fire when I've got some of this mud and grease off my hands. Sit down there and be comfortable."

'He hurried off upstairs and left me. When I told him that I wasn't nervous, it was the honest truth. Ronald is such a steady, reassuring person that you can't feel nervous in his company. I knew that when I went out to find him, and by this time my panic had quite subsided. While I sat there waiting for him, Alma came into the room again. It seemed as if she couldn't leave me alone until she'd satisfied herself exactly of what had passed between me and Mr Furnival, and hoped to do so just by hanging round. It was rather embarrassing, for neither of us had anything we could say to the other, and yet she couldn't tear herself away. Then Ronald came downstairs, shut the door behind him, and brought her to the point with his brutal, surgical directness.

'"Don't go, Miss Higgins," he said. "I want you to tell us all about Mr Furnival."

'"About Mr Furnival, sir?" she repeated. She looked round at that closed door like an animal in a trap.

'"Yes, Mr Furnival," said Ronald, with a sort of hearty brutality that he can do to perfection. "Come along now!"

'"But I know nothing about him," she said, "nothing at all."

'"Why, an hour ago," he told her, "you couldn't talk about anything else."

'"Well, that's just gossip, sir," she said; "what everyone knows."

'He wouldn't leave it at that. "But surely," he said, "you are such close neighbours, you must know more than anyone else. He's been kind enough," Ronald went on, "to invite us to see Cold Harbour tomorrow."

'Her eyes brightened. This was one of the things she'd been wanting to know. "Yes, sir?" she said. "Well, I should go if I were you. They say it's very interesting."

"'So you told us before," said Ronald. "Haven't you ever been there yourself?"

"'Oh, yes, I've been there," she answered. "Once."

"'Well, then," said Ronald cheerfully, "you can tell us what it's like."

'She shook her head. It seemed as if she shivered. "I don't know that I can, sir," she said. "It was a long time ago; I can't bring much of it to mind."

"'But you'd like to go there again, wouldn't you?" Ronald pressed her.

"'That I shouldn't!" This time she evidently spoke the truth.

"'Now that's a funny thing to say," Ronald persisted. "I suppose you frightened yourself with these stories about it being haunted? You didn't see any ghosts, did you?"

"'Of course I didn't," she said, with a feeble laugh. "I don't credit all that nonsense. Mr Furnival says–" she went on quickly, then stopped and picked herself up again: "I'm sure Mr Furnival will tell you what he thinks of it."

"'Why can't *you* tell us?" Ronald rallied her.

"'Because I know nothing about it," she said almost angrily. "I've told you that before."

'It was evident that the poor thing was now genuinely distressed by Ronald's questions. I felt it my positive duty to come to her rescue. "Dr Wake is only joking," I said. "You mustn't take him too seriously." She gave me one look of scared gratitude and retreated to the door. In another minute I think she would have burst out crying. "At what time would you like your breakfast, ma'am," she said piteously.

'"Are we making an early start?" Ronald asked me significantly.

'"No," I said. "We shan't start till the evening, after tea. I think nine o'clock will do for breakfast."

'"Bacon and eggs, ma'am?" Alma inquired tragically.

'"Yes, that will do," I said, as kindly as I could. "You needn't bother to come in again. We'll put out the light."

'She went out. By this time we were both awfully sleepy. Ronald yawned and began to unlace his shoes. Suddenly he asked me why I had decided to stay. "I don't know," I said. "Partly curiosity about those manuscripts; partly pity for the poor girl. You did bully her, you know."

'Ronald laughed. "Not a bit of it! I wanted to know what she could tell us."

'"She didn't want to tell you anything," I said. "You could see that for yourself.'

'"Obviously. As we said before, she's in love with him. That's what makes her secretive. As for bullying her, I'm just as sorry for her as you are. It's very awkward for a girl of that class to deal with a married man's attentions. And yet her life here with the old woman must be pretty deadly. I should imagine that Mr Furnival must be the only spot of brightness in her existence."

'The word seemed incongruous. "Brightness?" I said.

'"Well, of course, I'm quite in the dark," Ronald confessed. "I've never set eyes on the gentleman. You have; so you'll be able to tell me how he struck you."

'And then, quite unawares, I found myself echoing Alma's words. "I know nothing about him," I said.

'"You too?" Ronald laughed.

Chapter Three

Dulston

Evelyn Wake stopped suddenly. For half an hour we had been carried along the drowsy current of her voice, and the silence that followed was like that which rouses the sleeping passenger when he hears, instead of the thud of engines, a lapping of harbour water. Just so, serenely, she brought us into port and left us to awaken in silence, surprised to think how far we had travelled in our sleep. In place of that cosy parlour of the Fox, itself a focus of light upon the dark contours of Midland hills, we now regained consciousness of the Italian night, the faint stars, the white, high-sailing moon that now shone almost vertically upon herself and her listeners. Nobody spoke. We all sat waiting quietly for Ronald to continue the story. He rose and walked to the parapet to knock out his pipe.

'Curious,' he said, 'how extraordinarily innocuous it all sounds here: of course the stirring time is still to come.' He turned to me directly: 'To tell you the truth, we're rather looking to you to help us. Time after time since this business happened we've thought of you; for when we began to look at the map we saw that Cold Harbour wasn't five miles as the crow flies from your old home at Halesby. "He's bound to know all about it," we said, "and probably more than we do." That's one of the reasons why we've been keeping Mr Furnival's story hot for you; we felt that you'd be able to supply us with its opening chapter. Supposing we get that settled before I go on?'

'Of course you guessed quite rightly,' I said. 'I've known about Cold Harbour ever since I was a child, thirty years ago. In those days the house was empty. It hadn't been occupied for years. The Pomfret trustees couldn't let it.'

'Why couldn't the Pomfret Trustees let Cold Harbour,' said Wake quickly. 'Ghosts?'

'No, I don't think it was anything of that kind,' I told him. 'I'm talking of the nineties. By that time the Pomfrets, our local aristocrats, had definitely gone under. As the girl at the Fox told you, an ironmaster named Walter Willis had bought their big house, Mawne Hall. Cold Harbour, their dower house, was a bit too remote and old-fashioned and ramshackle for any of the other big business men to take a fancy to it. Since you've made the suggestion, I do seem to remember some sort of a ghost story, but nothing very definite; people in the Black

67

Country were far too busy getting rich to bother about things of that kind. The other Pomfret mansion, Mawne Hall, was always said to be haunted too, but that didn't prevent the Willises from keeping open house. The Pomfrets must have been rather a grisly family.

'But let's get back to Cold Harbour. I know, of course, that it is supposed to stand on the site of a Roman villa, but I don't think it had ever been excavated in my time. I thought it rather gruesome myself, because I was an imaginative child, and because it had stood for so long empty and neglected. But the curious thing is that though it was only five miles from Halesby I never visited it. That's a remarkable thing in itself, for in all that country it must be the only corner that slipped me. And that's all I can tell you about it. But Furnival – Humphrey Furnival – is a different matter altogether. I haven't heard of him for years, so I can't even be sure it's the same man. How old do you make him?'

'He has no age,' Evelyn Wake murmured.

'Anything between fifty and sixty-eight,' said her husband.

'Then I think it must be the same man. At any rate, thirty years ago he was in the prime of life. In those days he lived at Dulston, on the wrong side of what old Walter Willis used to call "the green fringe of the Black Country". And first of all, by the way, I can satisfy your wife's curiosity about his acquaintance with Martock. No doubt some Midland corporation sent him down to investigate the lead lodes on Mendip. He was a mining engineer.

'No ordinary one either. I know that in those days he had an enormous professional reputation. It must have been enormous for a boy like myself to have heard of it. I can't tell you where he came from, or what his beginnings were, but certainly, at the time I'm speaking of, he had made for himself a name that was quite unique, helped, possibly, by his godfathers and godmother, for the combination is one that you can't easily forget. I remember that it impressed me immensely when first I heard it and knew nothing else about him.

'But let us get down to details. I think you may have heard me speak sometimes of an old friend, a Dr Moorhouse; a curious figure, again; a bachelor, and an enormous influence in my life. He was a professor, as you know, in the medical school at North Bromwich, but long before I took to doctoring he had been forced to retire from that post by the smoke, which didn't agree with his lungs. When I remember him first he was still carrying on his work in the town, escaping every weekend to a cottage that he had taken on the high ridge between Pen

Beacon and Uffdown. I've never, to this day, known a creature more human and erudite at the same time: a great man, if only his health could have carried him through.

'For some reason or other – I shouldn't wonder if my boundless admiration had something to do with it – he took a fancy to me. In holiday time we used to go long walks together over the hills, and come back tired to tea at his cottage. A great viewpoint. Time after time from his front door I've seen those great Black Country sunsets of the kind that so impressed you; and later, when I cycled home to bed, I'd stop at a gate above Uffdown wood and listen to the nightingales, watching, at the same time, great jets of flame leaping from the throats of the blast–furnaces, and the serpentine fires of the pit mounds smouldering over Mawne, my head buzzing, all the time, with the fascination of the things he'd told me.

'But that's a digression, and your story is more important. In those days, and, for that matter, all through his life, my friend's chief interest was Anthropology. I think that was partly why he chose that commanding prospect to live with, because it offered his imagination so wide a field to brood on, reconstructing the life of the people whose bones lie disinterred and whose weapons he found upon the dome of Uffdown. And so, I suppose, he drifted into a loose association with Humphrey Furnival, one of the few moneyed men in the district who understood him, appreciated his learning, and shared his enthusiasms.

'I still remember the first day on which I met him. It was Saturday, a half holiday, and we'd planned to walk over and investigate some of the Arenig boulders at the other end of the range. It had taken my fancy, that idea of a vast glacier coiling like a slow snake out of Wales and depositing its alien stones on our own hills. Arenig ... what a savage and romantic name! I burst into Moorhouse's cottage, burning with eagerness, expecting to find him. On the hearth, astride, and warming his hands at the fire, stood an enormously tall gentleman in carefully creased cashmere trousers, black cut-away coat, and patent leather boots. Fierce blue eyes, staring at me under a tangle of red hair – like highland cattle, you know – and a flaming beard, beneath which – and this, I think, impressed me most – was a flowing satin bow of the kind that in those days was called "artistic", and a shirt and collar of Wotan blue.

'He just stood there and grinned at me, and all the time he kept on bending and straightening his knees as though he were performing some kind of physical exercise. He didn't speak a syllable until Moorhouse came in. Then he nodded at me and said,

71

"What is this, Moorhouse?" and my friend told him who I was. That seemed to satisfy him, for afterwards he took no notice of me. "Ready?" he said in a brusque, businesslike way, and out they went together, with me trailing behind, not on any Arenig adventure, but straight up on to the top of Uffdown.

'I'd never felt more cheated or "out of it" in my life. Moorhouse was too wrapped up in his visitor to take any notice of me, and this made me fiendishly jealous. They went at an enormous pace; I had to run to keep up with them; and all the time they were talking hard in their specialist's jargon that I couldn't understand, try as I might: the kind of allusive shorthand that experts use in the knowledge that no explanations are necessary.

'I can see them now, standing together on the dome of Uffdown. A bright, blowing day: on the hilltop a perfect flame of gorse, and all the border mountains as clear as if they'd been cut out of blue cardboard. I can see Moorhouse with his slow, leisurely gait, and my supplanter, Furnival, darting about from place to place like some strong-winged hawk, all fire and energy and hairy fierceness. He waved his arms and grinned and pointed, and at the end of each triumphant sentence came that laugh which froze the blood of your poor wife. Only I, as a child, shouldn't have called it sinister. It seemed to me just the expression of his triumphant energy, as if he were saying, "There you are! While you slow people go fuddling about with your theories, I can swoop and snatch the truth up from under your noses!" It troubled me to see my idol treated with such a want of respect.

'Little by little, picking up here and there a word that I knew, I gathered that they were talking about some battle in early history of which Ostorius Scapula and Caractacus were the heroes and this gorsy hilltop the scene. Later, when they made me read Tacitus for an examination, it all came back to me. The object on which Furnival expended his ghoulish energy was the probable site of the burial ground of this historical fight. Caractacus crossed the Severn at Buildwas. Ostorius, checked by the Uffdown reverse, followed slowly. Which way? Down there, by the Watling Street? In those days all the Severn basin was clogged with forest, only the greater hilltops, such as the Clees, lifting up like islands. "The way Ostorius Scapula went," he said, "was straight along the causeway to Cold Harbour, and so due north through Dulston and Wolverbury, keeping to high ground all the way, until he reached the road somewhere near Cannock. Ha?" And he burst out laughing. "Very well," he said, "the Britons buried their dead under the mounds that you've dug: the Romans, being decent people, carried theirs from the field of battle to Cold Harbour – never excavated, mind you! – and continued to shed their wounded as they died, all the way between there and Watling Street. Ha?"

'He pulled out a map; he and Moorhouse lay down together on the rabbit-bitten turf. "This," he said, "is the line of the Cold Harbour road. Good! Produce that northward to the Watling Street. You see it keeps to the hilltops all the way. Now *there*" – he made a minute cross with a pencil whose fine point ravished me with envy – "there, right on our line, mark you, is the site of the house that I'm building; and you may take it from me that the broken bones I've unearthed came from some poor devil who was wounded eighteen hundred and forty years ago within a hundred yards of the spot where we're lying. Ha?"

'He swept the map off the turf, folded it, and hurried off downhill again. We followed. I can remember very few of the arguments that Moorhouse advanced against his theory. I know he said that we weren't even certain that the battle had been fought on Uffdown. "An unbroken tradition," Furnival declared. Traditions were so unreliable. Tradition assigned every Celtic earthwork in England to the Romans. Furnival wouldn't have it. Tradition was as valid as any historical evidence not absolutely contemporary. He spoke with feeling of the Catholic Church. We had no evidence, Moorhouse argued, that the Cold Harbour road existed in those days. Admitted, said Furnival. The soldiers of Ostorius probably planted a grove at the point where they buried their comrades: *Colonia Arborum*. No need for that, Moorhouse replied; when you came to think that Cold Harbour was in the middle of what later became the great forest of Mercia.

'So we jogged down the hill, disputing, our progress punctuated by that hateful laugh of Furnival's. He clung to his thesis like a bigot; no reasoned argument could move him. It surprised me to find Moorhouse taking it with such good humour. If Furnival had spoken to me, I know I should have been hostile to him. But he didn't. As far as he was concerned, I didn't exist. I disliked him even more when we came back to Moorhouse's cottage for tea. He sat glaring at me, as I thought, across the fire, wolfing buttered toast piece after piece at an incredible rate. I'd never seen any one eat so fast; I'd never seen any one *live* so fast in every particular: gesture, speech, movement, thought. It was tiring to be in his company.

'When he'd finished eating, he sprang to his feet. "Glad of your opinion," he said, "and sorry we don't agree. But I shall convert you yet. You'll be able to see for yourself. When shall it be? I could have driven you over now, but the light won't last. What about tomorrow? Ha? Sunday?"

'I held my breath. I think I must have looked anxiously, reproachfully, at Moorhouse, and no doubt he saw me. He realized, kind soul that he was, that I'd been done out of my Arenig adventure, and didn't want to disappoint me for the morrow. "This young man and I," he began, "had planned..." I breathed again; but Furnival swooped into the middle of his sentence. "Plans be damned," he said. "The best plan is to come over to Dulston. I want the matter settled. Come tomorrow morning; I'll send the trap over for you. If you like, you can bring the boy with you. Dinner at one sharp. We don't have lunch in Dulston. Now make up your mind! I shall expect you. Ha?"

'And off he swept into the lane, where a solemn coachman with a big black horse in a gig, all shining yellow, was prowling up and down as though they too were on wires and itching to be off at top speed. Furnival leapt rather than walked towards them, sprang up into the box-seat, and took the reins. "One moment. Your overcoat!" Moorhouse called after him. "I never wear one; *was* one," Furnival called back. He waved his whip and gave the horse the lash. The great brute shot forward like an arrow. I saw the coachman clutching at the rail of the seat as they swung round the corner on one wheel. "Well, well," said Moorhouse, laughing to himself. "He's a passionate person. He must have driven thirty miles to find me. I hope he'll get home safely."

'Evidently he did, for next morning at midday the black horse, mettlesome as ever, was champing in the lane, waiting to whirl us over to Dulston. (I'm telling you all this in detail, because I don't want to interrupt your story again; because I want to give you everything I know about your hero, if that's what he is, with all the vividness that comes back to me out of a boyish memory.) Off we drove, at an enormous pace as it seemed to me, down through the woods and into the edge of the Black Country, We passed the gates of Mawne Hall, where you can still see the Pomfret arms, and shot out along the valley of the Stour, which Willis' works have now turned into an abomination of desolation. Then we climbed the side of the ridge on which stood the gigantic headgear of Fatherless Bairn colliery. In those days it wasn't called Fatherless Bairn; that's part of Furnival's story.

'There, a couple of hundred yards from the pit-head, stood a brand new house. Today you wouldn't think the house remarkable; examples of that sort of architecture are scattered over every suburb in England; but thirty years ago, I may tell you, it was the very latest thing in revivals: half–timbered gables, porches, fantastic chimney-pots, bow-windows, a jumble of all incongruous styles that was supposed, in those days, to represent a return to the picturesque.

'Of course the appearance of such aspirations in the middle of the Black Country impressed me, and Mr Furnival, who met us on the drive, was evidently proud and eager to demonstrate the mechanical contrivances with which it was fitted. He was dressed in the same clothes as those which had astonished me the day before; only, in place of the blue shirt collar, his chest and throat were encased in a starched front and a collar so high and rigid that he looked half-throttled by it. Above its brim his face seemed more sanguine and potent than ever. His lanky body oozed energy like a steam hammer. His mind leapt from point to point with an efficiency and exactness that made me feel dizzy. In ten minutes we had explored the whole of the house, a miracle of convenience, and found ourselves on the edge of the gravel-pit in which he had made his find. "But we will examine that after dinner," he said, and with that he looked at his watch, took a dog-whistle out of his waistcoat pocket, and blew it shrilly.

'For the moment I couldn't imagine what this performance meant, until, all of a

78

sudden, three children, two small, pigtailed girls and a boy several years younger than myself, came running up like dogs called to heel. "Gareth, Guenivere, and Elaine," he said by way of an introduction, to which they responded with timid smiles. "I expect they've been playing croquet. Croquet on Sundays, ha? Does that shock you, Dr Moorhouse? No? I might have known it wouldn't. *Ubi tres medici, ibi duo athei.* But we're not atheists here, nor protestants either. We keep to the faith of St Augustine. When they've heard Mass they have their liberty." He pulled out his watch again. The cover went back with a noiseless flick, mechanically perfect, like everything else in that house. The children stood by in silence. Then a brass gong thundered in the hall. "Dinner," he said, and led the way into the house.

'We had been rushed through the building so violently and entertained on the way by such a variety of mechanical devices, that I hadn't managed to "take in" anything else. Now we entered a room that was different from any I'd ever seen before. Its walls were draped, to the height of a man, with tapestry hangings. Over the Norman arch of the stone fireplace hung what I can now recognise as a pre-Raphaelite triptych, representing three aureoled figures on the verge of seasickness. "Burne-Jones," said Mr Furnival with a jerk

79

of his finger; and Dr Moorhouse nodded and said, "Ah," with a respect that I couldn't understand. Then we sat down at a black oak table, myself between the two crushed little girls with the romantic names.

'A moment later two women entered. The first, a tall and rather attractive figure, with masses of coppery hair and a white skin, took her place opposite to Dr Moorhouse, at Mr Furnival's left hand; the second and elder, a little woman with a pasty, patient face, dressed in a long *djibbeh* of dark blue satin, stole quietly to the other end of the table. Mr Furnival, who was already carving beef with a gluttonous efficiency, hardly noticed the arrival of either. I supposed that both belonged to the category of superior servants, until our host suddenly looked up from his dish and glared at the last. "Jane," he said, "this is Dr Moorhouse. Dr Moorhouse, my wife." The woman smiled timidly; Mr Furnival went on with his swiftly efficient carving; even his knife was more perfect mechanically than any I'd ever seen; and from that moment I don't think he addressed another word to her.

'Dr Moorhouse tried to do so, but whenever he attempted it Mr Furnival broke in with an irritable interruption. By the looks with which he raked the table from time to time, you'd have thought that he hated every one of us, and me particularly. Neither Mrs

Furnival nor the red-haired girl, whose name I now discovered to be Miss Penny – though whether it was her father's or merely an abbreviation for Penelope I couldn't guess – dared, apparently, to raise their voices above a whisper. The children didn't even open their mouths, and I was awed into following their example.

'But Mr Furnival, between his enormously rapid mouthfuls, continued to elaborate the thesis that he'd already expounded on Uffdown. On the table at his right hand stood an enormous beaker of beer, from which he steadily filled and refilled his tumbler. By the end of the first course he must surely have drunk a quart of it, with the result that his sanguine face grew redder and redder under the masses of fiery hair. Beyond this, he showed no signs of the volume of food and liquor that he was absorbing; and yet, as the meal went on, his body gave me more and more the idea of a high-pressure boiler, full of immense and increasing potential heat, and energy enough to blow the roof off.

'It couldn't go on for ever. By the time that the second course arrived these energies seemed to diffuse themselves into a blander mood. He stopped laying down the law about Roman Britain to Dr Moorhouse, and began to take notice of the tall girl on his left. He sat back in his chair, breathing noisily and deeply, and glancing sideways at her from time to time. She herself appeared to be unconscious of this scrutiny, but I took it in, wondering what it meant.

'By this time, I must confess, the sense of his diminished concentration had made me less frightened to observe him. I watched closely. His left hand was lying on the table. Slowly, with a sort of impish deliberation, he moved it, so that it touched hers. Miss Penny gave a sudden start and snatched her hand away. I saw a tide of colour rising under the milky skin of her neck; it swept into her cheeks, ears, forehead, until she was as red to the roots of her hair as Furnival himself. I imagined that nobody else had seen what happened, but I was wrong: Mrs Furnival also had seen: I caught the glance that passed from her grey-greenish eyes halfway. On her pasty face was a smile that I couldn't interpret, as if she had been forced to condone a bad joke. Mr Furnival's cackle broke the silence. He leaned over to Miss Penny and whispered something in her ear that made her look as if she'd like to hide herself under the table. So elated was he by this performance that he now leaned over to Moorhouse and repeated what he had said in an undertone. I couldn't hear what he said, but Moorhouse's face stiffened into a mixture of embarrassment and disgust, which told me that he had listened to something blatantly indecent. And again Mr Furnival laughed.

'With dessert appeared a cut glass decanter of port. By this time Mr Furnival seemed in the best of humours. He walked, or rather darted, round the table, filling the wine glasses, including those of the children and my own. They seemed to take it as a matter of course. For me, this was the first time I had ever tasted wine, and that, I think, is one of the reasons why I remember this dinner party with such extraordinary clearness. Miss Penny was the only one of us who refused it, and this gave Mr Furnival the occasion to whisper something that set her fiercely blushing again. "Well, if you can't take your liquor like a man," he said aloud, "you'd better go and fetch Gawain."

'The wine was sweet and insidious. It made me think that this was rather a jolly adventure after all. The strangeness of the room and that commanding figure at the head of the table no longer frightened me. "Who's Gawain?" I heard myself saying, but nobody answered me, and a moment later the blushing Miss Penny returned with a podgy infant of two, which Mr Furnival, embracing a new opportunity of contact, took from her arms. He settled the sleepy child on his knee, then dipped his forefinger in the glass of port and moistened its lips. The baby put out its tongue and licked them, like a kitten. "You see he likes it," laughed Mr Furnival, and I, by this time sleepy and complacent, watched him as he went on dipping his finger into the wine and giving it to the baby to suck.

'No doubt it was a painful and disgusting sight; I could see by my friend's cold face that he disliked it; but I, in my growing benevolence, and Mr Furnival, considered it the greatest fun in the world. The baby went on sucking at his vinous finger greedily; the other children lost their timidity and began to snigger; Miss Penny sat still in purgatory, and on Mrs Furnival's pasty face was fixed the same set smile. Time passed now without any clear impression. In a blurred vision I can remember the baby's head lolling over, Mr Furnival thrusting him, with a laugh of satisfaction, into Miss Penny's arms, myself rising to my feet, my brain spinning round like a paper windmill, and following an airy track in the wake of Moorhouse into another room smelling of tobacco, where a divan, heaped with cushions, restored my equilibrium.

'I was drunk, and cross, and awfully sleepy. Out of the confusion I heard Dr Moorhouse's voice, "You'd better lie down and go to sleep." I felt him tucking the cushions round my legs.

'I suppose I lay there for a couple of hours, sometimes sleeping, sometimes hazily aware of a murmur of voices, or stabbed half awake by the sound of Mr Furnival's laugh. Out of their murmurous talk emerged strange words that then meant nothing to me, but stuck in my mind as meaningless symbols to bring back the whole atmosphere of that adventure when I encountered them later in print. *Terra sigillata: hypocaust.* It's curious: even now the repetition of those two words can send a flare back into that lost chamber of my brain like a lit fuse.

'Of course, they were still talking about Roman Britain; and while I slept, no doubt, they visited Mr Furnival's last excavations. But I knew nothing of this. Nor did I ever see Mrs Furnival, Miss Penny, or the children again. Never in my life. When Dr Moorhouse came to wake me the sun had gone down. My head was splitting. Sometimes I wonder if, after all, it was only one glass. Through the cold evening Moorhouse drove back to Uffdown, dropping me at Halesby on the way. I went straight to bed, and heard him talking on the landing to my father. "I'm sorry," he said, "I'd no idea it would upset him like that. This man Furnival is a queer customer... Yes, curiously dynamic. I don't think there's a more striking personality in the Midlands."

'It was a queer incident, wasn't it? You, of course, will look at it from another point of view and in the light of your own experience.

From that day until one rainy afternoon many years later, when I was a medical student, and Moorhouse, dear fellow, had died with his work unfinished, I don't think Mr Furnival ever came into my mind. Of course, I knew that he was a prominent figure in the neighbourhood. His name was often in the papers as that of a pillar among the community who called themselves "Anglo-Catholics", and were called "Romanizers" by other people. I knew also that he was on the Council of the North Bromwich University and was counted something of an expert in education. Once, I think, I saw him driving furiously in one of those new perils to bicyclists called motor cars; but I don't think I ever heard of him in a way that arrested my attention until one day when, coming out from hospital to Halesby, I found myself forced into a first-class smoker.

'My companions in the compartment were two Black Country business men who had spent the day on 'change in North Bromwich. Their talk was of personalities rather than of prices, and neither would have distracted me from the anatomical textbook that I was reading if one of them hadn't said of a sudden: "Well, I suppose that's the end of Furnival."

'I pricked up my ears and listened.

'"I don't know about that," said the other.

"If you want my opinion, I think that Furnival's not only the best mining engineer, but the biggest brain we've got in the Midlands today."

'"He'll never live this down," said the first. "Old Joseph Hingston himself was at the board meeting. I've had it at first hand from him." He leaned over and went on talking behind his hand in a throaty whisper that was perfectly audible to me in my corner. Little by little I picked up the thread of the story. Furnival, it seems, had become consulting engineer to a new colliery called the Sedgebury Main, which, until the time of his appointment, had hardly paid its way. I knew the place well, for its headgear, topping the long ridge above Dulston, had lately become one of the landmarks of the neighbourhood. With his usual tremendous energy, Furnival had taken the show in hand, preparing a scheme of financial and mechanical reconstruction that took the directors of the moribund company off their feet and into his pocket, as the saying is. "Old Hingston," said the man in the corner, "says he had them properly hypnotised. The man's brain is uncanny, that's what he says."

'So hypnotised, I gathered, that within a month of getting his appointment Furnival had scrapped the whole of the colliery's original plan and convinced the board that he was going to make it the best thing of the kind in Staffordshire. In another six weeks he'd persuaded them to raise a quarter of a million of new capital to finance his developments, and so restored confidence in the undertaking that he'd quadrupled the market value of their shares. Nearly the whole of the new capital went on orders for improved machinery from America. Furnival promised them, and convinced them, that in three years this massive expenditure would be covered. There wasn't a flaw in his plans; the board just swallowed them whole. "I don't blame them either, from what I hear; but when it came to asking for new capital within six months – well, that was a bit thick, I admit. And yet the beggar carried them again! Personal magnetism, that's what I call it," said the man in the corner.

'I suppose he was right. I suppose, also, that the obedient directors were justified. Certainly Furnival had fulfilled the first part of his promise; in all the Midlands there was no mining undertaking that inspired such confidence in its skill and mechanical efficiency. Within nine months of Furnival's appointment, the Sedgebury Main started on its new career with the benedictions of all the biggest capitalists in the neighbourhood. Nobody was more assured of its success than Furnival himself, into it he had put the last ounce of his extraordinary brain. It was his masterpiece, and he knew it.

'A masterpiece in practice as well as on paper. The first five months' working fulfilled every promise that he'd made. And then, at the end of the sixth came the water; not slowly, insidiously, but in a savage flood that swamped the mine in a single night, and, with it, forty-seven human lives. It was a disaster in which there was no question of escape or rescue. I remember reading the bulletin in the *Courier*. In half an hour all was over with the Sedgebury Main and the half-million of money that had been put into it.

'The only person who took it calmly was Furnival. Nothing less than a disaster of this size sufficed to show his strength. For ten days and nights he concentrated on a scheme of salvage, as sweeping in its strength and confidence as the original plan. The directors met to consider it. For five hours on end he bullied them over it, but they'd had enough, and even Furnival couldn't bend them.

This was the meeting about which the fellow in the corner whispered behind his hand. "Furnival actually had the nerve," he said, "to ask for another hundred thousand, as cool as if it was twopence ha'penny. Of course, with the shares where they are they couldn't touch it. But that didn't stop him. 'Look here,' he says – and mind you, I've got the very words from old Hingston's lips –

'look here, if you haven't the pluck to go to the public for the money, I'll put down fifty thousand myself.' Like that!

'"But they wouldn't have it; and I'm not sure they weren't right: I think I should have acted the same. That pit's got a bad name, and even if they pump it dry, it's a name that'll take some living down before they'll be able to get men underground with any confidence. It's the women that put them off it, you know. But I must finish about that meeting...

'"When Furnival had made his proposal, old Hingston, who was chairman, asked him to leave the room while the board discussed it, and out he went. Well, as far as I can gather, there wasn't any discussion in the true sense of the word. There wasn't a man there that hadn't had his bellyful of the Sedgebury Main. Old Hingston saw which way it was going, so young George got up and proposed that they should realize what they could on the plant and reserves, and then close down. Carried *nem. con.* Then they sent out for Furnival.'

'"He came in, Hingston says, as if he were certain he'd done the trick. 'Take a seat, Mr Furnival,' said old Hingston, but he said he preferred to stand. 'The board has considered your proposal, Mr Furnival,' he says, 'and decided unanimously that it shall not be accepted. We're not going to throw good money after bad. There's nothing left for us but to close down permanently.'

"'Of course they were all wondering how Furnival would take it. Well, he stood there for a second as if he hadn't heard. Then he went down like a stone. They thought it had killed him. But it hadn't. Five minutes later he was sitting up again. 'I'm sorry this has happened,' says old Hingston kindly. 'I'm sorry you're such a lot of damned cowards,' says Furnival. 'You haven't the guts of a louse between you. I've finished with mining,' he says. So he got up on his feet – he wouldn't let them help him – and ran out of the room like a lunatic. Left his hat behind him as a souvenir. Yes, you may bet your shirt that's the last of Furnival."

'The train pulled up at the junction, and I left them shaking their heads over it. You can see the headgear of the Sedgebury Main to this day. They call it Fatherless Bairn. You must have noticed it, by the way, from Cold Harbour. And as for Mr Furnival; evidently the man in the corner was wrong. It wasn't the end of him.'

Chapter Four

En-dor

'No, it wasn't the end of him,' Ronald Wake repeated as soon as I had finished. 'It wasn't the end of him by a long way. But what you've told us, what we've been waiting for you to tell us – for in this case we've been driven to a good deal of speculation because of its delicacy – has been extraordinarily useful in filling in the background of the picture of what Mr Furnival's end was, or rather of what it will be if he fulfils our expectations. It's curious how this detached portrait of our host as a young man throws light on his later reactions. If we had improvised one, arguing backward to fit our own conclusions, I think our picture would have shown a general resemblance to yours, without, of course, the inspiration of its details: the gesture toward Miss Penny, the baby sucking port, the moment at the board meeting when he went down like a stone. Incidents of that kind are beyond the reach of invention.

'And I'm glad, in a way,' he went on, 'that you never actually explored Cold Harbour, because it would have deprived me of the pleasure of describing it. Of course, you never went there, just for the simple reason that on the plane of practical geography it doesn't exist. I was there a fortnight ago, and yet tonight, I assure you, I find it difficult to persuade myself that it had a more real existence than one of those landscapes that repeat themselves in dreams: countries of which the details, when you revisit them, are almost piercingly familiar, but which you recognise as phantasmal and peopled only by phantoms.

'Physically, as you know, the Cold Harbour district is a strip of sloping country between the main road that runs from the Severn to North Bromwich and the edge of the Black Country. From the south it is isolated by hills along the base of which straggles a remnant of the Mercian forest, now a preserve for pheasants. No road enters it from that side but the half-hearted cart-track by which we reached the Fox. On the north it is bounded not by black country – this is the point – but by a zone that was black a hundred years ago, riddled with colliery workings, scattered with pit mounds, utterly useless for farming or afforestation; abandoned; dead. You can see what I mean if you imagine it as a kind of no man's land; an area wrecked and untenable between the armies of Black and Green, a possession so long disputed and so unprofitable that both sides have abandoned it. The Black army has retreated, like a tide settling down into the Staffordshire colliery basin, and the Green, with a weakened purpose, has timidly re-established itself on the borders of the war-scarred area; as witness the minute oasis of the Fox, and Mr Moseley's farm, from which the labourers came in to drink their evening pint.

'We slept extraordinarily well. That wasn't surprising when you consider the variety of adventure we'd achieved in the last twelve hours. Alma gave us an excellent breakfast, and after that we went out into the yard and gave the car a good oiling to prepare her for a forced run in the evening. The morning was brilliantly clear, with a dew that seemed to have washed the sky clean of all suspended grime, draining it away into the sump of low-lying land beneath us. The hedgerows and coppices around the Fox were bright with purple elder bushes and busy with small packs of linnets and goldfinches pillaging their black fruit. While we fiddled about with the car, a robin came and sang on the red brick wall. It was like spring. Better than spring, in my own opinion. I don't think I've ever seen more blackberries on the brambles in my life; we could have picked them by the quart. But nobody seemed to want them. There *was* nobody to want them. As I've told you already, that patch of country only exists on maps.

'And I, of course, was too busy with my oily job to think of anything else. With Evelyn, who hates oil like poison, it was different. She hung about the yard, looking shrivelled with cold, although the sun was shining. I told her to go and pick blackberries, but she wouldn't. "I don't want to leave you," she said. The curiousness of the mood that had fallen on her was so definite that I ended by asking her what was the matter. "Nothing," she said, "it's really nothing. I don't think I like this place," she said when I pressed her. Of course I thought that was just rubbish, so when I'd finished with the car we went for a sharp walk together.

'It was still a gem of a morning; one of those days when your mind turns naturally to the idea of cubbing: leaves still on the trees, but the smell of them in the air when you stand waiting at the covert side with your ears strained to catch a whimper in the wood. And those woods, by the way, must be stiff with foxes, especially since our friend Furnival has quarrelled with the hunt. No wire, either. I suppose poor Mr Moseley can't afford it. We went for a smart walk towards the east, where a cart-track suggested that the farm should lie. It took us into another dip with a sandy stream at the bottom and straggling hazels so thick round us that we might have been miles away from anywhere. As for North Bromwich! But really the secrecy and silence of that hollow were quite incredible. And still, try as I would, I couldn't get Eve to talk.

'"Surely there's nothing wrong with *this*," I said. She shook her head. No, there was nothing wrong with it, but she didn't like it. "Well, my dear child," I said, "if it's as bad as that there's no earthly reason why we shouldn't cut our appointment for this afternoon. After all, I gather you left it open. All we need do is to leave a polite note with Mrs Higgins and say we couldn't manage it. Suppose we go right back to the Fox and slip away at once?"

'At this she became almost angry. If we went now, she said, we'd have wasted the whole morning for nothing. Besides, she wanted to see the Martock manuscripts, and she wasn't going to allow me to miss the chance of seeing Cold Harbour. "It's no use worrying me," she said – quite kindly, I'll admit – "I can't help feeling queer, can I? And if we leave it at that it'll be much better for everyone. Besides which, I've told Alma to prepare some lunch, and we'd have to pay for that in any case." This set me laughing, for if there's one thing typical in Evelyn's constitution it's her anxiety to get her money's worth. She saw the joke herself, so it didn't matter. And at three o'clock in the afternoon, or just after, we set out together for Cold Harbour. A matter of ten minutes: follow the road and you can't miss it, Alma told us. She stood in the doorway of the Fox watching us as we went, watching us out of sight.

'By this time the day had changed in a manner characteristic of the Black Country. I've told you already how in the early morning we got the impression that the sky had been washed by dew and all its impurities drained downward into the lower levels of the coal measures. One reason for this clearness was that the day before had been Sunday, and ninety per cent of the smoke-stacks were at rest. But all morning the chimneys of Dulston and Wolverbury and Darsall, and all the other congeries of red brick with uncouth names, had been disgorging their fumes of unconsumed carbon and sprays of steam, until a greyish yellow cloud hung over them. There wasn't a breath of wind that day; if it had been left to itself, the stuff would just have settled down on them like soup; but all the time fresh filth went on bubbling up from the bottom, so that the basin gradually filled, with the result that by midday its skimmings had reached the level of our sky. You couldn't see them, and yet they took every bit of colour out of the landscape, just as though we were looking through smoked glass. They were like a poison in our lungs; they made the air we breathed seem flat, devitalised, warm. We could taste their faint acridity with our tongues. All the time this thin, invisible poison came creeping up the slope of the hill. Evelyn spoke of it as a fog; we Londoners know the meaning of an honest fog; but this wasn't a fog; it was a blight!

'So we walked on through a landscape that was like a spoiled photographic plate. We followed the line of the Roman causeway between banks of rusty hazel. The surface of the road had been repaired with a dressing of slag that gave it a feeling of black sterility. The fields that we saw on either side of it, wherever the hedges straggled into gaps, had no greenness in them. They were dotted with mounds of ashes, on which no weeds would grow, and pits of dirty water. No trees but an occasional black and twisted hawthorn. In one field a huge circular boiler of a type that has long since been discarded lay on its side like a stranded buoy. No Man's Land, with a vengeance!

'And then, suddenly, Cold Harbour. Although we were prepared for it, it took our breath away. There were only three buildings: the church, with the manor house and the parsonage on either side of it. They stood huddled together, as if for protection, on the brow of the hill, which fell away from them into the basin beneath; and about them, as though to perpetuate the reason of the hamlet's name, ran a belt of magnificent beeches. All through the Cotswolds, on our drive westward, the beeches had shone like pyramids of flame. On those that surrounded Cold Harbour, not three days later, there was not a leaf left. The beeches in Cotswold had trunks that showed a sheen of steel and platinum; the trunks of the Cold Harbour beeches were black and dull as soot. They stood up stark naked and motionless, as though they were dead, a complete circle, dipping over the brim of the ridge like a fairy-ring; and as we passed within their circumference it seemed as though we were stepping out of this life and into another of ghostly silence. A fancy, of course. As a matter of fact, the deep felting of beech-mast and leaf-mould muffled our footfalls.

'First we passed the vicarage, a small house with pointed gables built of the local red bricks picked out with blue. The shrubberies on either side of the front gate were so overgrown that we couldn't see the lower story; but the upper windows were blocked by broken shutters. We judged that it was uninhabited. Then, within the boundary of a low stone wall, we passed the church, and that alone would have repaid us for our visit. As far as I could judge in passing, the tower at its western end was Saxon or early

Norman, and unusually massive for the period. The little graveyard was carefully mown and tended, and so full that it had evidently served, at some time, for a larger population. It ended abruptly against a high brick wall overtopped by the shrubberies of the manor house and the gable of its westernmost wing.

'We had to skirt this wall in order to reach Mr Furnival's drive gate, or rather the place where the drive gate should have been, for now there was nothing but a gap between two shapely stone pillars carved with the Pomfret bearings. And here our progress seemed quieter than ever, for the drive ran under a tunnel of horse chestnut trees which must have been very gay in spring, and the drift of their leaves was thick under our feet.

'One moment. In my hurry to reach the house I'm afraid I've forgotten something: at the level of the drive's opening the causeway, which we'd now followed all the way from the main road past the Fox, came to an end with a high holly hedge, so dense that we couldn't see beyond it. It seems a small thing to notice, but it finished so definitely, without even the continuation of a footpath, that we were conscious of being in the very bottom of a cul-de-sac, without any chance of escape, except along the narrow entrance of the Roman road, and, at that moment, I, at any rate, was aware of a sense of constriction, as though something unpleasant were crowding in on me and I felt the need of space.

'However, that's by the way. The horse chestnuts weren't quite as bare as the beeches; I suppose the beeches, being higher, protected them from wind. As we walked along beneath them, their yellow fans came floating down into our faces, and sometimes, without any movement to detach them, the seed cases fell with a heavy plop. We were awfully sensible there of the year's death. That place seemed two months later than the rest of the country. I suppose the trees had to fight against the blight of that poisonous air as well as time.

'The drive was a short one; a matter of forty yards at the most. As we came out of its tunnel we found ourselves flanking the front of the house. Nobody could see us there, so we halted to look at it. And really it was very beautiful. I can't tell you why. Probably it was nothing but the silence, the isolation, the unsuspectedness of the whole thing that gave it that effect. Architecturally its front certainly wasn't beautiful in the least, it hadn't, I mean, the advantage of being constructed in one style, like the Cotswold houses that we'd just seen. To be exact, it was a mixture of two. The wing nearest to us was half-timbered, with the bricks unwhitened; its level was sunk a little below that of the rest of the house, so that its long horizontal windows reached to within a little distance of the ground, and the single doorway, with its sandstone arch of late perpendicular, was made to look squat by the fact that one entered it with a downward step. The rest of the building was modern: a Palladian entrance porch flanked on either side by high windows with slender mullions.

'You see, it had no uniformity of style; but what it had was a uniformity of material. Apart from its porch, the mass of the building was constructed of small red bricks, whose clay might have come from the same clay pit and taken shape in the same moulds. What was more, they all seemed to be uniformly weathered, not, I suppose, by time, but by the acrid flames that had pickled them ever since the Black Country was black. When we came closer – I almost said crept, for there really was something stealthy in our advance – I noticed with the peculiar thrill that recognition gives one, that into the lower courses of the timbered wall a number of bricks of another shape had been built, and, what was more, built with a diagonal pattern. I saw thousands of their fellows only yesterday in those great aqueducts that go stalking over the Campagna. They were Roman bricks, laid in the Roman fashion. It was just as if a fragment of the villa's original wall had been built into the new house *en bloc*; and these, too, had weathered to the colour of all the rest.

'We kept the path close to the front of the building and approached the porch. The last of the Tudor windows reached just below the level of our shoulders. Its panes were latticed; some had the purplish sheen of eighteenth-century glass; some were of whorled bottle-glass, dense and sea-green; but all were so imperfect and aged as to distort by their uncertain refractions; and the little genre picture that we caught through them in passing had no need of distortion.

'It was that of a woman skinning a rabbit. She had brought it to the table under the window, I suppose, because that was the only part of her kitchen, or pantry, or whatever it was, that wasn't dark at this time of year. She didn't hear us approaching; thick leaves had drifted with wind over what, I think, was a flagged pavement skirting the house. She didn't hear us – she may have been deaf, too – but she did become aware of our passing shadow; and that, when it fell on her, made her jump backward from her unpleasant job as if she'd been shot.

'In this moment I got a quick impression of her face. The twisted glass may have been responsible for an illusion. It seemed to have the elongated distortion of an El Greco: greenish in colour (the glass again) and horse-like, with prominent teeth and eyes. I was glad that Evelyn missed it, for it was the sort of face one might dream about. Yes, it was definitely not a modern face. It had the grotesqueness of the Middle Ages, like the Lincoln gargoyles. I rather hoped, for Evelyn's sake, that she wouldn't open the door for us. It would be a bad beginning.

'Luckily she didn't, and Eve, to my astonishment, seemed less sensitive than myself to the peculiar quality – I shall have to leave it at that – which oozed out of the house's façade. We entered the porch and rang the bell. The wire scraped loosely, as if it were disconnected. We waited for two whole minutes of intense silence. Then the door opened cautiously, smoothly, like that of an hydraulic safe. The person who opened it stood behind it. For an instant it seemed as if it had opened of itself (by this time nothing would have surprised me), but in the next the opening agent revealed herself in the shape of an elderly woman, whom Evelyn can describe much better than I can.'

He paused, and with the smoothness of a competitor in a relay race, his wife picked up the thread of the story:

'A tiny woman of fifty,' she said, 'in a black satin dress, at least ten years behind the fashion, but very neat, fastened high at the throat with a cameo brooch. She wore a white muslin apron and a long gold chain round her neck, with an emerald crucifix at the end of it that must have cost a fortune. Her hair was half grey, the indeterminate sort of grey of hair that has once been fair. It was parted in the middle, and swept back tightly on either side above a very narrow forehead, so narrow that her head seemed to taper like an egg the wrong way up. What made it look even more like that was the fact that her eyebrows were thin and sandy, almost the same colour as all the rest of her face. She had a flattish, good-natured nose, and the sort of mouth of which you'd say at once that it showed a sweet, good, rather timid disposition.

'Her eyes were of a shade that's neither blue nor green nor hazel; a kind of muddy, neutral mixture of all three. What struck me most about them was their dreadfully puzzled expression. They weren't frightened eyes although they were timid; they looked you full and honestly in the face; but, all the time, they gave you the impression that the brain behind that narrow forehead was puzzled to distraction, that it couldn't possibly grasp the kind of life it had to deal with, or express the thoughts that arose in it. They made me most awfully sorry for her, anxious to explain her difficulties, whatever they might be, and to soften her loneliness. I was certain that she was lonely.'

She stopped, and after a moment Ronald

Wake continued:

'Well, there we were. For a second we just stood staring at each other. Then she spoke as dispassionately as if the words had no meaning for her. "Good afternoon," she said. "I suppose you are the lady and gentleman that Mr Furnival's expecting. Will you step inside? I'll go and see if he's in his study." She said something else, but her voice was so quiet and bemused that we lost it as she retreated and left us standing on the threshold.

'Then we had time to look at the hall. It was square, and patterned with oak beams and plaster. I'd guessed, as I've told you, that this part of the house was modern, but the rough staircase up which she went was certainly earlier, Tudor, I should say. The furniture was all old and good: four or five chairs, and a long coffer, on which stood a row of brass candlesticks ready for the evening, all beautifully polished. Up to a height of six feet or so the walls were hung with faded Italian tapestries; the very ones, possibly, that you saw in the dining-room at Dulston thirty years ago. And the whole place was full of the smoky light that reached it from that veiled sky of which we've already spoken. It was so extraordinarily quiet, mind you, that when one of the beams of the staircase gave a crack we felt as if something surprising had happened, and looked at each other. I saw that Evelyn's face was flushed.

'"Well, what do you think of it?" I whispered.

'"It's quite beautiful, isn't it?" she said.

'"Could you live in it?" I asked her.

'She hesitated for a moment, and I hung on her hesitation. '"Well," she said at last, "I think it could be made quite comfortable."

'"Do you?" I said. You see, I had put that question as a test, and I'll tell you why. This, mark you, is the plain, literal truth. From the moment I passed the threshold of Cold Harbour, the very instant, my skin had turned into goose-flesh from head to toe. Even when I speak of it now, in cold blood and thousands of miles away, that sensation comes back to me. I wasn't cold, in the ordinary sense, but I felt little shivering ripples running up from my feet, along my spine, over my cheeks, like the discharge of an electric current. I can't explain it. I'd never felt it before, and I've never felt it since, except in thinking or speaking of this story. And I could no more stop it then or now than...'

Wake paused and shrugged his shoulders inside his overcoat. Then he gave a laugh and continued:

'Evidently there was something about the house that reacted curiously on my nerves. I tried to get over it by turning my back on the staircase and looking out into the drive. A long strip of lawn, ending in a rose pergola, ran down toward the wall and the road, but these you couldn't see, for all the further end was a black shrubbery of hollies and old yews. The lawn was smooth and carefully tended. On either side of it lay wide herbaceous borders, hazed with the milky hues of Michaelmas daisies in clumps, and brightened – if one can use that word – by dark-flowered dahlias. But there I found no relief. An autumn garden has a sadness when the sun is not shining, and here it seemed as if that blight in the sky had effaced every colour that disputed it; and beyond all, like sentinels set around a prison, the black, stark beeches kept watch, guarding the sadness within their circle From all influence of the outer world where things were sweet and sane and shared in the illusion of life. And a silence... No robins here, I thought; they wouldn't have the heart to sing. The only mitigation to my hopelessness was the fact that Evelyn evidently didn't share it; I'm still puzzled to imagine why.

'The woman, whom I had taken to be some kind of housekeeper – Alma had told us, you'll remember, that Mrs Furnival was an invalid – came downstairs again. She had elegant brilliant buckles on her black satin shoes. Her face looked like a plaster mask against the darkness of her clothes and of that sombre background. She seemed as worried and preoccupied as ever.

"'I've told Mr Furnival," she said. "Will you come upstairs into the library?"

'We followed her to the first floor and turned into a room that occupied the front of the further wing. Its latticed windows commanded the length of the garden, the high skyline of beeches, and showed us the last kind of interior you'd have expected in such a remote place. That sounds like a contradiction: I know that Cold Harbour is only twelve miles from North Bromwich, with its million odd inhabitants. What I've tried to imply is that the place seemed to have a spiritual isolation of its own. That road, those circling beeches... I won't enlarge on it; you must just take it from me or leave it. We'll get back to the room.

'Obviously, to begin with, it was in the taste of a man of culture. There was nothing in it that wasn't beautiful. A man of erudition, I might almost have said, for the furnishing had been chosen by an eye that was skilled in the details of the period it suggested, and sensitive to incongruities. It was the room, to put it shortly, of a man learned in the Middle Ages, one in which the face of the woman I'd seen through the kitchen window might have taken its place without offence. Perhaps Mr Furnival had chosen her for the job with a sense of her appropriateness.

'My eyes – you know my weakness – went at once to the book shelves. Mr Furnival's interests covered a wide field; and yet, even in that first moment, it was easy to recognise their general direction. Fine printing and binding evidently delighted him. Then I remembered the tapestry downstairs, the skilfully selected furniture. This man, I thought, is what you might call a "Mediaevalist". My eyes began to examine the other shelves in search of confirmation, when I suddenly realized that my eagerness had made me impolite to the woman in black satin on whom I'd abruptly turned my back. I slewed round with an apology on my lips, but she had gone. Nobody there but Evelyn. "Isn't it stiflingly hot?" she said, and I was just wondering whether it would be fair to tell her of my own uncomfortable condition when Mr Furnival entered.

'You'll remember that when I asked Eve to tell me what he looked like the night before, she couldn't do it. It had struck me as funny at the time, but now it seemed more curious than ever, for Mr Furnival wasn't the kind of figure you could easily forget. He came into the room briskly. He still carried with him the quality that you noticed in his Dulston days, an *aura* of intense physical and spiritual energy. I was conscious, I mean, of a compelling personality to which his appearance didn't contribute. At Dulston, twenty years before, you speak of masses of red hair low down on the brows like the fringe of a Highland steer, and a tempestuous beard. You gave me the impression of a caricature of Bernard Shaw; I shouldn't wonder if the master's example hadn't something to do with it. At the back of his head the hair was still there, a fringe of unruly white; but the brow and scalp as far backward as the crown were now completely bald, and his forehead, which you never saw, now showed itself in a high benevolent dome rising smooth above bushy eyebrows. The eyes themselves were deep-set, small, and very blue. His chin was pointed and clean-shaven; his moustache straggled downward. He had a set of white, ill-fitting dentures, but you only saw them when his lip and moustache twitched upward in that characteristic laugh; and, indeed, the huge, smooth forehead was so conspicuous that I could scarcely look at anything else.

'Now for his clothes. Black patent boots, to begin with. Then grey, home-knitted stockings and greenish knickerbockers. The boots came so high on his legs, and the knickerbockers so low, as to exaggerate the bulk and elongation of his figure. Then a black coat, green with age and very greasy, a ready-made tie and a two-inch stand-up collar, fringed and dirty, showing the stud behind.

'But when he spoke, as he did, in a cultured voice, these unsavoury personal details didn't seem to count. It was only when I compelled myself to look at him, at his cold, blue eyes, his false teeth, and, above all, his hands, long, and apparently sensitive, but with bitten fingernails, that I escaped the spell of the voice's persuasiveness. In the dark, I'm prepared to believe that I should have found him charming. In that dim and lovely room there were moments when the voice had its way with me. And not only the voice; for here, as you've suggested, was a man of vast erudition, a lively, exciting mind, and, as far as we were concerned, a nature hospitable and benevolent. I felt, in fact, rather ashamed of the gusts of dislike that passed through my mind as involuntarily as the shivers that still went on wrinkling my skin. There was no reason, it seemed, for either, and yet their existence made me sympathise with the disquietude that had troubled poor Evelyn the night before.

'He came into the room, as I say, carrying with him that aura of energy. The little, shrunken woman crept in gently behind him. He took my hand with a firm grip. "Dr Wake," he said, "pleased to make your acquaintance. Mrs Wake and I have met already." He laughed for the first time. I agreed with Evelyn; the laugh was unpleasant. "I'm sorry to have kept you," he went on. "I was in my study and my wife couldn't find me." The woman behind him gave a faint smile; evidently it was she that he referred to. She passed us and began to speak in whispers to Evelyn. He stood in front of me, sturdy, sanguine, smiling, examining me with his keen, elusive eyes. The silence was unpleasant.

'"It was kind of you to ask us," I said, "though I had no idea how much we should have been missing if we hadn't come."

'"Not at all, not at all," he said. "You must give me credit for knowing that you'd appreciate Cold Harbour. It isn't often that such people as yourselves come near us. I sit here like a spider, and when they come I'm on to them! Ha? We're very lonely here. My wife is an invalid" – he spoke the words almost with satisfaction – "and I am not on friendly terms with the people of our own station in the neighbourhood. I have no use for them, and they have no use for me, with their motor cars and their damned ostentation. Overfed, ignorant, bursting with money. Ha?"

'He went white as he spoke. The laugh with which he ended his sentence was full of hatred. I felt that he'd make an uncomfortable enemy.

'"Well, money has its uses," I said. "The contents of Cold Harbour, for instance, and

113

the house itself. You're a lucky man to have found a place like this; and the place, if I may say so, is lucky to have found a master who appreciates the spirit of it."

'The compliment made him smile. You could see the pride and pleasure burning in him like a red coal. "I flatter myself that you're right," he said. "There's nothing like it in the Midlands. It's unique. I know it, and I'm devoted to it. It's a combination of everything that I want: beauty, isolation, leisure. Unfortunately, Mrs Furnival doesn't agree with me. Ha?"

'When she heard her name, the little thing in black satin gave a jump and looked anxiously toward us; but Furnival offered no explanation, and she caught nothing but his laugh.

'"We'd better go into the garden while it's light," he said. "Come along!" He pulled a check cap on to his head. Now that his baldness was hidden, you might have taken him for a man of fifty. He went downstairs, talking rapidly all the time. The women followed us. I pointed to the tapestries in the hall as we passed through. "Florence," he said. "Yes, Eugene Muntz liked them. Perhaps you've read his books? I knew him well. In those days I knew everybody. Now I know nobody personally, though I manage to keep pretty well abreast of the times."

'We passed out into the garden. Really it

114

was a relief – I can't exactly explain why – to feel the unpleasant pressure of that low roof no longer on the top of me. I looked behind to see what was happening to Evelyn. She and Mrs Furnival were descending side by side in silence. Furnival caught my glance. *"They're* all right," he said. "Trust the women to chatter. Ha?"

'But even the garden was melancholy: on the grass our footsteps made no sound, the quiet, black shrubberies pressed in upon us, beyond them the circle of beeches stood on guard. Do you know what a ghost hedge is? The Romans planted them round certain tombs to keep evil spirits from wandering out into the world again. The idea of a ghost hedge came into my mind when we stood in the middle of Mr Furnival's lawn with the black beeches round us. It seemed to me that there was reason for one; that the atmosphere within that hedge was curiously, definitely evil. I've got to a point, you see, when words are quite inadequate to express my meaning. Words, after all, have been evolved to deal with ordinary experience, while this experience was extraordinary and I make no pretensions to any skill in language. Far more definite than any thought I could formulate was the evidence of my horrified skin and the feeling of hatred – that, at least, is the right word – which now swept over me: hatred for the house, the garden, the presence of Mr Furnival himself.

'All of which, I told myself, was nonsense. In another moment we were talking quite normally and politely about the pains which he had taken to give a feeling of space to the narrow strip of garden which stretched between the house and the road. In this conversation there was nothing sinister. We stood in a little circle, while he spoke with enthusiasm and his own surprising vividness of what he had done. "In my fifteen years," he said, "I've changed the whole aspect of the garden. And with my own hands. Great fun it was too! You see, I took a leaf out of Shenstone's book. The eighteenth-century poet, you know, who used to live under the edge of the hills between here and North Bromwich. He was cramped in the same way, and found it difficult to produce effects of distance, so he planted his avenues as I've done: dark trees, masses of yew and holly and cypress in the foreground, graduating down to paler leaves in the distance. You see? Now, if you'll follow me to the other end," – we did so – "you'll see exactly the opposite effect. That brings the house right on the top of us. Ha?"

'It was true. There it stood, with its dark, grimy brick, a steely light reflected from its windows. It seemed to rise up in front of us monstrously, malignantly, as though it hated us. And God knows I hated it too. If this place were mine, I thought, I'd never rest till I'd got rid of it. I stood there looking at it, so absorbed in hatred that when Furnival took my arm I felt as if he had guessed my feelings.

'"But all that's unimportant," he said. "This is what I want to show you. We found it quite by accident when I was digging holes in which to plant the poles of my pergola. At a depth of three feet, the poles struck what I thought was rock, six of them, one after another, at the same depth. I nearly lost my temper, and gave it up. Lucky I didn't. When I dug down to see what it was all about, we struck the pavement. Here it is. You see, I planted the roses all round it and trained them over to act as a cover."

'He led the way to a circular pit that I had imagined to be an ornamental tank or fish stew. Three feet below the surface, as he had said, lay a small but perfect square of mosaic. Round the margin a key-fret pattern, in the centre a circular medallion, a human figure surrounded by a ring of birds and beasts. "Rough work," he explained. His voice became almost tender as he spoke. "You see, the *tesserae* are almost all of local material. The red ones are just baked tiles; the chocolate colour is the local sandstone; that yellowy white must have been brought here from the Cotswolds; it's oolite. As for the figure, it's quite an ordinary one, a reach-me-down, so to speak: Orpheus and the animals. Some of the books try to suggest that this is a Christian motive, symbolical, you know. But that's all my eye. I have evidence to show that the occupants of this villa, or whatever it was, were not Christians. The place, in fact, has never been remark-able for Christianity. Ha?"

'"There's a biggish church," I suggested, "and Saxon at that."

'He laughed again. "Quite right," he said, "quite right. But that's another story. We'll have a look at it later."

'He left the pavement reluctantly, and held us back for a moment to contemplate the face of the house again. "You've no idea how it grows on one, this building," he said, with an almost pathetic anxiety that we should appreciate it. "The wing on the right—"

'"That's Tudor," I said.

'"Pre-Reformation," he corrected me. "What do the names of reigning houses matter? The central fact of English history is the Reformation."

'He spoke so emphatically that there was nothing more to be said about it. It seemed to annoy him that I didn't take up his chal-lenge, but as I refused to be drawn, he went on talking about the beauties of that horrible house as he saw them. I could see them, too; but that didn't affect my firm conclusion that the place was a bad place, and ought to be destroyed. Curiously enough, I felt that he knew this as well as I did; that he wouldn't insist so desperately on its other qualities if he hadn't been aware of this one.

'So I pulled him up short in the middle of his rhapsody. "Isn't there some story," I said, "about the house being haunted?"

His mouth twitched up into the shape of a laugh. "Who told you that?" he said. At that moment my eye caught Mrs Furnival's. I don't think I've ever seen such a degree of misery in the eyes of a living creature. She stood there, rapt, her hands clasped before her – such white, soft, helpless hands! "Ah, Alma," he went on. "Poor little Alma at the Fox. These people's lives are so empty that they have nothing else to think about."

'"But it *is* haunted, isn't it?" said Evelyn timidly. "Don't spoil my illusion by telling me there's nothing in it."

'"There's enough in it," said Furnival vindictively, "to have turned my poor missus into a Papist. That's something, anyway." As he laughed he looked at the poor woman as though he could kill her. She answered him with a pale, pathetic smile, but the misery was still in her eyes.

'"Do tell us," said Evelyn, persuasively.

'"I know nothing about it," said Furnival. "I've never seen, felt, or smelt anything at Cold Harbour that wasn't perfectly normal.

I can't be more definite than that, can I? Ha?"

'But Evelyn stuck to her guns. "Perhaps other people–" she began.

'"Other people?" he said. "Only a lot of neurotic women and priests. If people are gullible enough to accept a conglomeration of nonsense like the Roman Catholic dogmas, they'd accept anything. Don't you agree with me?"

'"But if a lot of people have ... experienced things," Evelyn persisted, "surely there must be something in it? Do tell us ... just one incident."

'He smiled at her. In spite of his scathing words, I could guess that where women were concerned he was anxious to please. "Very well," he said, "I'll tell you. But please understand that I take no responsibility. I consider the whole business absolute nonsense. Do you know what a Poltergeist is? Of course you don't; they didn't exist; but Mrs Furnival's friends believe in them, and you know what I mean. Well, the fellow we've got here, according to my missus and the priests, is called Jerry. That's our private name for him. The priests love him, and he loves priests. Some years ago we had one of these gentlemen staying here–"

'"He belonged to the Church of England," Mrs Furnival mildly suggested.

'"At that time, yes," said Furnival with a

smirk, "but Jerry turned him Papist, too. Well, this poor fellow – his name was Lowe – was positively hagridden on his last visit here; if you believe him, that is. Jerry would never let him sleep. One night he went to bed as usual and folded up his clothes on a chair at the foot of the bed. Now, Mrs Wake, do you know what a man's braces are like? Just where the straps that go on the buttons at the front come off there's usually a closed metal buckle. Very well. And on a man's drawers – pants is the polite word – there are little loops through which the straps of the braces pass before they button. Now, when Mr Lowe woke up in the morning he found that Jerry had run the loop of the pants through the buckle of the braces so that they were fixed like links in a chain. That's a small thing to be frightened of, isn't it? But Mr Lowe was so upset that he changed his trousers and brought the ones Jerry had tampered with down to breakfast. We all tried to undo the loop. Of course we couldn't. Then my little daughter Elaine said, 'Let me have a try,' and the thing came adrift in her hands. Oh, yes, Mr Lowe might have had quite a lot of fun with Jerry if he'd had a sense of humour, but he took it all too seriously. Said he'd never stay in the house again, which was no loss to us, and wrote me an insane letter. I've got it still: one of Jerry's best testimonials. He implored me, whatever it might cost and however inconvenient it might be, to leave – what did he say, Jane? 'a house that was evidently under fire from hostile influences whose power we were unable, to measure'. Quite in the grand manner. And all that because of a pair of braces! Ha-ha!"

'Mrs Furnival shook her head but did not speak. "And is that really all?" Evelyn asked.

'"Not quite all," said Furnival. "There's another story of a girl who came here as governess to my children ten or twelve years ago. She was a methodical creature, who always put her watch on the bedtable when she wound it up at night. And every morning when she woke up she complained that it was moved to some other place. It got on her nerves, poor dear. 'Well,' said I, 'why the devil don't you put it under your pillow?' So she did. Next morning I asked her what had happened. 'My watch was all right,' said she, 'but the candle that I'd blown out on the bedside table was moved to the top of a high wardrobe. I couldn't reach it, even with a chair.' Of course every one said, 'Jerry'."

'"We always tried to make a joke of him," said Mrs Furnival gently, "for the children's sake."

'"Exactly," Furnival broke in with some irritation, "as you see, it's all so trivial and childish and unimportant that nobody should have made a fuss about it."

'"What happened to the governess?" Evelyn asked.

'"She left us. The poor thing couldn't stand it," murmured Mrs Furnival.

'"And here we are," said Furnival suddenly, "wasting the precious light over superstitious nonsense. Pull yourself together, Jane, and take care of Mrs Wake while I show the doctor my treasures."

'We walked up to the house again. I felt like an animal being driven into a butcher's pen. I wondered if Evelyn shared my feelings and was prepared to refuse to leave her; but when I looked round I saw the two women following us quite happily, talking in an undertone together. And Mrs Furnival had taken her hand. So it seemed all right. As we re-entered the house, a new set of shivers ran up my spine. I determined to fight against it. Jerry, at any rate, I told myself, had nothing to do with that. Indeed, if his were the only sort of possession to which the house was subject, there seemed very little to worry about. So Furnival himself had suggested; and I, like most medical men whose training has been concentrated on physical signs, was inclined to be sceptical. I don't suppose I should have thought much more about it if it hadn't been for the exaggerated eagerness with which Furnival had tried to turn the poor Poltergeist to ridicule, combined with the misery that had come into his wife's eyes when the matter was first mentioned. As for my own shivering discomfort, I think I should have put that down to the dampness of Mrs Higgins's sheets.

'Furnival led the way up two flights of staircase, three wide steps at a time. He was as nimble and full of bursting energy as a boy. Extraordinary, for a man of his stature. Then he darted in front of me along a dark passage to the foot of another stairway. "That's the room," he jerked over his shoulder, "where the parson lost his trousers." The walls of the passage were so dark that no door could be seen, and before I could ask him anything more I stood panting on the landing outside his study.

'"Isn't this a room now?" he said to me. His eyes positively glistened with pride. "Can you imagine anything better for a man of my tastes? This view over the Black Country. So vast, so sombre. Ha? Isn't it worth a hundred sentimental landscapes? Stormy sunsets beyond the Clees; and then, at night, you know, with the furnaces spouting and pit fires smoking, it's like looking down into hell from the battlements of heaven. Quiet, too. No women's voices. Ha?" He swaggered with his hands in his pockets: he was like a boisterous schoolboy. "Doesn't it fit me like a glove?" Then his eyes blazed: "And that's what the Missus wants me to leave. I'll see them all damned first! See them damned first!" he repeated with a laugh that was like a scream.

'Then, just as if he were ashamed of showing so much feeling, off he switched into another key, suave, urbane, too, too polite for words. "Now, Dr Wake, what can I show you? As you see, there are plenty of books. In my young days, when I was richer, I was something of a collector. First editions here. Manuscripts ... and that reminds me; poor Mrs Wake, who's downstairs being bored by my wife, wanted to see Martock's. Here they are, all the lot of them. A queer devil, Martock: I very nearly saw him die. If I'd stayed another night I might have had that pleasure. Deathbeds of men of genius; what do they see? Ha? But business, business!"

'I stood there listening to him, turning over the pages of that manuscript that Evelyn would have given her eyes to touch. I didn't read a word of it. I'd seen nothing until he snatched the book out of my hands. "Volumes of Art Criticism," he went on. "Years of futility. You can't teach men to see beauty; either the faculty's there or it isn't, and if people haven't got it by birthright, it's no good teaching them to pretend they have. That's what it amounts to. No acquired knowledge is worth a damn; but I suppose stupid people have to acquire it for purposes of showing off. And how I hate 'em! I wonder if you know a beautiful thing when you see it. Ha?" He thrust a small statuette into my hands, and stood challenging me with a stare; but before I could answer he'd snatched it away. "Modern," he snapped. "Mestrovic. Ancient or modern, beauty is just the same. All through the arts, all through the ages, every one of them. And who'll find the common aesthetic basis? Not me, for one. But I know, Dr Wake, I know."

'I can't attempt to keep pace with the spate, the whirlwind of talk that swept over me. I can't do justice, either, to what it contained. I don't suppose, as a matter of fact, that what he said mattered much. It was the man himself. By this time it had begun to rain; a black squall darkened the sky and thrashed the windowpanes, so that the room grew dim; and in the dimness this extraordinary creature's mind smouldered and glowed and flamed like a furnace. I imagine he didn't often get the chance of flaming before an audience and now seized his opportunity. When he came close up to me I could almost feel the palpitating heat of his brain. Amazing...

'I must have spent at least half an hour there listening to him and peering at the lovely things he showed me: Greek, Roman, Egyptian. That long, irregular room was more inspiring than any museum, because,' he hesitated, 'because each of its beauties seemed to catch fire from the ardent spirit of its owner. Fire played between them and him as between two magnetic poles.

'Then, suddenly abandoning his treasures, he began to talk of religion, or rather of comparative religion. In this department his library was enormous, and when he spoke of it you would have imagined that he had no other interest in life. We spoke of black magic. "Now, that's a ticklish subject," he said. "If you want to study it, here's your chance. It's played a big part in the history of your learned profession." He showed me three shelves crammed with curious books on the subject. "I hope you approve my arrangement," he said: "witchcraft, psychic research, and insanity, ha?" and from these we drifted away to Mithras and his cult in Roman Britain.

'I told him that I had seen the Mithraic grottoes on Hadrian's wall. He nodded his head impatiently: of course, he knew more about them than I did. "But talking of Roman Britain," he said, "we've wandered off into so many fascinating byways that we've forgotten all about the things in which you're principally interested. This spring I had a busy time excavating a series of graves placed, as you'd expect them, along the sides of the road where it enters my property."

'He led me in the dusk – the sky was still

dark with storm – into a large curtained alcove. The whole room was so full of irregularities that I've forgotten its shape: a number of rambling attics of different levels knocked together. In this alcove stood a black oak table, like a carpenter's bench, littered with lamps of red pottery, green glass, glazed Samian, and little white clay figures. He passed them by contemptuously.

"This is all funerary junk," he said. "No bones: all the burials were pre-Christian. There's nothing really worth looking at; nothing, I mean, that you can't see better specimens of in the museums. Of course, for me, it has the sentimental interest of a private discovery; but I don't advise you to waste your time on it. Ah, there's one thing here." He handed me a dagger, heavy but slender, covered with a green patina. "Bronze," he said, "Celtic. Feel the point of it. In spite of two thousand years, it's still up to its job. I shouldn't like to get that point under the ribs, ha? Of course, I've cleaned it up and shaped it a bit. My sacrificial knife, I call it. That's rot, of course; but all the same I found it near to this."

'He pointed to an object which looked to me, in the darkness, like an oblong chest set up on end and covered with a piece of black velvet. He stood contemplating it with affection.

'"I'll tell you how I got it,' he said. 'Central

heating, that's the explanation. Last winter we had to put down a furnace and a boiler underground. The best place for it seemed to be a disused scullery at the old end of the house. There wasn't any cellar beneath it, so we had to dig down under a paved floor. I wasn't expecting anything, but in a place like this one has to be always on the lookout. And this is what we found; nothing else!"

'With a gesture that was almost theatrical, he swept off the black velvet cover and lit a candle that stood on the end of the bench. Then he stood waiting for me to catch the fire of his controlled enthusiasm.

'"It looks to me like a votive altar," I said.

'"And that's what it is!" he laughed. "Rough work: the local Permian sandstone, badly used by weather. No decoration; only the plain inscription. Can you read it? No; the light's too bad; but that doesn't matter. It's Greek. I'll translate:

'Thou seest me, an altar of Astarte. Gaius, Centurion of the Twentieth Legion, *Valeria Victrix*, set me up.'

What do you make of that?"

His laugh was so shrill as to be positively embarrassing. I felt that anything I might say in reply would sound feeble and inadequate. "It's remarkably interesting."

'"Interesting?" he screamed. "I should just

think it was! Do you realize that there's only one other altar to Astarte in Britain, at Corbridge on the Wall? But that's nothing. Who the hell was Gaius? And what was the Twentieth Legion doing here?"

'I pulled my wits together. The Twentieth Legion, I told him, was stationed at Chester: its badge, a charging boar, was often seen on monuments there. "Quite right," said he. "The Twentieth was at Deva; but the Cold Harbour tombstones all relate to the fourteenth. Now I'll tell you something. When Suetonius went east to deal with the lady whom the English persist in calling Boadicea, he reinforced the fourteenth legion, of which we have evidence on this spot, with a *vexillatio*, shock troops, of the Twentieth. And when the lady Boudicca, as I call her, had been dealt with, the centurion Gaius must have been left here with the legionary detachment to which he'd been seconded. And here he set up his altar to Astarte, the Goddess of Groves. Now do you see light? Ha?" He rubbed his hands in ecstasy. "Remember the name of the place: Cold Harbour, the Colony of Trees. Why not the Colony of the Grove? Have you seen the great circle of beeches that surrounds the house? I don't suggest that the beeches are Roman, but what I do believe is that they have replaced, or their ancestors replaced, a circle deliberately planted by this Gaius; that this is the one place in Britain, apart from that isolated fort on the Wall in which the Syrian Mysteries were celebrated."

'"It's a pretty theory," I admitted, rather grudgingly.

'"Theory?" he snorted. "I tell you it's a fact. I *know*."

'He made the whole thing so dramatic that I couldn't help smiling. "No doubt," I said, "your library in black magic has enabled you to obtain an interview with the centurion or perhaps with Astarte herself?"

'With him it was no joking matter. He said nothing, but he glared at me with the same look of insane hatred that I had already intercepted on its way to Mrs Furnival in the garden. I assure you it was most uncomfortable; I didn't know for a moment what would be the end of it, when suddenly his mouth twitched up into another laugh.

'"Let's go downstairs," he said, "and see what the women are doing. What about a whisky and soda before tea?"

'I refused as politely as I could, but that didn't prevent him mixing a stiff drink for himself. On the landing it seemed to me that I heard Evelyn's voice, but there was no sound of footsteps and nothing to be seen, and so we moved down the stairs in silence, returning to the room in which he had received us.

'From the moment when we had left

Furnival's study, neither of us had spoken, and now it seemed as if this strange silence must continue. Furnival himself stood with legs wide apart in front of the fire, a sturdy, prepotent figure; and I, without knowing what I did, found myself standing in front of a sort of lectern, on which the beautifully printed seventeenth-century Bible lay open before me. I don't know how it was, but, as I turned the pages, my eyes fell on a single verse that seemed to detach itself from the rest and force itself on my attention. I can't tell you to which of the books of the Bible it belongs, and at this moment I can't even be certain of quoting it accurately, but this is, more or less, what I found myself reading:

"There shall not be found anyone among you that useth divination, or an observer of times, or an enchanter, or a charmer, or a consulter with familiar spirits, or a necromancer. For all that do these things are an abomination unto the Lord..."

'And as I read these words – I find it quite impossible to express the feeling exactly – it seemed as if all the influence that had shivered my skin to goose-flesh rushed upward into my brain, so that I lost consciousness of every blessed feeling but an overpowering murderous desire to destroy Furnival as he stood there toasting his calves. Before that I'd been puzzled by him; if I'd disliked him the dislike had been quite indefinite, but now my whole brain seemed to be swept up into a positive conflagration of hate. I looked up from my book. Our eyes met. He answered with a normal, innocent smile. But that made no difference. Once or twice during the war I caught myself seeing red, but nothing like that! God only knows what would have happened if at that very instant Evelyn and Mrs Furnival hadn't entered the room.'

Chapter Five

Mrs Furnival

He stopped, and the voice of Evelyn Wake continued:

'You left me at the point when we all came in from the garden together, and Mr Furnival carried Ronald off upstairs to his study. He's told you that he didn't like leaving me. Well, I'm sure I felt it more than he did; not because I was frightened by the stories about "Jerry" – I'm not the sort of person who sees ghosts, so those things don't worry me – but because he seemed to be dragged away from me by something invisible, like the undertow of a tide.

'But in any case, quite apart from any question of good manners, I couldn't have followed him. Mrs Furnival clung so tightly to my arm with her little, podgy fingers, just as if she, too, were frightened of getting out of her depth. I'm not much of a swimmer myself, but I felt bound to give her my moral support, whatever good it might do her! Why? Well, to begin with, she was a woman, and married to that white-haired monstrosity; I was sorry for her, and liked

134

her most awfully. It seemed queer that she should have found it comforting to take the arm of a stranger like myself. It showed how lonely she was, and rather flattered me as well: it gave me a sense of responsibility and trust that took some "living up to".

'As Ronald has told you, she had been whispering to me in the garden, but there was nothing at all mysterious in that. She just went on talking innocently, like a child, about the flowers – she really loved flowers – and her husband's skill in gardening. Evidently she was tremendously wrapped up in him in spite of his weirdness. It was, "Mr Furnival says this", and "Mr Furnival does that", all the time. Of course, she may have been trying to make me think she was happily married, though any one with two eyes could see she wasn't. Women *do* talk like that; particularly with other women. But, honestly, I don't think she was clever enough to pretend. For better, for worse, she was devoted to him, and thought that there was nobody like him on earth. As far as that goes, I think she was just about right. There wasn't.

'But, weak and spare and pitiful as she seemed, there was something very sweet about her that compelled me to be gentle. For instance, no woman who wasn't an angel could have put up with the digs that he kept on giving her about her religion. When people go to the trouble of changing their faith, it stands to reason that they must feel strongly about it, and yet she showed no resentment when he made fun of her conversion. The only time that she appeared to be distressed was when he spoke about the haunting of the house. Then Ronald says he saw her eyes go miserable. I didn't notice her eyes, but her hand tightened on mine, oh! so pathetically, that I felt I wanted to take the little thing into my arms. And even then she reassured me with a smile.

'Well, there we were, standing in the hall, and Ronald swept away from me. When the men had disappeared, we followed them upstairs at about a quarter their pace. Mrs Furnival went very slowly, pausing for breath: she said something later on about "her poor heart". At the top of the first flight, she led me into that long room where all the books were. The fire had burned up brightly: it was very cosy. It smelt as if they had been burning cedar, I told her.

'"Ah, that's incense," she said. "Mr Furnival must have thrown some on the fire. He's very fond of it."

'"How contradictory!" I said. "Just now he seemed very bitter about your having become a Catholic."

'"Oh yes," she said. "But Mr Furnival is a deeply religious man all the same. He always serves at the Eucharist. He's an Anglican

Catholic, you know, and Anglicans are awfully fond of incense." All through this she was moving aimlessly about the room, pulling the chairs from one place to another, and patting the cushions. "Come along, my dear," she said, "let's make ourselves comfy. We shan't see the gentlemen for another hour: I know what Mr Furnival is when once he gets talkin' about books and that."

'She made me lean back in an easy chair facing the fire. Then she pulled up a big satin pouff and perched beside me. After that, there came a long silence that made me want to get up and shout to make sure that I was myself. Everything there seemed so unreal. I wonder if you understand?

'No. Of course you don't. And yet I can't tell you how thankful I was when she began to talk. By this time she had got hold of my hand again, and as she spoke she kept on fondling it.

'"I know it must sound odd to a stranger," she said, "the way in which Mr Furnival talks about my conversion. But you mustn't judge him harshly; it isn't his fault. Mr Furnival is a man with a very strong mind, much stronger than mine. He's so much cleverer than anyone else, you see, that he finds it impossible to put himself in the place of stupid people like myself. He doesn't realize that if I *hadn't* become a Catholic I couldn't possibly have gone on living here. I think my mind would have given way, my dear; and if I weren't here to look after him, heaven knows what would happen to him! You see, he is so wrapped up in his studying and investigations that he has no time to think about his own comfort; and he has such a practical, sunny nature that he doesn't see what a terrible house this is."

'"But if the house is as terrible as all that,' I said, 'why don't you persuade him to leave it?"

'"My dear," she said, "you don't realize what you're saying. Mr Furnival adores it; he's bewitched by it. I think he'd rather sacrifice his life than leave Cold Harbour. He can't see anything abnormal; he simply *can't* see it; he's blind to it. That is his terrible misfortune. That is the awful, awful danger!"

'Her words didn't mean much to me: her behaviour all along had been so queer that by this time I felt sure that she wasn't quite sane. I told myself that nothing that she said really mattered for that very reason, and that it was my duty to let her go on talking for the good of her soul, so I made up my mind to sit through it and keep my end up until Ronald returned.

'"Please be patient with me," I said, "if I seem to be dull, but really I don't understand you. Why is Mr Furnival in danger? What sort of danger is he in?"

'She hesitated. "In danger of his life," she said slowly. "But that's nothing to the danger of his immortal soul. If God would only give him the power to see! If my prayers could help him to see for himself! But he won't. He can't. They've hardened his heart. He's possessed, my dear. Possessed. And nothing that I can do is strong enough to release him. Nothing but a miracle or the power of some living saint can do that. It's too terrible ... terrible!"

'"But what, exactly, is terrible?" I asked her.

'"The house, and the dreadful influences in the house," she said. "You know what Mr Furnival said to us in the garden: that he'd never seen, heard, or felt anything? When we joked about Jerry? It's a silly name, isn't it? But it was the best I could do. I invented it myself, as I told you, so as to conceal the awful reality from the children. Thank God! they've all grown up and left us now and found safe places to live in. It was the happiest day I've known in Cold Harbour when the youngest left us. That's a funny thing for a mother to say, and yet I say it from the bottom of my heart."

'"But, after all," I said, "the things that Mr Furnival told us – about the governess' candle and the clergyman's braces, you know – didn't seem to me so very dreadful as all that. We've often heard tales of that

139

kind about houses before. And people just laugh at them, as you did. Honestly, if that's all you have to complain of–"

'"Oh, my dear," she broke in, "you don't know what you're talking about. Of course, that's nothing ... *nothing*. It wouldn't frighten me a bit if that table in the corner were lifted up this moment and placed in front of the fire. Things like that – oh, well, they're nothing at all to me. But this house – what a blessed thing it is for you that you don't feel it! – this house is full of other influences: not poor, dead memories whose shadows we can see, but forces of active evil. Just as Mr Lowe said in his letter: 'hostile influences whose power we are unable to measure'. You remember how Mr Furnival made fun of that? But Mr Lowe realized the seriousness of it; he knew something about it. Perhaps he knows more about it now that he's gone. He was such a good man."

'She stopped, and I made no reply. I suppose that was what encouraged her. From that moment her story came gushing out like water from a sluice. Nothing that I said could have stopped her, so I thought I'd better let her go on. It was so monotonous and steady that I scarcely listened to her at first; I began to feel sleepy.

'"It began twenty years ago," she said. "At that time we were living seven miles from here, over at Dulston. I say seven or eight miles, but really, my dear, it was quite another world. You see, in those days Mr Furnival was in business. As you see him now, you wouldn't think that he had ever been a business man, would you? But whatever he put his hand to, there'd always be the same cleverness: people often told me, in confidence, what a remarkable man he was. We were very happy in Dulston: all the children were born there, you see, and the house was one that we'd built for ourselves – so cheerful, and clean, and easy to work.

'"Then Mr Furnival had a great blow. You see, his mind worked faster than the others', and that made them jealous of him. Anyway, things went wrong, and the directors wouldn't back him up. For a short time he was very ill; I really feared that he was going out of his mind, but then his brain's so very strong that I doubt if anything could do that. He lost a lot of money, too; we had plenty to spare, thank heaven, so that didn't make much difference, but we were forced to leave Dulston, which was a dreadful pity, I'd become so attached to the house and that.

'"You see, when Mr Furnival had got over his blow, he said, quite naturally too, that he'd never put all his strength again into work that wasn't appreciated. He'd finished with work, he said, and I agreed with him, as I always do, though it did seem a pity, too, for a man in the prime of life like him. He just set off one day on his bicycle – he was a great cyclist – and I heard no more of him for a fortnight, after which he wired for us to join him at a place called Lapton Huish in Devonshire, where he'd taken half a farm on Lord Habberton's estate.

'"Such a lovely spot it was, too! The farming people were so kind to us, in spite of being dissenters, and the children had the time of their lives, what with country air and scalded cream and that. Mr Furnival furnished a room of his own that he crammed full of books, he used to spend his time in study and taking long walks and rides through the country. He knew much more about the churches than the people themselves. And yet he wasn't happy.

'"You see, he's so energetic, my dear, that a quiet life of that kind couldn't content him. He might have spent his time in educating the children, but he preferred to let them run wild. That was his theory, you see; of course, it was difficult for him, with all his learning, to put himself on their level, and, after all, health is the only thing that matters when highly strung children are concerned. They took after him in that.

'"Of course, I knew that Mr Furnival, being what he is, wouldn't put up with such a quiet life for ever. All the time he was looking round for something more in his line, as you might say, and at the end of five years, the happiest years of my life, I think, he came and told me that he'd taken a long lease of a house in Worcestershire, of this house, in fact, and back we all came.

"'I didn't like it from the first. Naturally, it was a strain to begin housekeeping again after so long an interval. But one's duty lies with one's husband, and he was mad on it; quite his old self, in fact. I remember the first day we drove up here. It was an autumn afternoon like this: not a leaf on the trees – it's the fumes from the Black Country, you know, that make them fall so early – and the garden in such an awful tangle because the place hadn't been occupied for years. Oh, my heart simply sank within me when I saw it, for it was so cheerless, such a contrast to Lapton, where the dear children had almost lived in the sun. Mr Furnival only laughed at me. Well, I thought, it's a mercy anyway that he's got over his blow, and really it was a treat to see the pride he took in it. It made a young man of him again.

"'We all put up at the Fox for a month. In those days, poor Mr Higgins was alive, and Mrs Higgins made us very comfortable. While we were there, Mr Furnival and the children used to spend all their time up here. It seemed strange to me that they didn't notice the difference from Lapton; but novelty, of course, is everything to children, and it was my duty to make the best of it, though you can't conceive how hard a task that was; it's impossible for me to tell you how I hated Cold harbour even then.

'"To begin with, it was so dark. I begged Mr Furnival to put in the electric light, but he said he couldn't afford it – something about fire insurance – and that it would spoil the character of the place. Then I hated those trees: the beeches that you see through this window. They seemed to shut the place in so. I asked him to have them cut down, but he wouldn't hear of it. And then I didn't like the house being next to the churchyard – it's just the other side of this wall, you know – because a thing like that couldn't possibly be healthy for the children, though, of course, it was an advantage having the church so near. Mr Furnival and myself quite agreed on that, for although he's so naughty about my conversion, he's really a deeply religious man in his own way.

'"Still, I went on feeling unhappy. Mr Furnival said it was the change of climate, and made me see a doctor about it, but I knew for certain it wasn't that. It was only when I came to Cold Harbour that I was miserable: I was quite contented as long as I could stay on at the Fox. I used to tell him that I felt sure there was something wrong with the drains, but he wouldn't have it. It was the place he'd been looking for all his life, he said, and, after all, he came first, didn't he?

'"One evening, I went back to the inn so wretched that I simply had to tell Mr Higgins about it. He seemed to understand at once. 'Why, don't you know,' he said, 'yonder old place is haunted? I thought everyone in these parts knew that.'

'"I told Mr Furnival what he had said, and that made him quite angry. 'What, you call yourself a Christian,' he said, 'and allow yourself to be frightened by pagan superstitions?' Of course, he was perfectly right. I knew I had only shown him my lack of faith; but the vicar who lived at Cold Harbour then was a dreadfully low churchman and wouldn't hear confessions, so I couldn't get any spiritual comfort from him. Shortly afterwards Mr Furnival quarrelled with him, as was quite natural, and the living was never filled until Mr Lowe came.

'"So, at the end of a month or rather more, we moved here. I tried to be as cheerful as I could. I took a tonic that the doctor had given me, and nothing happened, I'm thankful to say, for several months. Of course, I felt just as dreadful as I knew I should, but Mr Furnival was so pleased and excited, and the dear children, thank heaven, seemed so insensitive to the awful feelings I had, that I persuaded myself I was suffering

145

from the lack of faith that Mr Furnival had pointed out to me, and tried my very hardest to make the best of it. I never referred to my own discomfort if I could avoid it, and then, naturally, not in the presence of the children.

'"That wasn't easy, I can assure you. We kept on having reminders that the place wasn't what it should be. We had great difficulty, for instance, in getting servants, and then, after a year or two, Rose, an old servant who'd been with us at Dulston, insisted on leaving without any explanation. This made Mr Furnival very angry. The next one had no complaints to make, so he insisted that we should dispense with a second servant, he said that we'd spent so much money coming into the house that it was our duty to economise, and really I'd no objection to that, because there's nothing like work for filling your mind. She's still with us. She's one of the lucky ones like Mr Furnival. She's been with us thirteen years, and we feel that it's better to put up with her temper than to run the risk of – well, you know what I mean.

'"Of course I was unlucky. From the moment that we came into the house I began to have experiences: nothing of the kind that have happened since, but still experiences that were disturbing until you got used to them: the things that had driven poor Rose – that was the housemaid – away.

Within a week or two I had realized that we had company. I mean that ours were not the only spirits in the house. At first it gave me a great fright to see a woman dressed like a nun coming down the stairs, and a strange man with a cassock in the kitchen passage. Of course it *was* frightening, but it soon became clear that I was the only person who saw them, and that they, poor things, were just as harmless as shadows.

"'When I told Mr Furnival, he was only amused. He said they were heirlooms and increased the value of the house. Some years later, my eldest daughter, Guenivere, told me that she had often seen them too, but had been afraid to mention it, because she knew that her father would laugh at her. It's such a pity! The children were always afraid of him, but I suppose that's often the case, and Mr Furnival has always lived, as they say, in a world of his own. Still, my heart bled for poor Guen when she told me. It's unjust, isn't it, that a child should experience such strange things? She told me that she and Elaine had names for all of them, under which they used to mention them in their prayers. Pathetic, isn't it? Enid hadn't come to us at that time. Did I mention her before? I don't believe I did. She was my little stepsister who came to live with us when her poor mother died. Of course, I felt like a mother toward her, myself, and Mr Furnival was devoted to her too, almost more than to our own. Yes ... she was one of the lucky ones.

"'Now I've gone and lost the thread. My memory's dreadful nowadays. The phantoms? Ah, yes, how stupid of me! After a time, I grew so used to them that now when I meet them I take them quite as a matter of course. What I never could get used to, and never shall, was the feeling of other presences behind all this: presences and influences too. I'm afraid I'm not clever enough to express it. Mr Furnival could do so in a moment, but then he, of course, has never felt them.

"'After a bit we began to have visitors in the house, and then I knew how real they were. You might have thought that it would make it easier to know that I wasn't going mad, as I'd often thought I was. *You* don't think I'm mad, do you? But it didn't. It just proved that I wasn't. It couldn't be possible that half our visitors were going out of their senses. I was almost thankful when Mr Furnival and the low church clergyman at the vicarage quarrelled, and he decided to give the living to Mr Lowe, who understood our ways. The man who left was really a very unpleasant person apart from his beliefs, he left the vicarage in a dreadful state, and as he hadn't any money, Mr Furnival generously paid for all the dilapidations. While the repairs were going on, Mr Lowe came to stay with us in the house.

"'That was the time when Jerry began his tricks. I expect it sounds irreverent to talk of a spirit like that, but we're so used to him now, and he really *is* so harmless, that it seems quite natural. It's just like having a defective and mischievous child in the house: we don't really take him seriously. You see, it isn't as if he were our own. But, of course, it was very trying for the dear abbot – Mr Lowe, I mean – and for poor Miss Hemus. You remember the story about the watch? It got on her nerves so much that she had to leave us, and after she'd gone we never heard a word from her. I often think of her, and wonder where she is. But that's what happens: when once people have gone from us they don't seem ever to want to think of Cold Harbour. They pass right out of our lives. Yes ... I'm forgetting. Miss Hemus had some sort of disagreement with Mr Furnival. She wouldn't tell me what it was about. Education, I expect. That's a thing in which I don't consider myself qualified to interfere. But that's another funny thing: part of the influence of the house, it does, actually, seem to make people fall out with one another. Isn't that dreadful? Don't you think so?

"'Let me see, where was I? Oh, Mr Lowe, of course ... I don't think Jerry's antics seriously upset him, though he was the person who had started them. Of course, they were an inconvenience to him, but he was a man of very strong faith and bore them with great dignity, and if that had been all I think he would have held on till the end. The terrible thing was that the more he despised him, the more outrageous Jerry became. Mr Furnival thought it all a joke, and I'm sure that was the right attitude, in a way, for all our sakes, though poor Mr Lowe couldn't see it.

'"And then one day Mr Lowe came to me in this very room and sat down in the chair that you're sitting in. 'Mrs Furnival,' he said, 'I can't go on being hagridden in this manner. I've come to the end of my tether. I thought that I was secure in the Armour of Light, but I was mistaken. I've now reached a point when I can't stay another night in this house.'

'"It came as an awful shock to me, my dear, because I'd been counting so much on his goodness and strength as a support to myself. I begged him to reconsider; but it wasn't a bit of good. 'No, Mrs Furnival,' he said. 'I've made up my mind. I've come to the conclusion that the salvation of my soul is at stake: the risk is too great. And if you take my advice, you'll do the same. It's your duty to yourself and your children to leave Cold Harbour.'

'"I told him that that was quite out of the question; that we'd only just moved in at an enormous expense, and that I knew Mr Furnival was devoted to the place, and wouldn't listen to the idea for a moment. 'That is what I feared,' he said, 'and in some ways that appears to me the most terrible feature of the affair. Mr Furnival declares that he feels nothing, and I believe he speaks the truth. *Why* does he feel nothing when all the rest of us are weighed down with horror? Because they won't let him, Mrs Furnival; because he, poor man, is already in their power.'

"'I saw there was no moving him. 'Well, Mr Lowe,' I said, 'we must do the best we can. I'll try to put up a bed for you somewhere in the vicarage. It'll have to be downstairs, for the paper-hangers haven't finished with the bedrooms.' He shook his head; the poor man's eyes were full of tears. 'No, Mrs Furnival,' he said. 'That's no good. I shall never live in the Vicarage. I am going into retreat near Oxford. This morning I wrote a letter to Mr Furnival resigning the living. I've told you that my soul is not safe here within the – now, what did he call it? – the radius of the house's activity. Even in the church itself I'm not safe,' he said.

"'I asked him what he meant, it seemed such a terrible thing to say. 'You're forcing me to confess my own degradation,' he said. 'Well, it's best that you should know the worst. This is the truth. During the whole of the last week I have felt this evil influence growing on me, and now, to my shame, the devil has got the better of me, of *me*, Mrs Furnival, a priest in Holy Orders. For the last thirty-six hours I have been unable to pray.'

'"After that he broke down completely. I tried to comfort him, but what could I do? 'Let's pray together, Mr Lowe,' I said. "When two or three are gathered together in My name..." 'God bless you, Mrs Furnival,' he said, 'you're stronger than I am.' Of course, it wasn't true, for Mr Lowe was a real saint; but we knelt down together on the hearthrug here, with no sound but the clock ticking in the corner, just as it is now. And after a few moments up he jumped. 'It's no good,' he said, 'it's no good. I am lost. How can I expect to pray in this accursed place when even the church will not protect me? I must go now, at once. I've left the letter to your husband in my bedroom. Will you be kind enough to give it to him?' I promised to do so. I didn't know what I was saying, his face was so truly terrible. And he went. He went straight out of that door, and I never saw him again. We heard that he went out as a missionary to Africa, the Universities Mission I think they call it, and died of blackwater fever some years later. But don't you think that is dreadful? Perfectly dreadful?"

'She waited for me to answer, and naturally I could only say that it was. In the interval, she sat perched on her pouff, with her soft hands clasped in front of her, and a face that was absolutely blank with misery. I forced myself to break the silence.

'"That letter," I said, "was the one from which Mr Furnival was quoting just now?"

'"Yes," she answered. "That was the one. Mr Furnival was positively enraged by it. You see, he *couldn't* understand: it wasn't really his fault. And he wrote Mr Lowe a violent, scathing letter in reply, which Mr Lowe acknowledged. Then Mr Furnival sent the correspondence to the Bishop, but what could the Bishop do? It *is* dreadful, isn't it? But not as dreadful, not nearly as dreadful, as what followed.

'"Miss Harrow. Old Doctor Harrow was the rector of Lapton, you know. Dear, dear. I'm forgetting Muriel. She was a second cousin of Mr Furnival's. Such a dear! You can imagine what a relief it was to me to have another lady with me in the house. It was a pleasure to see her here with her high spirits, joking all the time with Mr Furnival, who's always at his very best when young girls are about. I loved watching them together; and yet, from the moment she arrived, I was frightened to think how they would receive her. Fortunately, it seemed as though she were going to be one of the lucky ones, and everything went quite well until the following Sunday.

"'I ought to have told you that after his disappointment in poor Mr Lowe, Mr Furnival took no steps to fill the living, he made arrangements with the Rector of Halesby to send over his curate to Cold Harbour twice a week for the necessary services. Well, Muriel went to church in the ordinary way on Sunday morning. Of course, Mr Furnival and myself had driven over to Stourton for early service before breakfast, as we always did, but Muriel had been brought up in a very Protestant household, and went to communicate here. For some reason or other, I stayed at home that morning. When she came back, I was arranging the flowers on the table over there. Of course, from the moment she entered, I saw that there was something the matter. She was in a state of such violent feeling that she could hardly speak. 'Aunt Jane,' she said, 'I want to speak to you.' 'Yes, my dear,' I said. For the moment I thought that Mr Furnival had said something to her that shocked her. He's so naughty, you know, and sometimes says things that seem outrageous to women in a joking way. But it wasn't that. Unfortunately...

"'"Auntie,' she said, 'you know I wanted to stay to communion? All through the service this morning I felt queer. I thought I should have to go out, but Cousin Humphrey persuaded me to stay. Then, at the end, just when I was on the point of taking the Holy Sacrament, I couldn't.' Oh, I wish I could tell you how deeply I felt for her! 'My dear Muriel,' I said, 'what on earth do you mean?' 'I mean that I couldn't,' she said, quite sharply. 'Just as the priest held the paten in front of me, it was as if something black – something black – came between me and the elements. I couldn't touch it, and he passed on in front of me. What will he think of me, Auntie, and what can it mean?'

"'I tried to console her. 'You must have had a little fainting fit, Muriel,' I said. 'No, no, Auntie,' she said, 'it wasn't that. It's worse than that. I know that I shall never be able to communicate again. It was the devil, Auntie, and he's stronger than God. What's more, I don't believe there *is* a God!' 'Oh, Muriel!' I said, 'you can't, you mustn't say such dreadful things!' But she went off, laughing; and from that day to this the poor child has been an absolute infidel. Now, isn't that dreadful? Don't you think it's perfectly dreadful?"

'By this time I was beginning to sit up. At first I'd felt, as I've told you, that the poor thing's brain was touched, and that I'd have to put up with her ramblings. But she didn't ramble. The whole story that she went on pouring out was so connected and clear and the way she told it so steady and matter-of-fact, that my head began to whirl. I wished to goodness she'd come to an end of it and take me back to Ronald. I looked about me for an excuse. Those manuscripts of Martock's! But now that she'd got me, she evidently meant to stick to me. "Don't you think it's perfectly dreadful?" she said again. I had to answer her, she waited so pathetically for my reply.

'To say the least of it, I admitted, it was very strange. "But your own children," I said, "were they affected in the same way?"

'She sighed. "I'm coming to them," she said quietly. "In one way or another they were all unlucky, all except dear Enid, thank God! Fortunately, soon after we came here, I persuaded Mr Furnival to send Gareth away to school. Naturally, he had to come back for the holidays, and I suppose it was then that they got hold of him. I shall never believe that his own nature was wicked. Never. It's a very tragic story, my dear. He brought disgrace on us. If you don't mind, I'd rather not speak of it; and please, please don't mention his name to Mr Furnival, or refer to him in any way!"

'I promised her that I wouldn't.

'"When Gareth went to school," she went on, "I was left at home with the three little girls. I think I've told you already that they were just as conscious as I was of the bad things in the house, and that they kept it all to themselves. The only thing we ever talked about was Jerry: of course we couldn't attempt to conceal *him*. But the others... You see, the poor mites didn't know that we knew about them; they went on living in a dreadful little world of their own, and that was so bad for them. I mean that it made them secretive and strange – not like ordinary children – and as Mr Furnival could never bear to have his studies interrupted by their noise, they used to go about the place like little ghosts themselves, whispering to each other in corners.

'"When I realized, later on, how this dreadful blight had lain over all their childhood, I could have died with pity. And yet I'd thought, all the time, that I was acting for the best. And it was no good consulting Mr Furnival about it. He couldn't, he wouldn't believe a word I said."

'She waited, as though she were anxious for some confirmation, and I hastened to assure her that she could not be blamed. "It's sweet of you to say that, my dear," she said. "You see, it was not until Guen was fifteen that I had any idea that they knew. I suppose that the dear innocents imagined that all human life was like life at Cold Harbour. They couldn't make comparisons. We never went away to the sea in the summer like other people; I didn't dare to leave Mr Furnival alone at the mercy of them, so to speak, and he became more and more wrapped up in Cold Harbour every year. The only times at which I left the house were those when I went up to London on business or shopping excursions. I used to catch an early train at the junction and return the same night.

'"In the winter, of course, that meant starting before it was light, and Guen, who was a perfect little housewife, used to come into our room and call me at six o'clock in case I overslept. Mr Furnival never wakes before eight: he's a very heavy sleeper. You see, he has nothing on his mind. It's very wonderful for him, isn't it?

'"Well, one morning about ten years ago – yes, that must be right, for I know that Guen was fifteen then and now she's nearly twenty-six – I'd planned to run up to town for the day and do some Christmas shopping. When you have children, particularly in a house like this, you *do* feel that Christmas should be made a festival of brightness, and Mr Furnival loves all the old customs too. You've no idea how dreadfully dark this place is at that time of year. What with the smoke and that, we often never see the sun for weeks at a time, and at half past six in the morning, which was the time you have to start for the junction if you want to get back the same evening, it's so dark that you'd think you were at the North Pole. So I always used to get Guen to run along and make sure I was awake at half past five.

"'That morning, luckily, I woke early, and lay in bed waiting for Guen to come, and thinking over my shopping list. I looked at my little travelling clock and saw that it was half past five, but I didn't get up. I thought it would spoil Guen's pleasure if she came in and found that I'd waked by myself, so I went on lying there till twenty to six, and then, of course, I knew that I couldn't waste any more time if I were to catch the train. So I just crawled out of bed and lit a candle and began to dress very quietly so as not to disturb Mr Furnival. It makes him cross to be wakened, as you can imagine, when there's no need for it.

"'So the time went on. By six o'clock I'd finished dressing, and still no Guen. I had plenty of time to spare, so I thought I'd give the children a surprise by making an early cup of tea and taking it to them in their room. I was just on the point of going downstairs to the kitchen when Guen arrived. At that moment my back was turned to her, and anyhow it was too dark to see her face, but, of course, I knew that it was she.

"'Is that you, Guen darling?' I said. 'Do you know it's just on six? I couldn't wait for you any longer. Did you oversleep?' 'No, Mother dear,' she said, 'I didn't oversleep. I woke at five o'clock.' 'Then why didn't you call me, darling?' I said.

"'I turned and saw her standing in the doorway, such a poor, white, shrivelled little thing. I knew at once that something was wrong and guessed the reason; but, of course, it wouldn't have done to admit it. 'I couldn't come, Mother,' she said. 'I'm awfully sorry, but I couldn't!'

"'I went over to her and kissed her. 'My dear child,' I said, 'it's nonsense to say you couldn't if you were awake at five.' Her little face was like ice; I could feel how cold her body was through her nightdress, and when I'd put my arms round her she gave way entirely and began to sob so loudly that I had to beg her not to wake Mr Furnival. 'What is it, my darling?' I said. 'Tell me why you couldn't come.' It seemed, for a moment, as if she wasn't able to form the words, she just went on wailing, 'I couldn't, Mother, I couldn't.' My own heart went as cold as her poor little body. I led her out into the passage, for Mr Furnival's sake, and there, at last, I managed to get her to tell me, 'You won't believe me, Mother darling,' she said, 'but it's true, it's true. I couldn't come to you because there was a dead body, all covered with blood, lying on the carpet between me and the door.' Then she began to cry again.

"'Of course I tried to persuade her that

she had imagined all this. I said that she must have been dreaming, and things like that; but I knew in my heart that she was speaking the truth. By that time I should have taken the awful thing she'd seen almost as a matter of course: I was getting used to them, you see, but I'd no idea, until that moment, that the children were suffering in the same way. That was what upset me, and though I didn't think it wise or right to ask her there and then if she'd had experiences of that kind before, I knew quite well that she had; for the thing that upset her wasn't so much the awfulness of the apparition itself as the fear that I should be cross with her. You can see what that meant, can't you?

'"Oh, it was dreadful! I couldn't bear to think of leaving her to go to the station, but I knew it would never do to take her seriously, so I just told her again that she'd evidently had a nightmare, and that, of course, I wasn't in the least bit angry with her. And all the time that I was doing this I could see by her eyes that she was only pretending to agree with me, and that her little brain was full of all sorts of secret horrors that she'd determined to keep to herself. I was lying to her, and she knew it and was condoning my lies, and I felt that this agreement actually separated us, and that we could never be quite natural with each other again. If you had children of your own, you'd realize how perfectly dreadful that was.

"'Dear, dear, I shall always remember that awful day's shopping in London. I don't know how ever I got through it, because, all the time that I wandered about Harrod's buying things like crackers, I was wondering, hoping against hope, that the other poor darlings had escaped. I kept asking myself whether it wasn't my duty to try to find out, and yet I couldn't bear to think of putting any idea of the kind into their minds. Even if they hadn't seen anything, I wondered if Guen had told them; but of course I knew that it would never do to ask Guen if she had. That would have implied that I believed her, and I'd quite determined never to admit that.

"'So it went on and on. Guen never spoke another word, and I used to try to persuade myself that what she'd told me on that morning was just an isolated accident. I used to watch the children playing. It comforted me to see that they seemed quite normal and happy, and when the days began to lengthen I felt more contented, for then they all ran wild about the lanes and were able to escape from the house.

"'As far as I was concerned, the spring made no difference. It used to cut me to the heart to see the way Mr Furnival went about the making of the garden. Even when the beds were full of flowers, they seemed sad to me. I used to go out in the evening with him to look at his roses, and every one of them seemed to me alive – of course they were alive, that's silly – seemed to be looking sideways at things that were there and that we couldn't see. Like dogs, you know. Mr Furnival would never have a dog in the house, and when people brought their dogs here you could see that they hated it.

'"It was a wonderful summer that year. All through the first half of June there was no rain, and the children were getting so used to living out of doors that they begged me to be allowed to sleep in hammocks on the lawn. Of course, I was only too glad of the excuse to get them outside the house at night, when things generally happen, but Mr Furnival was all against the idea. He would be, naturally: he's very conservative in his ideas of religion and politics and everything else. But though he's so often stern with the children, and says harsh things about them to tease me, he's really so tender-hearted that he never refuses anything in reason. Apart from leaving Cold Harbour, you understand; but that, poor darling, isn't his fault.

'"They do say, I know, that it is not good for the nerves to sleep in the moonlight, but that always seems to me superstition. You mustn't think, from what I'm telling you, that I'm a fanciful woman in the ordinary

163

sense: I'm not. Anyhow, we decided that all three of them, Guen, Elaine, and Enid should have their little hammocks hung out on the lawn, in front of the house. They were all very excited about it; they'd never done anything of the kind before; it was just a jolly new adventure for them.

'"At about nine o'clock I went out and kissed them good night – or rather I kissed Guen; the other two were asleep already. 'If you get nervous, darling,' I said, 'you must call me.' 'Oh, I shan't be nervous *here*, dearest,' she said. It was only in little allusions of this kind that we ever came near to the subject, and, in spite of that, she seemed so happy that I went in to bed quite contented, and fell asleep almost at once so soundly that I never heard Mr Furnival come up an hour later.

'"Just after midnight, I woke for no particular reason. I lay wide awake for about five minutes, wondering why. Then, all of a sudden, I heard a most dreadful scream. I knew it was one of the children, so I jumped out of bed at once and ran on to the lawn. There they were, all three of them. My poor little sister was crying by herself, while Guen was trying to comfort Elaine in her sweet, motherly way. The poor child – Elaine, I mean – was almost dead with fright. 'She's seen something, Mother,' said Guen. 'She's had a horrid dream about blood. She

164

thought she saw blood gushing out of the front of the house.'

'"Then the most curious thing happened. Elaine, who in the ordinary way was the sweetest and gentlest creature, flew into the most dreadful passion and hit Guen in the face. I never saw a child so transported. 'I *didn't* dream it, Guen,' she screamed. 'You *know* I didn't! I saw it. I saw it with my eyes wide open. She's a liar, mother: she knows I saw it.'

'"Really I didn't know what to do with them. All three of them were crying. Elaine was struggling like a little mad cat in my arms, and kept on saying the most dreadful things about poor Guen, words that I'd never even suspected that she knew at her age. I had to be quite stern with her, though she was still nearly stiff with fright. I took them all into the house again. Elaine had been shouting so loudly that she'd woken Mr Furnival, and, of course, he didn't mend matters by saying, 'I told you so,' though really he was quite justified. When things had quieted down a little, I took Elaine into my bed, and there she lay beside me, still cold and stiff. She never slept a wink that night. Now don't you think that was too dreadful?" she ended, breathlessly.

'"You see, all the way through from the very first," she went on, "there has been this element of blood in the things you see. Once

I arranged with a friend of mine to send a friend of hers, a medium, down here for a bit, and she said just the same. 'Blood,' she said. 'In this house, Mrs Furnival, I can see nothing but blood.' And later, of course...

"'But Gladys Harrow. I haven't told you about Gladys, have I? Oh, well, there are so many, you can't remember things in order, She was the granddaughter of old Dr Harrow, the rector of Lapton, down in Devonshire. It was no sort of life for her at Lapton: you see, her grandfather was nearly ninety-four, in spite of the damp, when he died. The rectory was in a dreadful state of disrepair, and so gloomily furnished that we used to invite Gladys out to the farm with us. Mr Furnival took a fancy to her, and treated her almost like a daughter. But then we left Lapton, and in the change and confusion she sort of dropped out of our lives, until, one day, we had a letter from her to say that she was taking up a gymnastic training at some college for ladies near North Bromwich.

"'Of course, we were both delighted. Mr Furnival loves to have young people about the place, and I knew it would be a great treat for me, too, because, since we'd been at Cold Harbour, I'd scarcely seen a soul. I couldn't call on people who had been rude to Mr Furnival. But that's beside the point. We invited Gladys to come over for a long

166

weekend at her half-term. She was so strong and healthy and full of spirits that it was a treat to see her; she'd always been an athletic, daring sort of girl, ready to ride bareback or to walk over to Dartmoor by moonlight, or go out swimming in Start Bay. I think that was what Mr Furnival liked about her; he loves a tomboy. Even in the old days at Lapton he was always daring her to do some mad thing or other, and, what's more, she wasn't often beaten.

'"Well, that evening, these two started their old games, Gladys challenging Mr Furnival to perform all sorts of complicated gymnastic movements which seemed quite outrageous for a man of his age. But you've no idea how strong and supple he is; I wish I could say the same for myself. I watched them performing here in this room, and all the time I was wondering if Gladys was one of the lucky ones or not. Whenever we had visitors, that was the first thought that came into my mind; but in this case, somehow, there seemed so little to fear that I decided not to warn her, particularly as I'd put her to sleep in the room under Mr Furnival's study, in the new part of the house.

'"When she came down to breakfast on Saturday morning, I asked her how she'd slept, and she answered with the queerest sort of look. 'Oh, all right, thank you,' she said, 'but I wish Mr Furnival hadn't spent the night walking to and fro in the study over my head.' When she said that, Mr Furnival burst out laughing, and told her that he'd gone to bed ten minutes later than herself, and slept soundly the whole night. I wished, in a way, he hadn't told her; but, of course, it was quite true, and afterwards we said no more about it.

'"But next morning, Sunday that was, she didn't wait to be asked. She turned on him right away. 'I believe you're trying to frighten me,' she said, 'but you needn't think you can do that.' I asked her what had happened. 'Happened?' she said. 'Why, Mrs Furnival, he's been moving the furniture about all night. I think he might put off his spring-cleaning until my bedroom's empty; I could fall asleep this minute.'

'"I felt that it was now really time to say something, but Mr Furnival gave me a look that stopped me. 'You must have imagined it, Gladys,' he said, and that quite upset her: I suppose the poor child was irritable with want of sleep. 'Imagined it?' she said. *'I'm* not imaginative; you know I'm not. What's more, if you do it again tonight I shall come upstairs and catch you out.' 'All right, Gladys, that's a bargain,' he said, turning the whole thing into a joke.

'"But *I* knew it wasn't a joke. All that night I'd been worrying about her; I had guessed, by that time, that she was one of the unlucky ones, and as I lay there in the dark I heard Mr Furnival tossing from side to side in his own bed, and so knew for certain that he had nothing to do with it. During the morning I suggested that I should change Gladys' bedroom, but she wouldn't hear of it. 'You needn't think I'm frightened,' she said. It was really rather a point of honour with her not to be.

"'That evening there was a moon. After Sunday supper, Gladys and Mr Furnival went for a moonlight walk in the lanes. I sat there waiting for them till close on ten o'clock, and when I heard them come into the hall I went down to scold them for being out so late. Gladys looked so pale and tired that I advised her to go to bed at once. 'I think I'd better,' she said, 'I slept so badly last night. No more tricks, now!' she said, pointing her finger at Mr Furnival. He laughed and shook his head; then he kissed her good night, as he always did, having known her since she was almost a child, and she went upstairs.

"I waited with him in the hall, watching him as he unlaced his boots. There was a knot in one of the laces, and the light was so bad – just candles, you know – that he couldn't see to undo it. So I went down on my knees to help him with it; he's so impatient when a thing like that thwarts him he only loses his temper and makes it worse.

There was I, on my knees, just saying that I hoped to goodness they'd leave poor Gladys alone that night, when we heard a most dreadful scream, and a moment later Gladys herself came flying downstairs like a whirlwind. 'Has it torn me?' she cried. 'Has it torn my face? It has! I know it's drawn blood!' She kept her hand up to the right side of her cheek so that I couldn't answer her. Mr Furnival got up in his stockings and took hold of her arm to steady her, but she seemed as if she couldn't bear him to touch her. 'Don't ... *don't!*' she screamed. 'Can't you leave me alone?'

'"Oh dear, I can't possibly tell you how horrible it all was: to see that fine, strong, self-reliant girl reduced within five minutes to a state of terror bordering on madness. For that's what it was. At last I managed to drag her hand away from her cheek. It wasn't torn, as she had imagined, but the skin was all red and inflamed, and you could just make out four long streaks, as if it had been scratched by fingernails. 'It *is* torn ... I know it is!' she said. We could do nothing with her, she cried and laughed so dreadfully. She implored me to take her away, right away out of the house, and really I don't know what would have happened to her reason if we hadn't done so. I hope I shall never see a human face so deformed by terror again.

'"It was awkward, too; the Vicarage had

been empty for more than a year; there was nowhere to take her, except the Fox, and I knew that the Higginses went to bed at nine o'clock. Besides, it seemed so strange to take one of our guests there to sleep at that time of night; we'd always been so anxious that the local people shouldn't have anything to talk about. But there was simply nothing else to be done. Mr Furnival volunteered at once to take her along to the inn, but that made her lose all control again; she seemed to have it firmly fixed in her mind that he had something to do with it, and clung to me so desperately that I had to go with her myself and explain things as best as I could to Mrs Higgins. Heaven only knows what they thought of it; but, luckily, by the time we had reached the Fox she had quietened down a little, and I was able to tell them some lie or other, much as I hated doing it.

'"At first she begged me to sleep with her, but, about midnight, she allowed me to return. I promised to send her things over to the inn next morning. She'd quite determined to go back to college on Monday. 'I couldn't bear to see that dreadful house again,' she said, and, of course, I quite sympathised with her. Poor child, she was such a fresh, bright creature, and we both loved her so. We've never seen her again nor heard from her to this day. That is what usually happens. But don't you think that it was perfectly dreadful?"

'Mrs Furnival stared at me with those puzzled, entreating eyes. This time I couldn't answer her. I could only let her clasp my hand, and she clung to it in a way that nearly made me cry. There wasn't much to choose between us in that way. It was quite a relief to both of us when she went on:

'"By that time," she said, "I had realized that I couldn't keep my reason if I went on fighting in the dark. I think I should have lost it a long time before if it hadn't been for the support which my religion gave me. Poor Mr Lowe had been a great help, but when they'd driven him away, I felt too dreadfully unprotected. His going had been a great blow to Mr Furnival, too. I think I told you that he shut up the Vicarage and arranged with the Rector of Halesby to send his curate over twice a week; but the curate, I'm afraid, was a young man without vocation, in whom one couldn't really confide.

'"Then came the fire at the Vicarage: I don't think I told you about that? Mr Furnival believes it was caused by some tramp getting in through one of the kitchen windows. That may be so, but, anyhow, it made the place so uninhabitable that he couldn't afford to have it put right again, and so there was no more question of having a resident priest, which made things worse than ever for me. The struggle seemed endless, and little by little I began to lose the power of praying, just as Mr Lowe and Muriel had done. So, in despair, I went one day to the Oratory at North Bromwich and had a talk with Father Westinghouse. That really seemed to give me the courage and faith that I wanted; I felt that I must have something strong and definite to support me, and, thanks to him, I became a convert to the Faith. Father Westinghouse was just on the point of leaving, but he put me in touch with the Abbot of St Chad's, who took charge of my initiation.

"'Mr Furnival was furious. I can't tell you how furious he was. That was the first and only difference we had ever known in all our married life. I'm still puzzled to think why he should have felt it so keenly. You see, he himself is a most devout Anglo-Catholic; he's told me times without number that he considers the Reformation the greatest blow that Christianity has ever suffered in England; and yet there's a point beyond which he seems unable to go. It's a curious thing in a man who's so truly good as he is, and one who prides himself on being so thoroughly logical. But there it is! I sometimes wonder if they have anything to do with it. I know him so well that I can't believe his real self capable of the cruelty that he showed to me about my conversion. Still, that's a long time ago, and now he knows that I can never change back again I think he's reconciled to it, though he's often dreadfully rude to me before strangers. I'm afraid you noticed that; but you mustn't think hardly of him.

'"And I can't tell you the new strength and happiness it gave me. Of course, I should have been happier still if he'd allowed me to bring up the children in the Faith, but I knew that was out of the question. Little by little we began to go our own ways in matters of religion. He's so much in sympathy with what you might call the decorative side of religion that he made no objections when I fitted up, with my own money, a little oratory in a recess at the top of the house. And, though he pretended to laugh at it, he actually made me a present of a beautiful Byzantine crystal chalice, which shows how soft his heart is beneath all his scoffing. My little oratory was a great joy to me. Whenever I was too terrified, or felt my reason shaking, I used to go there and pray. It was the one place in the world where I felt myself really safe.

'"And, indeed, about that time, I needed all the support I could find. That summer I lost my little boy, Gawain. He was only eleven. Appendicitis. I don't think they understood the disease in those days as well as they do now. You see, Mr Furnival is a great believer in homoeopathy, and, as the doctors told me afterwards, appendicitis

174

isn't a thing that yields to that sort of treatment. They operated on him in North Bromwich. Mr Lloyd Moore was a very great surgeon, they tell me, but he came in just too late. It was the first blow of that kind that we'd ever had. For a time I simply couldn't believe it; it just stunned me. But now I sometimes wonder if it wasn't a dispensation of Providence that he should have been taken away before all these dreadful influences had a chance of playing on him as they did on poor dear Gareth.

'"That came a few months later. He was expelled from school for a reason that's too terrible to mention. Mr Furnival is so very strict in moral matters that he would have nothing more to do with him. He even refused to let him come home again. I suppose, from the strictly moral point of view, he was right, and yet I always feel that whatever wickedness Gareth may have committed, it wasn't entirely his fault. I'm convinced that *they* had something to do with it. The boy wasn't naturally wicked. Nothing but the evil, corrupting influences of this place could have made him do what he did, he went into the army as a common soldier. Five years later we heard that he had died of sunstroke in India. I often go up into his room. You mustn't mind if I cry a little...

'"Two in one year ... oh, how it broke me! I think even Mr Furnival began to realize then

175

that nothing but my conversion could have saved my reason. In speech, he was still always very harsh about it, but you can see for yourself what a kind heart he has behind his prejudices: he allowed me to ask the Abbot to come over and dedicate my oratory. He came with his chaplain, and brought a consecrated altar with him.

'"That was a great joy to me, although, naturally, I was a little anxious as to how Mr Furnival would behave to him. As a matter of fact, I needn't have been nervous. Nobody can make a more charming host than Mr Furnival when he's a mind to, and he was delightful to both of them. At night, he and Father Vincent used to sit up in the study discussing questions of ritual and tradition that were far too deep for me in my poor, dazed condition. The Abbot told me himself, in so many words, that Mr Furnival's was the most remarkable brain he had met for years.

'"I can't tell you the confidence that the presence of such a holy man in the house gave me, until – I think it was on the second morning. Then he took me aside and told me solemnly that all the things I'd said to him about the house were true. It was too ghastly to hear him repeating, word for word, everything that poor Mr Lowe had said years before. You'll hardly believe it when I tell you that he, too, found it difficult to pray: and if ever there were a saint on earth, he was one!

"""There's no doubt in my mind,' he said, 'but that this house is in the possession of evil forces. I have made an attempt to exorcise them in the usual way, but must confess to you that I have failed. I've failed, Mrs Furnival,' he said, 'and all that I can do is to adjure you most solemnly, as you value the salvation of your immortal soul, to leave this place.' 'In that case,' I told him, 'I must leave my husband. Surely you would not advise me to do that?' 'I believe that that is your duty,' he said.

"'I put it to him. 'Wouldn't it be worse than cowardice,' I said, 'to desert the man I loved and my sweet children – for Mr Furnival would never let them go – to leave them exposed to the most awful spiritual danger while I saved myself?' He only shook his head. 'In any case,' he said, 'I'm sorry to tell you that I myself dare not run the risk of staying here another night. I've used every power that the Church has placed in my hands. I've failed; and it would be presumptuous on my part to continue to fight this battle with weapons of my own choosing. As it is, I shall feel bound to undergo a long penance after contact with influences so impure.'

"'I pressed him to advise me, but he wouldn't. He'd spoken his final word. 'At any rate, Reverend Father,' I said, 'you will do me one favour before you go, and that is to say Mass in the Oratory for the last time.' 'I can't refuse you that,' he said. 'I only hope, dear daughter, that the Blessed Virgin will open your eyes to the peril against which I've warned you. I'm afraid that I can do nothing with your husband: his heart is so full of heresy and pride that no word of mine can soften it; but, if you like, I will tell him what advice I have given you.'

"'Of course, I knew that this would only lead to disaster, so I begged him not to. An hour later we all went up to my little oratory to celebrate Mass: Father Vincent, his chaplain, and myself. I took the opportunity of a moment when Mr Furnival was out of the house. You see, although he was far too considerate to make any fuss, I knew that it would irritate him. I remember going upstairs, so full of peace and hope, in spite of what the Abbot had told me; for really it did seem as if the consecration of that little oratory had sweetened the whole house. I knelt down and prayed that it might always be so, while Father Vincent and his chaplain prepared the elements. It seemed as if they were taking an unusually long time over it, but that didn't trouble me. In the middle of one of my prayers I heard a little cracking sound, but I took no notice of it, and didn't open my eyes. Then Father Vincent came over and touched me on the shoulder. I can hear the sound of his voice at this very moment. 'Mass cannot be said this morning,' he said. 'You had better go. The chalice has broken in my hands.' Now don't you think that was dreadful – perfectly dreadful?

'"No. Dreadful isn't the word. There's no word for it. And that was how he felt it too; you could see it in his face. Then, suddenly, my feelings changed. It seemed to me like a direct challenge from all I'd been fighting against for three years, and I knew that I'd got to accept. I spoke to him quite sharply, forgetting for the moment where I was and what *he* was. I said, 'If you'll wait a moment, Reverend Father, I'll see if I can mend it. We can't, we simply can't, give in like this!' And that, in spite of my boldness, which he'd every right to resent, seemed to hearten him. 'Very well,' he said, 'I'll hold the chalice till you come back, but don't be too long away.'

'"So I ran down to Mr Furnival's study and found a stick of sealing-wax and a box of matches, It was only the base of the chalice that had snapped off in his fingers, and luckily none of the wine was spilt, so, when I came back, he and the chaplain were able to mend it between them and go through with the Holy Office to the end. Perhaps it was only nervousness that made his hands tremble – some curious strain, you know; but in spite of my feeling that we had turned a defeat into a great victory, I couldn't get him to stay in the house any longer. No doubt he was right; he had done everything that the Church ordained. But though he continued to advise me by letter, he never came to Cold Harbour again. I sometimes think it was only because of his outstanding saintliness that the evil powers made their efforts against him. I suppose a great saint has to withstand the greatest temptations. And after that victory my little oratory seemed to me a greater refuge than ever..."

'She broke off suddenly. It was curious. I couldn't be certain whether she'd lost the thread again or finished. Then I guessed that she was praying, and didn't dare to interrupt her. At last I ventured to ask if that were the end.

'"The end?" she said. "Oh, no. There *is* no end to it. That happened nearly eleven years ago. During that time I've had my share of purgatory. All through those years I had to watch the children growing up; that was a sorrow in itself. There couldn't be any happiness in this house. I tried to make things easy for them, but something was always bound to go wrong. I watched their natures changing, but I was quite powerless, and Mr Furnival would only laugh at me when I told him that things were going wrong. Guen and

Elaine, the two unlucky ones, made most unsuitable marriages. It turned their father against them: he's so very particular in social matters, although he calls himself a socialist. I couldn't blame *them*, I knew they were quite justified in taking any step that would get them away from home. Unfortunately, neither marriage turned out happily. I'm afraid their early experiences had left their mark on them. You see, as the medium told us before her dreadful quarrel with Mr Furnival, the influence of the house is definitely evil."

'"You've said that before," I told her. "I wish you'd explain what you mean by 'definitely evil'?"

'"It's evil," she repeated. "I can't say more."

'"But do you mean," I said, "that it makes you want to do evil things yourself?"

'"Yes," she said. "That's what I do mean. I feel that some day I may do something really dreadful. I feel it more strongly every year, every day. Except for the blood that is the worst part of it."

'"The blood?" I said. By this time, you see, she was getting rather incoherent. "Oh, I'm so sorry," she answered. "Of course you don't understand. My mind runs on so. I'm so used to it myself that I take it for granted that other people know. Naturally, living in an atmosphere of this kind, I wanted to learn as much about it as I could, and Mr Furnival is really just as interested as I am. He has quite a number of books on the subject – his 'spook-books', as he calls them – and when he is out of the house I sometimes creep up to his study and read them.

'"In that way I found out that the thing most to be dreaded in these cases is what they call 'materialisations'. All the time I'd been congratulating myself that nothing of that kind had occurred, but during the last year – the last two years – it's come, in just the form which might have been expected. The medium said that she felt blood all over the house; on several occasions the poor children have seen it; but during the last eighteen months I've done more than that. I almost hesitate to tell you. I've not only seen it: I've touched it... *Touched it*."

'At this point the poor thing must have seen some shade of incredulity in my eyes. As a matter of fact, the conviction had suddenly come back to my mind that all the horrors she'd told me were just delusions. That was what Alma meant when she said that Mrs Furnival was an invalid. The woman was mad. It was extraordinary, and quite in keeping, too, how she tumbled to my suspicions. Her voice lost that reasonable gentleness which had been so persuading. It became harsh and frightening.

'"Ah," she said, "you don't believe me? I'm

182

only telling you the solemn truth. Everywhere in this house there's blood: actual blood. On my mirrors, on the carpets, everywhere. I spend half the day going about the house wiping it up."

'While she spoke I was thinking hard. I'm not quite a fool, you know, and this really was too steep. I pounced on her like anything. "This blood," I said. "Have you ever thought of having it analysed?"

'"Analysed?" she said. "But how *could* I get it analysed?"

'"Your husband," I suggested, "could send it somewhere."

'"Oh, but I couldn't dream of telling *him*," she cried. "I've given that up long ago. He gets so upset that now I know better than to mention anything. He thinks that all the trouble is over, and it's much, much better that he should think so, for he's quite incapable of seeing for himself."

'"If you can touch it," I said, "surely he can see it."

'"Oh, but I couldn't, I couldn't!" she cried.

'"Well, I think, for your own sake," I said, "that he should be told."

'She shook her head piteously. "My dear, you don't know Mr Furnival," she said. "And you don't realize the truth of what the medium declared – though I knew it quite well before she told me – and that is that it's

183

all directed against *him*, and centres in him. He's so possessed by their influence that he's incapable of believing. That, as I've told you, is the most dreadful part of it." She moved away from me, her voice hardened again. I could see that my little scientific suggestion had made her mistrust me. "We'll talk no more about it," she said. "It's very kind of you to have listened to me so patiently. Wouldn't you like to see the house?"

'Of course, I said that I'd be delighted, which wasn't true, for though I didn't believe in her "materialisations", I knew that I wasn't proof, by a long way, against the unpleasant feeling of the house. My cheeks were still burning, and I wanted, dreadfully, to get in touch with Ronald again. That feeling of separation... There seemed to be more in it than brick walls or plaster panels; it was spiritual more than physical; I felt almost as if he were dead. It made me shiver. And then, during the last few minutes, the relation of me to Mrs Furnival, and Mrs Furnival to myself, had changed. At the beginning of her story, even in spite of the extraordinary things she'd told me, I'd felt quite safe with her; but now the sudden change in her voice made me a bit scared of her company. I knew this was perfectly beastly of me; I was ashamed of it; and yet I couldn't help it. I felt, all the time, that any minute she might do or say something frightening and unaccountable. Even when she spoke kindly to me, her ideas seemed so incoherent that I felt she was talking and living on a different plane from myself, that her mind wasn't quite normally human like my own. Of course, it *couldn't* be – after all that.

'So we began to wander over the house together, and I hated every step of it. I wondered how I had ever been such a fool as to tell Ronald that I thought it could be made quite comfortable. Comfortable! Why, there wasn't a brick or a panel of it that wasn't tainted. I thought: "That must have been what Ronald meant when he looked at me so closely: what an innocent, insensitive little idiot I was not to see that for myself. If I had realized it, I should never have allowed myself to get separated from him like this."

'Anyhow, there it was. I'd landed myself, and had to put up with it. Mrs Furnival took my arm and led me along the passage. I think there must have been something wrong with her heart as well; the only sound that I could hear was a sort of wheezing when she breathed. That corridor was simply beastly, but not nearly so horrible as the rooms. The first one she showed me was empty, with all the furniture draped in yellowish dust-sheets. On a nail over the head of the bed hung a football cap with a tarnished tassel. "This was Gareth's," she said. "The room's never been used since his day." "Then why on earth," I wanted to say, "haven't you cleaned it up and moved all this ghastly furniture?" But I couldn't speak; and after she'd stood there for a moment, glancing round and sighing to herself, she led me out of it and into another.

'"This was the room," she said, "in which poor dear Guen saw the body on the floor." I had to look at the place where she pointed. I felt that I could have screamed out loud, but she just went on talking in the same placid, dazed, inconsequent way; and after a few moments we escaped again into the passage, which now seemed quite homely and comfortable. She opened another door.

'"Now, *isn't* this a delightful room?" she said. "You see it faces east, and on a summer morning the sun comes streaming in at this window." She hobbled over to the curtains and killed a clothes moth. Ough! that room, which she'd described as delightful, was really as dank and foul as a burial vault. "It has such charming memories," she said. "It was here that little Babs slept when dear Enid came to stay with us last summer. Such a darling little thing!"

'It made me quite furious to imagine the crime of putting a child into such a sepulchre, and then it suddenly struck me that she'd never mentioned Enid's marriage.

I told her so. "Enid? Ah, *dear* Enid!" she said. "Enid is my little stepsister. Curious, isn't it, at my age? We do love her so! She was the only really lucky one of the whole family."

'I'd heard all this before. Evidently she didn't remember that she'd told me. "I really don't think I could have gone on living here if it hadn't been for Enid's good luck. She was only eighteen when she was married. So young; but such a nice man! Unfortunately, his profession compels him to live abroad. She's taken a cottage down in Devonshire, not far from Lapton. Of course, I should have loved to make a home for her here, but with a baby it wouldn't have been wise. It was so delightful to have them with me in the summer and to see her still unaffected."

'She went on sighing over the charms of Enid and her baby as we climbed the stairs. But I wasn't thinking of the baby nor of Enid. Ever since we had left the rooms in which Gareth had been – how shall I put it? – corrupted, and Guen had seen the bloodstained corpse, my mind had been hot on a new trail, and just as she stood wheezing in the last step I found myself blurting out, all of a sudden: "Mrs Furnival, do you sleep in the same room as your husband?"

'An extraordinary question! I knew, as I spoke, that she might easily have been offended. But she wasn't. She only stared at me mildly as she got her breath, and then said, with a faint, charming smile: "Well, I do and I don't. Our room is just over here on the right. I'll show you." "Thank goodness," I thought, "I haven't upset her." We entered the bedroom. It was long and low, with two windows that made it seem lighter than any of the others; lighter and more ... possible. On the walls, print hangings of a pattern that I'd always loved. Now I can never bear to see it again. There were a pair of cold, chaste-looking little beds, standing side by side, and between them, completely dividing the room into two when it was drawn, swung a thick, brocaded curtain. "What on earth is this for?" I said.

'"Now you'll understand," she answered, "what I meant when I said that I do and I don't. This curtain ... Mr Furnival always has it drawn at night. You see, he says I snore, and I dare say he's quite right, though I can't imagine that the curtain makes any difference. When *he* snores I can hear him plainly. But then, I suppose it's his fancy, and really it makes no difference to the sense of companionship. I mean, that if either of us were taken ill in the night, the other would be available. And it *is* a nice room, you know."

'I agreed with her; not because I thought it was anything but horrible, but because, from the moment I set eyes on that sinister curtain, I was convinced, without taking the trouble to reason it out, that all the horrible things she told me were not directed against, but centred *in*, this man of whom she always spoke so tenderly. My mind went scurrying back through the incidents one by one, trying to find out how far Mr Furnival could establish his alibis apart from this poor thing's evidence.

'I'll admit that I couldn't go very far; I was up against difficulties as soon as I started; but all the same I felt positive, instinctively, that I was right. "We've slept in this room for fifteen years," I heard her saying. "All through these dreadful troubles, we've never been separated. I don't think there are many married people who could say as much as that."

'We passed out on to the landing again. I kept saying to myself: "I'm right, I know I'm right." She stood with her hand on the knob of another door. "This is the room," she said, "in which poor Mr Lowe had such a bad time. We call it Jerry's room. You'd like to look inside it, wouldn't you?"

'As a matter of fact, I hated the idea. At this point, all my fear and distaste seemed to come to a climax. I knew that if I entered that room something would happen. I couldn't imagine what. I didn't expect to have my face torn, or anything like that. I just felt that if once that door were closed behind me she might tell me something more horrible than anything that had gone before, or I might find myself trapped alone with Mr Furnival, or that, perhaps, she might take the opportunity of breaking down, or being affectionate to me, which would have been just as bad. And so I simply dug in my hind legs and stood still on the landing, while she gazed at me with her sad, puzzled eyes. I wouldn't give an inch; so, at last, she just opened the door a few inches, peeped inside it, and left it.

'"But I *must* show you my darling oratory," she said.

'And there I couldn't refuse her. It evidently meant so much to the poor thing. It stood at the top of another flight of stairs, wedged into a kind of triangle made by the slope of the gable: a little cupboard of a place with a heavy oak door. She went quickly up the stairs, in spite of her shortness of breath, and unlocked this door with a wrought-iron key. I stood below her on the stairs, I could just see a light burning, and a crucifix with a painted plaster Christ, and down the stairs incense came drifting.

'"Yes, very nice," I forced myself to say.

'"Do come in and look at it: it's so sweet," she said.

'I couldn't. I simply couldn't. I can't explain myself. If I'd been able to reason, I could have told myself that this was the one place in the whole house that was absolutely free from sinister influences, so that I ought to have been thankful to enter it. But somehow I couldn't reason. That crucifix, so lifelike, so still... Do you know, it simply terrified me? I suppose I was just about coming to the end of my tether, and that place suggested, more than anything else she'd shown me, the ghastly things that it had been planned to counteract. I hated the incense, too, not just because I always dislike it, but because it seemed to me – the thought's a horrid one, but I can't help it – like the smell of disinfectant in a mortuary that's been put there to conceal ... others.

'I ached to find some way of escaping without wounding her. "Yes, I'm sure it's a great comfort to you," I said; "but don't you think it's time we found my husband and Mr Furnival? It gets dark so early, and I'm afraid we shall have to go soon. Besides, Mr Furnival promised to show me some manuscripts."

'She closed the door reluctantly. "Of course, we must give you tea before you go," she said. "I'm afraid I've wasted the whole afternoon in talking to you. You'd forgive me, my dear, if you realized what a comfort it's been. Yes, we'll go downstairs."

'We did so, slowly. She seemed tired. At the top of the first flight she paused. "I think

I saw them go in there," she said. "Hadn't I better look inside?"

'By this time I really couldn't bear any more opening of doors. I stood, burning, with my back to her while she did so. "No, I must have been mistaken," she said. "How curious!"

'Down we went, step by step. Every minute I felt happier at getting nearer to Ronald. It was just as if we'd been separated for ages. Like the end of the war. At the bottom of the second flight she stopped again. The landing was deadly silent. She seemed to be listening, staring at a closed door on the left.

'"Why," she said suddenly, "I believe they're quarrelling! How perfectly dreadful of them!"

'And still not a sound. Evidently either she or I had gone mad. She hurried forward to the door and opened it, and I saw the interior of the library in which we had sat talking. There was Ronald, standing at the lectern, looking up from that open Bible toward Mr Furnival. And there was Mr Furnival, his legs wide apart, in front of the fire, stroking his smooth chin.

'As I came in our eyes met. We didn't speak a word, but it seemed to me as if our minds were in a state that made words unnecessary. His mind challenged mine. "Well, what do you think of it all?" it said.

And mine answered his with words that jagged through my brain like lightning, and split the middle of my skull on their way out: *"You* are the devil in this house." I felt as if I had shouted them.

'Then he came toward us, rubbing his hands and smiling. "So here you are, at last," he said. "Better late than never! When once these women get talking, Wake... Ha? Well, Mrs Furnival, what about a spot of tea?"

'Ronald took my arm quietly. It was like heaven to feel him near me again. To know that he was alive. And that I was alive. And sane. We all went down to the ground floor together.'

Chapter Six

Mr Furnival

'And sat down to tea,' Ronald Wake continued, 'at a round table in the window niche of what, I suppose, was the Furnivals' dining-room. I'm afraid we've been describing the rooms at Cold Harbour like house-agents. Looking at it from one point of view, the house is half the story; and, in any case, this part of it was so different from all the rest that I mustn't pass it over. In shape, it corresponded with the library on the floor above, but in its decoration and the feeling that it gave us, nothing could have been more different. No dark ages, no languid pre-Raphaelites there! The panels blazed with pictures which seemed to have been chosen for their gaiety and vividness. All modern. Over the fireplace there was an opulent, flaming thing by Brangwyn. Renoir: Matisse: Laura Knight. A curious, exciting mixture: against that background they shone out like old glass.

'Furnival saw that the contrast had taken me aback. "This is what I call my kill or cure surprise packet," he said, with a sweep of his

194

hand. "There's nothing like a bit of kaleido-scope for a change, particularly at meal-times. It gives one an appetite. Ha?"

'Certainly there wasn't anything wrong with his. He sat down at the table between us, and began to wolf great slabs of rich cake at an enormous rate, chaffing poor Evelyn on the smallness of hers, which was per-fectly normal. He seemed so cheerful that you'd have thought he'd had another drink on the way down, though, of course, I knew that he hadn't. The idea of drugs passed through my mind. I looked at him with medical eyes, and decided no.

'"I'm a real Midlander in one thing," he said, "and that is that I fancy my spot of tea as much as a schoolboy. What's more, talking makes one hungry. I should have thought that you, Mrs Wake, 'ld be famished after an hour of my wife's gossip. Now, do have another piece of this cake, or I shall be forced to finish it."

'Evelyn shook her head. By this time I guessed that something had upset her. I couldn't ask her what it was. I just wondered if she were suffering from the honification of goose-flesh that still rippled up and down my spine. I tried to help her out. "Perhaps you haven't been talking?" I said.

'"Not talking? You trust my wife!" said Mr Furnival, laughing with his mouth full.

'"Yes, we've been talking all the time," said

Evelyn in a subdued, significant voice. He laughed again, but I could see he knew what she was driving at. He glanced quickly from her to Mrs Furnival, then screwed up his eyes and stared her full in the face. "Well, Mrs Wake?" he said.

'"I only want to know what you think of it," Evelyn answered, as calmly as you like.

'"What I think of it?" he repeated. "That's very mysterious. What I think of *what?*"

'"Of the house, and the things that happen in it," she said.

'"Oh, that's easily answered," he said. "I don't waste my time; life's too short for that, my dear lady. I don't think of it at all."

'"You'll have to, sooner or later," she said.

'They went on sparring for a minute or two like this. It was a curious situation for me: you see, I'd heard none of the stories that Mrs Furnival had told her, and hadn't any clear idea what Evelyn was driving at, though I could see by her grim face that she was determined to pin him down. And Mrs Furnival didn't help us with a word. She just sat there, perched behind her tea things, like a starved sparrow in the snow. Then, little by little, putting together Evelyn's questions and Furnival's replies, I began to tumble to the meaning of her catechism. Incident by incident she was taking him through the whole list of horrors that Mrs Furnival had confided to her; inch by inch Furnival was fighting the suggestion that he could be in any way connected with them. Even to an outsider the contest was good sport. You can imagine me in the position of a stranger who drops into the law courts in the middle of a case about which he knows nothing and has to pick up the threads of argument as they appear.

'They began with Jerry. Furnival was prepared to admit that the Jerry phenomena existed, but not, for a moment, that such things were unusual, or necessarily unpleasant. The records of "that sort of thing" were full of poltergeists. Possibly she'd heard of the Wesley case? Yes, the famous Wesley, the great Nonconformist. He had been troubled with a spirit of this kind to whom he'd given a nickname. "As long as Jerry doesn't keep me awake," Mr Furnival said, "he's welcome to his antics! Luckily, he prefers the parsons."

'From Jerry they passed on to the visions that had troubled the two children: the bloody corpse on the bedroom floor, and the stream of blood that had gushed out of the stones of the house. "It's no good asking *me* about things like that," he said. "If you want to get at the root of them, you'd better interview the cook. She's the person responsible. Indigestion. Nightmare. Have you ever yet heard of a highly strung child – they get that from their mother, not from me – who hasn't suffered from imaginations of that kind?" Evelyn stuck to her guns. Imaginations, yes: of that kind, no. Nightmares were freakish things, but these visions were consistent. "Well, supposing I admit that," said Furnival, "it takes you no further. All nightmares have their origin in impressions received during waking hours. In this case, no doubt, the children had heard their mother talking." Mrs Furnival, still fixedly smiling, shook her head. She knew better than to dispute him. "But, Mrs Furnival," Evelyn contended, "wouldn't have spoken of anything she hadn't experienced herself?" "Ha! Wouldn't she?" he cackled. "A woman who upholds the Apostolic Succession is not to be trusted, in my opinion, on any question of fact."

'The sneer evidently pleased him. He went on chuckling for a moment or two. Mrs Furnival didn't turn a hair; I suppose the poor thing was used to it; and Evelyn renewed her attack. The hagridden Mr Lowe? Why Mr Lowe, he scoffed, was no better than his poor, deluded wife! A credulous, superstitious, weak-minded fellow of the stamp of which Roman Catholic converts were made. He refused even to discuss Mr Lowe. "Moonshine, my dear lady, moonshine!" Muriel and her refusal of the sacrament? That was another case of the same kind. Women and effeminate priests!

With all respect to Evelyn's own sex, the facts were significant. No healthy, normal male had ever been troubled in Cold Harbour, nor ever would be. It was no good talking to him about the Abbot of St Chad's and his broken chalice. The chalice was a thousand years old, and made of crystal. After all, there *was* such a thing as the law of averages; and in the ordinary way that chalice should have been broken ages ago. No doubt Mrs Furnival's stories had made the wretched fellow tremulous with fright. Unconscious muscular tremor. What about the hazel twigs that snap off short in the fingers of the water diviner? The chalice broke, in short, in obedience to some natural, physical law; its time had come, and there was an end of the matter! "There's nothing," he went on, "in all that Mrs Furnival has been silly enough to tell you, that can't be explained along the same reasonable lines."

"'You're forgetting Miss Harrow," said Evelyn slowly. "I should like to know how you explain that."

"'Ah, Miss Harrow..." he laughed softly. "Yes, that, I'll admit, was a curious case. Very remarkable. It all happened in a moment. We'd come in from a walk in the moonlight, you know. I was just sitting down in the hall outside here, taking off my boots–"

"'Yes, I've heard about the boots," Evelyn interrupted. "Mrs Furnival told me. I think those boots are a significant part of the story."

'He pulled her up sharply. "Now what do you mean by that?"

'"Because they give you an 'alibi'," she said.

'His mouth twitched up into a grimace. "So you think I need one, Mrs Wake? Well, there it is, isn't it? in any case." He laughed again, to himself. "I suppose we shall have to saddle Jerry with that. We've admitted Jerry, haven't we? And if Jerry is capable of moving furniture and playing tricks with a parson's braces, we may as well give him credit for scratching Miss Harrow's face. Certainly something did scratch it. The marks were quite plain; and as for terror, I must say that I've never seen a human being in such a blue funk in my life. Yes, Mrs Wake, I'll grant you Miss Harrow, but I'm damned if I'll grant you anything else. Would you like me to establish my 'alibi' in all the other cases? If you attach any importance to it, I think I could do so, with my wife's assistance. Well, well, I congratulate your husband. You're a very wide-awake young woman."

'He looked at her with a teasing, challenging smile which made me so conscious of the antagonism between them that I felt it my duty to break a silence that might have ended in plain-speaking. Evelyn is dreadfully direct, and, after all, the man was our host.

"'Of course,' I said, 'I'm rather in the dark about the details of the things which you're discussing; they all sound to me extremely unpleasant, whatever may have caused them. Uncanny things seem to have happened in this house to a large number of very different people, and, naturally, one would feel more comfortable if they could be explained. There's just one point that strikes me. I should like to know if the house has always had a bad reputation of that kind.'

"'Now that,' said Furnival, 'is the impersonal question of a man of science, not of an amateur detective. I quite agree with you. And the answer is, yes. I didn't know it when first I took the house. The Pomfret trustees, or rather their solicitors, didn't tell me so, though it may have had something to do with the low figure at which I got the lease. But it is a fact that Cold Harbour has been said to be haunted for the last hundred years. The farm labourers in the district know quite a number of tales about it; I've heard them discussing it in the Fox; but I'm afraid they're all of a very conventional pattern, and don't help us much. Except as an 'alibi',' he added, with a mischievous glance at Evelyn. 'You see, I've only been here fifteen years.'

"'Then there's another point,' I went on.

201

"It seems to me curious that none of the incidents we've been discussing have been connected with servants working in the house. That strikes me as strange."

"'Right again," Furnival admitted. "It *is* curious."

"'There was Rose," Mrs Furnival put in gently.

"'Rose was a neurotic little donkey," Furnival snapped. "Rose would have been all right if you'd left her alone. I always told you so."

"'She said that she saw things," Mrs Furnival mildly protested.

"'Rose is the only one," said Mr Furnival irritably.

"'Still, Rose counts," I suggested. "And it really does seem that a certain percentage of the people who come to the house are liable to unpleasant adventures. I think you've mentioned nine cases of the kind, not counting Mrs Furnival and yourself?"

"'You needn't count *me*," he snapped. "I've told you already that I've never felt anything abnormal, and I don't believe that any normal person does. Still, it is a fact, as you say, that a certain proportion, say sixty per cent, of our visitors do. And that" – he laughed softly – "does make entertaining rather difficult."

'He put it so whimsically that I was forced to laugh too. Altogether his temper appeared to be improving so rapidly that, in spite of Evelyn's continued, dark disapproval, I felt there was something to be got out of him.

'"I should like to know," I said, "how you explain all this."

'"I don't explain it," he answered shortly.

'"You haven't any theory?" I persisted. I knew, in my bones, that he had. Whether he believed in his theory was another matter.

'"Well, if you want a theory, I'll give you one," he said. "But you must realize that I offer it entirely without prejudice, as the lawyers say–"

'"Quite, quite; that's understood," I told him.

'"Very well," he said. "It's understood that what I'm going to tell you is merely romantic moonshine. You have to give the women a fable to play with."

'He settled back in his chair, preparing to enjoy himself, putting the tips of his fingers together, staring up at the ceiling as if he expected to find his inspiration there. And certainly there or somewhere else he found it. Looking backward, I confess myself in agreement with your Dr Moorhouse: "amazingly dynamic ... the most striking personality in the Midlands": and all this, mind you, not because of his personal appearance, but in spite of it, and in spite of a prejudice on my part that by this time amounted to – well, loathing's the only word. Evelyn's spoken already about his voice. I don't know, even now, that I should call it beautiful; but as for persuasiveness, I should say that no living orator has ever affected me more deeply. A voice of gold. Not that: a voice of crystal, and in the crystal the flaw of that demoniac laugh. Anyhow, it's a waste of time to talk about things that can't be heard. This, more or less, is how his explanation, his apologia, went.

"'I think,' he said, "that when you asked me if Cold Harbour had a bad reputation in the past, you were very near hitting the right nail on the head. Of course, you didn't mean what I mean. You only wanted to know if there were any ghost stories connected with it, and I answered that there were, meaning just the ordinary super-stitious rubbish that accumulates round every building with a long record of human habitation. There are very few old houses, in fact, that haven't gathered some accretions of that sort. But if you'd asked me, more generally, if I thought there was anything unusual in the position of the house and its history, apart from local superstitions, I should have been forced to say 'yes' again: as a matter of fact, mark you; and not for one moment admitting any of the psychical implications that some people would attach to it. You know my position already. I'm a complete sceptic, or rather a complete agnostic in these matters. I only offer you the material, the turnip and the candle out of which to build your bogey, if you want one, as most people do.

'"Very well. We'll start a few thousand years ago. Imagine yourself for a moment standing on the terrace at the back of the house. There may have been buildings there then; I don't know. I should think that very probably there were. Now run your eye over the prehistoric landscape. The outlines of the hills you see today must be very much as they were: Pen Beacon and Uffdown behind you; westward, the Clees and the Wrekin – no Uriconium in those days; north and east, the line of the high Midland plateau: a regular amphitheatre of hills, a tremendous cup – saucer is better – in the bottom of which lies thick, impenetrable forest. The Mercian forest, they called it later; but I'm speaking of a time before the Saxons came.

'"And now comes a curious point. This little knoll on which Cold Harbour stands is a key position. Possibly I'm not using the term rightly: I know nothing about soldiering. But my point is this: from Cold Harbour you can command every important station of the Neolithic religions extant in this part of the Midlands, from the stones on Pen Beacon to the circles over in Shropshire. There's no other site in this part of the country of which you can say that. It's the visual, if not the geographical centre of all of them; and in those days, of course, there was no smoke to hamper one's vision. For that reason I like to think that Cold Harbour was in those days a pagan centre of importance. I can't prove it: all this is sheer theorising, but I think there's a case to go to the jury. Ha?"

'He waited for my approval. "As long as this doesn't form the basis of your argument," I began.

'"There *is* no argument," he protested. "I'm merely offering you suggestions on which to build your blessed theories. If the day were clearer, I could show you what I mean. But let that pass. Let's skip a few hundred years. At this period of the world's history, centuries don't go for much. Now we're in the period of the Roman conquest: our old friend Boudicca or Boadicea, ha? And now we have something to go on.

"At that time our friend old Gaius, Centurion of the Twentieth Legion, set up his altar to Astarte. Seeing's believing, ha? Why did old Gaius take the trouble to set up his altar here? We've touched on that already. Because he found a grove here ready made? Possibly. But there's one curious thing about the Romans. They had, as you know, a habit of adopting to their own uses not only the deities but the religious sites of the people they conquered, and my opinion is that this old boy stuck up his altar here because he knew, from local gossip, that it was an important religious site, a place where other people, who knew a deal more about the nature of the country, had celebrated religious rites for centuries.

'"Or again: Gaius may have been playing for safety. He may have thought to himself: 'Now here's a spot that has been saturated for centuries incalculable with the power of old gods and goddesses who may play the mischief with a poor foreigner like myself. Damned if I won't put a little reasonable religion into it on my own account.' Probably he thought he'd better be on the safe side both ways. And in any case, he stuck up his altar, just as my wife stuck up her oratory; because, for some reason or other, the place frightened him. He was what she'd call one of the 'unlucky' ones.

'"At any rate," he went on, "here you are, in the first century, with at least two layers of religion, and pretty ugly religions at that. You know for yourself what Astarte worship implies. You've read Frazer? It's a subject that you can't discuss before ladies, ha? How long it lasted, I can't tell you; probably, in some form or other, for hundreds of years. Anyhow, the odds are that when the Saxon Christians invaded Mercia, it was still persisting in some form or other.

'"Why? Ha! There you think you've got me.

207

But you haven't: not by a long way. By this time we're entering the period of recorded history, and can argue from known facts. The facts are these. In the Saxon period, call it the eighth or tenth century AD, the people of this district felt it incumbent on them to build a church. Did they build it to cope with the religious needs of a large population? Not at all. At no period in history has this bit of country been important from that point of view. All the human activities of the district at the time of the conquest were centred in Halesby, just about four miles away. From that point of view, there wasn't, and never has been, the least need for a big church at Cold Harbour. See Domesday...

'"Why did the Saxons take the trouble to build one then? Obviously for the identical reasons that made Gaius stick up his altar and my wife her oratory. Fear: the need of protection. The Saxons came along and settled in Halesby, and when they'd been there a bit they began to hear whispers about that queer place in the trees at the foot of Pen Beacon, nasty, uncomfortable stories of the kind that I'll bet my shirt that chatterbox Alma has been telling you at the Fox. And some old priest, who had a high sense of religious sanitation, said to himself: 'This isn't healthy; I'm not going to have my congregation corrupted by mysteries of that kind; this is a powerful thing, and we must deal with it.' So he dealt with it, according to the rules of the game, with book and bell and candle and aspersions of holy water, just as the Abbot of St Chad's did for my wife. First of all, by way of precaution, he put up the stone cross, the remains of which I'll show you in the churchyard later; and then, to make a clean sweep of it, he got to work on the church whose tower is still standing. And I dare say he died imagining that he'd scotched Cold Harbour for good and all. Anyhow, my point is this: that the Saxons found material here for heroic sanitary measures, and took them.

'"Now we'll skip another century or two. Monastic history's a very ticklish subject; the old monks had a way of letting their pens run away with them, and their records are just about as trustworthy as historical novels. Still, I suppose there's a basis of truth in them. Well, in the Middle Ages, according to the Worcester records, this particular piece of ecclesiastical property fell into the hands of the Abbey of Halesby. Cistercians. If you have time to look at the ruins on your way, it's just barely worth while. They never had much to do with Cold Harbour, probably because the ugly stories were still hanging about it. What they did was to turn this building – or rather the east wing of it – into a house of correction to which they banished members of their community who'd misbehaved themselves. According to the chroniclers, there must have been some pretty bad hats among them. I can't tell you what they did; but in Halesby there have always been traditional stories of their misbehaviour. Shenstone, the poet, must have got hold of some when he wrote about the Abbey's dissolution, and the country people here are convinced that some of these malefactors were bricked up in the cellars of the house. I dare say they were. The parson we had here, Lowe, always maintained that the place had a bad effect on his morals. I don't know what it made him want to do, but he was a weak-kneed fellow of the type that always appeals to my wife in any case.

"'And so it goes on. It does seem a fact that a certain number of people have always regarded Cold Harbour as a pretty hot spot; and history, up to a point, bears them out. Before the Reformation, they took measures accordingly. Then there was a good, sound, healthy religion, that had experience of those things, and knew how to deal with them. But after the Reformation, the English Church set up to be superior to superstitions, and kept the devil as a sort of Nonconformist bogey to frighten children with. They didn't seriously believe in the powers of evil. They were such damned fine fellows. They thought that as long as they read their Bibles and said their prayers at bedtime, nothing could touch them. What they called their strength, and I call their ignorance. And so, little by little – this is pure theory, mind you – all the old influences began to wake up and raise their heads, and said to each other: 'These fellows think themselves just too clever to live; isn't it about time we showed 'em?'

'"And so they jolly well did. To some purpose, as my wife and her friends will tell you. Not that for a fraction of a second I'd admit it myself. Still, there's your explanation, if you really want one."'

For a moment Wake hesitated.

'Mr Furnival left off suddenly, just like that. I wish I'd been able to give you the least impression of this apologia of his. Unhappily, it's quite beyond me. I've given you the substance along with an occasional phrase, generally a colloquialism, that has stuck in my mind; but what I can't give you is the infinite persuasiveness of his voice, which made the mere act of listening a sensual pleasure, and the feeling of knowledge and power that lay behind what he was saving. His theory, in point of fact, was just the sort of thing against which the doctor in me instinctively rebels; but the atmosphere that he conveyed with it was so strong that he almost carried me along with him. I looked at the others. There, on my left, was Mrs

Furnival, pale, shrunken, always smiling. Opposite to me, flushed, bolt upright, stiff with alertness, sat Evelyn. I smiled across at her. Apparently she didn't see me. Her mind seemed concentrated on some inward struggle. For one horrid moment I thought that she was ill. Then, suddenly, she slewed round face to face with Furnival and spoke:

'"I don't believe a word of it!" she said.

'The words took my breath away. It isn't usual to speak quite so emphatically to one's host. Mrs Furnival's face fell as though she feared some exhibition of violence. For an instant, Evelyn and Furnival stared at one another. Then up went his moustache and out came a cackle of laughter. *"Brava!"* he said. "You don't believe a word of it? Neither do I! I think, you know, that you and I should be friends."

'I held my breath. That, pretty obviously, wasn't what she had meant. I knew her habits of directness, and couldn't guess what she'd say next. Luckily for all of us, she made no reply, and I myself butted in with an attempt to save the situation.

'"In any case," I said, "historically speaking, it's an interesting record, and, of course, it is just possible that past history may have something to do with your trouble."

'"*I* haven't any trouble," said Mr Furnival quickly.

'"But by your own admission," I said, "a certain number of people have. You yourself put it down at sixty per cent of all your visitors. Well, that's a considerable proportion. In a court of law you'd say that there was a case for investigation."

'"Investigation!" he scoffed. "I've told you, it doesn't affect me."

'"But it does affect your guests," I said. "They certainly don't like it."

'He laughed. "Well, then, they'll have to lump it," he said.

'"That's all very well," I told him, "but I don't think you're consistent. You're in love with the place; you've treasured every fragment of its history; you're interested in everything that belongs to it; and yet you cut out the most interesting thing about it, from a historical as well as a scientific point of view. Don't you want an explanation?"

'"Not in the least," he said. "I tell you again, it doesn't affect me."

'Mrs Furnival shook her head. "It does affect him," she said, "it *does*..."

'Mr Furnival jumped up nervously on to his long legs. His white hair seemed to bristle. He looked as if he could kill her. Then, apparently, he changed his mind and sat down again.

'"I should like to investigate it myself," I said.

'The words seemed to prick him on the

raw. "Investigate... investigate," he repeated. "My dear sir, you're talking through your hat. There's nothing to investigate, and no one competent to do it."

'"Have you ever heard of the Society for Psychical Research?" I said. 'There are a number of people with a large experience of this sort of thing who would be only too glad of the opportunity of examining your evidence."

'"I tell you there *is* no evidence," he persisted.

'"Oh, nonsense," I said. "There's a cloud of witnesses. Mr Lowe, the governess, the Abbot, Miss Harrow, your cousin, to say nothing of the children and Mrs Furnival herself."

'Once more he jumped up from his chair. "I say there are no witnesses," he almost screamed. "Mr Lowe is dead and buried somewhere in Africa; the Abbot of St Chad's has gone to Australia, begging, the others are scattered all over the world. And as for my wife" – he spoke with a laugh of the most bitter scorn – "surely you, as a medical man, can judge by this time just how much *her* evidence would be worth!" He controlled himself, and went on more quietly, "Besides, in any case," he said, "you've got to realize that all this is ancient history. Since we've been living alone in the house without visits from her neurotic friends, there's been nothing to worry about. Until you came here today we haven't even mentioned the matter for months. Upon my soul, I thought it had died a natural death."

'He spoke soberly, like a man with a just grievance. All through his outburst I had been watching Mrs Furnival. The insult that he had thrown at her – for he had practically suggested that she was insane – seemed to pass over her head as though it were quite an ordinary thing. Behind her pallid smile I saw the contest in her puzzled mind reaching its climax. Probably she had taken new courage from her talk with Evelyn and our sympathetic presence. I saw her struggling for words, like a creature that has lost the habit of speech. Then, pulling all her courage together, she spoke:

'"It's not ancient history, Humphrey," she said, "not by any means. During the last year I've never mentioned it because – well, because I knew what you would say, and I couldn't face it any longer. Jerry's as bad as ever. Every week, every day, it grows worse and worse. Of course, darling, you don't realize it. I thank God, for your happiness, that you don't. But it can't go on like this. It's reaching a point when it can't go any longer without something terrible happening. I know what we have to expect. All these materialisations. The blood..." She put her hands to her eyes.

'At first Mr Furnival had listened to her with a mocking smile, but when she came to the word "materialisation" his face changed. "Ah, that's it!" he cried. "That's it, is it? Now I see where we are. Jane, you've been ferreting in my spook books. You needn't deny it: you've given yourself away. And, by God, if I catch you doing that again ... if I catch you..."

'The poor creature only shook her head from side to side, automatically, like a bear in a cage; and Furnival, realising, apparently, the indecency of his outburst, tried to pass it off as a joke. "Well, I ask you," he said, "what in God's name can you do with a woman like that?" He burst into a cackle of unnatural laughter. "Blood, indeed!" He turned to me. "Doctor, do you ever allow your good wife to read medical books? Of course you don't! You know as well as I do that in five minutes she'd imagine she'd got cancer and diabetes and Addison's disease, whatever that may be. And it's just the same here. If they hadn't cost such a damned lot of money, I'd burn every one of them. And now you'll see why I lost my temper when you spoke of investigations. Anything to keep her mind off it. Don't you agree with me. Ha?"

'I didn't. The possibilities of the case and its mysteriousness were still buzzing in my head. But evidently he wished to change the subject. He took my arm with a hearty, hospitable gesture. "If you want to see the church by daylight," he said, "you'd better get a move on. There's that Saxon cross. I don't know if you're an authority on such things – you seem to have dabbled in most – but, in any case, I'd like to have your opinion. I'm inclined to think it's our greatest treasure."

'He opened the door. The women passed out in front of us. The hall was dim and dank. As we entered it, I had a momentary vision of Mr Furnival taking off his boots by candlelight. My mind was prepared to see the unfortunate Miss Harrow flying downstairs with her hand to her torn face. Then Furnival suddenly vanished from my side and took possession of Evelyn, leaving me behind with his wife. We followed the others into the garden. On the threshold she turned and gave me a look, the most beseeching that my eyes have ever encountered. I told myself quickly that she might be distraught, as Furnival had suggested. But that wasn't what I saw. Nothing but the harrowed glance of a soul in torment entreating help that it was beyond my power to give. I don't think I have ever felt more deeply touched by any contact with humanity. Don't forget that I'm a doctor, and that doctors, in spite of the mask which necessity compels them to wear, are more sensitive to suffering than you laymen. In that moment I felt that I would sacrifice anything to give this woman comfort; but all that I could do, in fact, was to take her thin arm.

'"It *is* perfectly dreadful, isn't it?" she whispered. "Don't you think so? You see *he* is the object of it all: it's all directed against him. 'Under active control': that's what the medium told me. And I know for myself that it's true.

'"You and your wife have been so kind to me," she said. "She is the greatest dear, isn't she? How silly of me: I forgot to ask you. Are you a Catholic?"

'I confessed that I wasn't. "What a pity," she said. "That is the only thing, isn't it? You'd know, if you were in my shoes. And yet, in a way, it's fortunate, after all the awful things Mr Furnival has said about us. He doesn't *mean* them, you know. I think the words are put into his mouth from outside."

'We entered the churchyard. I felt that my opportunity was slipping away from me. "This blood," I said: "is it actually a fact that you have not only seen it, but been able to touch it?" She looked at me wonderingly: "Of course it's true," she said; "really I'm not as imaginative as Mr Furnival makes out. I'm a very ordinary woman." "In that case," I said, "don't you think it's your duty, next time this occurs, to send the blood for analysis to North Bromwich. I'll give you the name of the Professor of Physiology; he's a friend of mine." She shook her head. "My dear doctor," she said, "can't you see that that's quite impossible? How could I do such a thing without Mr Furnival knowing? If he did know, he'd never permit it. And if he didn't ... why, that would be deceiving him. Oh, no, I couldn't dream of it. Besides, it's to be expected. For the moment I can't remember the name of the book. Dear, dear, my memory's simply awful, but–"

'The voice of Mr Furnival interrupted us: "Come along, doctor, or the light will be gone!" She pressed my arm gently. "You'd better go," she said. "I don't know how to thank you." Tears came into her pathetic eyes. Meanwhile, Evelyn–'

'Meanwhile I,' Mrs Wake continued, 'had managed to get in a few words with Mr Furnival. Hating him like hell. He'd made it clear from the first that he didn't want to talk about the one thing that interested me, but I wasn't having any of that. "Has it ever occurred to you," I said, "that all the things about which we've been talking may have a serious effect on your wife's health?" He stared at me and laughed. "Well, naturally,' he said, "it can't be very good for her. That's what I try to impress on her."

'"I want to tell you," I said, "one curious thing that happened when we were coming downstairs."

'He took my arm with a familiarity that made me shiver. "Now this, you see," he said, "is undoubtedly Saxon work." But he couldn't put me off like that. Somehow I managed to get my arm away from him. "Just as we were standing outside the door of the library, or whatever you call it," I told him, "your wife stopped and said to me: 'Why, I believe they're quarrelling. How dreadful of them!' I thought I ought to tell you."

'I waited for him to reply; the hatred was simply boiling up in me. The light was so bad that I couldn't see his face. Then he burst out laughing, in that horrible way of his, and turned round and called to Ronald to hurry up if he wanted to see the cross. "I think your wife's a bad subject, doctor," he said. "You'd better take care of her!" Bad subject, indeed! Go on, Ronald.'

'We had a good look at the cross in the twilight,' Ronald Wake went on. 'Naturally, he knew a good deal more about it than I did. As a matter of fact, I didn't listen to him. By that time I'd had enough and more than enough of Cold Harbour and everything about it. My only anxiety was to get away, partly for my own sake, and very much more for Evelyn's. Without exchanging a word with her, I could see that she was near the end of her tether. I thanked him, formally, for his invitation and all he had shown us. I think he guessed my real feelings. At any rate he seemed quite willing to let us go.

'We walked back together through the graveyard to the gate in the garden wall. We passed the front of that abominable house. The windows seemed to watch us lazily as we went. In front of the door Furnival halted.

'"It's just occurred to me," he said, "that poor Mrs Wake has never seen the Martock manuscripts after all. That's your fault, Jane. Don't you think we'd better just run up to my study and have a look at them?" I glanced at Evelyn. Even in the dusk I could see that nothing would induce her to do so. "I think we're too late already," I said. "I'm sorry." "Why not let her speak for herself?" he said. I heard Evelyn murmur, "No thank you," in the strangest voice. Furnival laughed. "In that case there's no point in standing here and catching our deaths of cold. Ha?"

'We shook hands, with other vague words of thanks. His was a good, firm handclasp. And I shall never forget the pathetic softness of his wife's. It seemed to me like a callous and ghastly betrayal to leave her standing there on that damnable threshold. "If ever you're in London," I said, "St Margaret's Hospital will find me. Our name's in the telephone directory." She thanked me, pathetically, and we went. I heard the voice of Furnival calling after us. "Never mind about the Martock manuscripts," he called. "We'll have a look at those next time."

'As if there would ever be one!

'We walked away beneath the ghostly autumnal trees. We went like ghosts, the leaves were so thick under our feet. It was as though death hung in the air. Something worse than death. I know death, and this was infinitely worse. Evelyn was tugging at my arm, like a child who is cold and wants to run. I knew what she meant. We began running together. Down the drive, into the road, running away from Cold Harbour, and feeling, all the time, the house behind us, lying there, like a stony monster, crouched, ready to strike. When once we were past the ghost hedge of beeches we both slackened our pace instinctively.

'"Tell me quickly. What do you think of him?" Evelyn said with a kind of gasp.

'"A devil or a criminal lunatic," I said. My voice trembled ridiculously.

'And we didn't speak another word until we reached the lights of the Fox. There Eve turned suddenly and looked at me. "Why, Ronald, what's the matter with you?" she said. "Your face, I mean."

'Then I burst out laughing. I knew that she had seen what I had felt from the first moment. "Your cheek," she said, "it's all

222

funny, shrivelled, drawn-up, like goose-flesh!"

'"And has been, my child," I said, "ever since I set foot in that house." "While I'm burning – in a fever!" she said.

'We found Alma waiting for us with a kettle on the boil in case we hadn't had tea. We didn't want any tea, but the girl hung round us as though she couldn't bear to part with us until she'd heard how we had fared. As we got into the car and handed her her tip, she plucked up courage and spoke.

'"You didn't tell me, ma'am, what you thought of Cold Harbour and Mr Furnival."

'For myself, I thought it better to say nothing, but Eve's feelings were so much on the surface that she couldn't resist the chance.

'"I think he's possessed by the devil, Alma," she said.

'"You're not the first as has said that, ma'am," said Alma eagerly. "Did you catch sight of Mrs Furnival?"

'Well, that question I thought best unanswered; so I let in the clutch, and away we went. Five hours' hard driving. It wasn't until we reached the lights of the Uxbridge Road that we spoke more than a casual word to each other. All through the night Cold Harbour kept us company. "Hagridden" was Furnival's own word. We sat there quietly, thinking and thinking, and when I put up the car in Wigmore Street my silly face was still drawn up with the Cold Harbour goose-flesh. We lay awake all night, talking. We had to get it over somehow. And yet, even when we had talked the matter through and through, it seemed to both of us as though the whole course of our lives had been changed, as if they'd been thrust out of their normal, peaceful orbit by a blow from something dark and invisible whirling out of space. We looked at each other anxiously at breakfast to make sure that we were the same people. I think we're sure of it now. But only just.'

Chapter Seven

Symposium

'And is that the end of the story?' I said at last.

'The end? Well, hardly that,' Ronald Wake replied.

During the latter part of his narration his voice had taken on an emotional tone that was new to my ears, a strange quality, reinforced, as it seemed, by the silence of his wife and the intentness with which we listened to him. Now he was himself again; and the change, I must admit, was reassuring.

'The end,' he went on, 'is a matter that needn't immediately concern us. What Evelyn and I have tried to do is to give you an accurate and intimate account of our experience, an experience, of two hours at the outside, which impressed us both more than anything else in our lives. We've tried to express it as fully as possible. Naturally, coming to you at second and third-hand, it must have lost a good deal of its force in the telling; but the facts, as far as we know them, are there. The facts, I mean, from which we've drawn our conclusions; and before we let you know anything of the sequel, we're both of us anxious to know what you make of them. We want to empanel you as members of a jury of Godfearing men, sitting in judgment on Cold Harbour and its inhabitants. After you've delivered your verdict, I'll tell you what, up to this point, we'd made of it ourselves. It's possible that you'll disagree with us and each other, and that'll only make it more interesting.'

'Very well,' I said, 'we'll do what you wish. On the face of it, the case belongs more to Mr Harley's province rather than to mine; it's one in which the parson takes precedence of the novelist, and so I think he'd better have first "go". No interruptions. That's agreed? Go on, Padre!'

'That is just as you wish,' said Harley; 'still, I think you're right. The problem is a spiritual problem, and, in my opinion, should be judged by religious standards. At the present moment, I admit, my head's rather in a whirl. We live so materially in these days that any invasion of the spiritual finds us unprepared. Finds *me* unprepared, I should have said. That's a sad confession for a clergyman to make; but there it is. Still, I've been trying to look at it from the point of view that the Church adopts toward phenomena of this kind, and that has simplified it, as, of course, it always does.

'To begin with, I feel that we have no right

to be surprised by anything you've told us. Shocked, yes; for it's all very dreadful, as that poor woman suggested. But not surprised. We are taught to believe in the eternal survival of all human spirits; and our experience, in all its records from the Bible onwards, has confirmed this belief. It's silly and thoughtless to ask Christian people if they believe in ghosts, because Christians can't disbelieve in them. So I don't think we've any right to reject any of the terrible things that Mrs Furnival told you, even if hers were the only evidence before us.

'And, of course, it isn't. Part of the evidence is traditional, and for that reason a good many people would refuse to admit it. I don't agree with them. Traditions may twist the form of things, but they do, as a rule, preserve the substance; and when, as in this case, tradition is reinforced by the experience of living men and women, then tradition, in my opinion, becomes of the highest value.

'Let's take it for granted, then, that Cold Harbour has been haunted, as the saying is, for a great number of years, and is haunted to this day, by the spirits of its former occupants. Next, not because of any theological dogma, but because it does seem a matter of recorded fact, we believe that the spirits of the righteous who have found rest in God, are never concerned in these manifestations, are never "earthbound", as the phrase goes.

Whenever cases of this kind are investigated to the extent of arriving at an explanation, we find that the spirits concerned in them are those of men and women who have died violent deaths with some weight of sin or anxiety on their minds that has been sufficient to exclude them from the peace of heaven.

'And this case confirms that universal experience in the highest degree. All the apparitions of Cold Harbour seem to be associated with the scenes of blood and violence and horror that one might expect. But here we can go a step further: at Cold Harbour there appear to be a number of influences at work whose forces are definitely and actively evil; and as they are evil, so, proportionately they are potent. In me the mere appearance of these unhappy beings whose shadows have persisted at Cold Harbour would have inspired not dread, but pity. We know that such things are permitted, and that they are powerless to harm. Sometimes, by the exercise of religious rites and prayer, they can be put at rest. But the spirits that possess Cold Harbour, or some of them at least, are not of this category. The evidence of poor Mr Lowe and the Abbot of St Chad's, and the very terrible story of Mrs Furnival's niece, Muriel, all show that an active spirit of evil and darkness, desperately opposed to the light of Christianity, a hostile and jealous spirit, has been allowed to exercise its power in that place. And that is the only part of the story that is serious from my own point of view. How serious, I find it difficult to imagine.

'Of course there's nothing new in that, though, fortunately, it is the first case of the kind that has ever come to my notice in modern times. The early history of Christianity is full of such occurrences. We've no right to believe, for instance, that the temptation of St Anthony is a fable when the temptation of Our Lord in the wilderness is on record. The youth of Christianity was full of contest. It had to fight its way, step by step, against the powers of darkness. In those days they were so apparent that nobody dreamed of disputing the existence of the devil in all his multitudinous forms and devices.

'For two thousand years that process of cleansing has been going on, and in these days the Powers of Light have triumphed so completely that the dark powers have sunk beneath our cognisance. I don't mean that the work of the devil is not apparent. In the hearts of men, as any clergyman who hears confessions must realize day by day, the struggle is continued with an unceasing bitterness. What I mean to say is, that in these days the contest is usually waged beneath the surface of ordinary sensual consciousness,

229

with diminished prospects of success, and therefore, possibly, with increasing subtleness. If you want a parallel, the difference between the spiritual war of today and that of two thousand years ago is the difference between a charge of pikemen and a wave of poison gas or bombs of noxious germs. The powers of darkness fight no longer in the open, but secretly, and at long range.

'That is the experience to which we've been accustomed; but in this case, it seems to me, the old conditions of warfare have been renewed. The enemy has taken courage and come into the open in a desperate attempt to regain his old position.

'How this has happened I can't say. It's possible ... Dr Wake, no doubt, will correct me if I'm wrong. An idea has just come into my head. Isn't it a fact that germs of disease sometimes seem to lie dormant and innocuous in the bodies of certain people, and then reappear, full of renewed virulence, in an epidemic?'

Wake nodded solemnly. 'Quite right: carriers.'

'That's just what I was thinking,' Harley continued. 'By Mr Furnival's own showing, Cold Harbour has been for centuries an infected spot. I think he used that very figure when he talked about the Saxons' cross and the Centurion's altar. First, the unimaginable rites of the Stone Age, the worship of dark spirits that gained power, as all spiritual forces do, from the devotion of human beings; then the abominable cult of Astarte, which historians tell us was one of the most powerful forces of antiquity; then the super- stitious survivals which the Saxons had to fight against; then, some hundreds of years later, the concentration on the same spot of heretical or recalcitrant monks, the very dregs of the old monastic system: who can wonder that the germs of evil clung to such a place, finding, in generation after generation of its occupants, some individual "carrier" in whose soul they might flourish with a sort of subdued virulence? Awaiting the day when they might burst forth with the power that they have now assumed? Isn't that possible? Isn't that reasonable to suppose?

'You see, I find myself arguing into line with Mr Furnival. I don't know any reason why I shouldn't do that. I think Dr Wake treated his theory rather cavalierly. One could see that he was influenced by his dislike of the man's person and personality. But that, in a case of this kind, seems hardly fair. Of course, you may answer that Mr Furnival himself gave you the impression that he was arguing with his tongue in his cheek. That doesn't influence me. Mr Furnival, as I see him, is a man who prides himself, with good reason, as far as such things are a matter for pride, on the possession of a rational and, scientific

231

mind. That, in my own opinion, is a disqualification in considering matters of this kind. But he, like most modern people, thought otherwise; and when he expounded the theory that his heart suggested he was ashamed of it. A very natural and a very human failing in these self-conscious days. And yet everything that you've told me about the man, and particularly his wife's account of him as a creature full of deep religious feeling – though his words don't always sound to me like those of an Anglican – incline me to think that beneath the rationalist surface which he took pains to show you, his heart is that of a mystic and a believer, which pride in his own intellect and erudition have hardened. Laugh as he may, I believe that Mr Furnival's theory is the product of his heart and of his conscience. Within the depth of these, he believes it himself.

'Naturally he was reluctant to speak of such things. In these days very few of us dare to do so. And, as he suggested to you himself, in a moment of self-distrust, his great anxiety was to keep away from the mind of his wife all references to a subject which had played such havoc with it. That, I admit, was not a courageous attitude; but in some ways it was excusable, particularly when you remember that he himself has so far been immune from, or, at least, ignorant of the evil influences at work. I even think that Mrs

Furnival may have been right when she believed that it was part of the policy of these influences to keep him in ignorance, playing on the weakness of his intellectual pride to attain their object. It seems to me a subtle and devilish way of retaining their power over the place to convince its owner that they don't exist. From every point of view, I think that Mr Furnival is to be pitied. If only some heavenly revelation could open his eyes! That is the solution to which our prayers should be directed: the only solution that, at present, occurs to my mind.'

He stopped. For a little while we sat on in silence. Then I spoke.

'Supposing, Padre,' I said, 'that Mr Furnival's eyes should be opened to the enormity of the present conditions, what would you advise him to do?'

Harley rose from his chair in the shadows, a dark, lank, prophetic figure, curiously different from the shy, boyish creature that we knew.

'There's only one thing,' he said. 'It seems that all ordinary means have failed to remove the infection. As long as that house stands it will remain a danger to human souls. I should destroy it. I'd burn it to the ground.' He relapsed into his chair. Ronald Wake turned to me. 'Well?' he said.

'To tell you the truth,' I began, 'you've put me in an awkward position. I must warn you, to begin with, that I'm going to disagree with your other juryman, and I want to make it clear before I express my differences that there's more in them than a natural disinclination to accept supernatural explanations for the things that you've told us. I may as well confess that I'm prejudiced by the fact of my early encounters with Mr Furnival. Mr Harley has given us a very plausible and humane explanation of Mr Furnival's attitude which I can't accept, because whatever virtues Furnival may possess, I'm convinced that simplicity isn't one of them. So that, even if I felt inclined to accept Furnival's own theory at its face value – which I don't – I know quite well that I'd be bound to turn it down simply because it happens to be his.

'I don't claim that the impressions of childhood, which are all I have to build on, are infallible; but I do hold to the conviction that in Mr Furnival we're dealing with an extremely complicated personality, who mustn't be judged by the standards of good faith that Harley has applied to him, and it seems to me that Furnival's attitude must be the key to this extraordinarily intricate situation.

'Not that I find any fault with the historical basis of his theory. I've no doubt in my mind that he's correct in his details. It's more or less his own subject; he's studied it deeply, and is far too conscientious an artist – that's the word – to weaken his story by introducing anything of doubtful authenticity. I'm willing to take it from him that everything points to Cold Harbour having been a religious site for more than two thousand years. I accept his explanation of the Astarte altar, the Saxon cross, the incongruously elaborate church. I'm ready to believe that in the Middle Ages Cold Harbour became a penitentiary for the abbey at Halesby. I admit that the place has deserved a bad name all through its history, that it's been, as he called it, "a pretty hot spot".

'I'm even ready to admit that this unsavoury history may have had something to do – I won't put it more definitely than that – with all these ghostly phenomena. But as for explaining them completely, that's another matter altogether.

'Of course we don't know much about ghosts. Mr Harley would tell you that we're not meant to know much about them; but that's a point of view that my scientific education won't let me accept. It's my belief that in years to come the founders of the SPR will be regarded with the reverence that science owes them. At present they haven't managed to do more than collect a mass of evidence which establishes the existence of phantasms, and phenomena of the kind which the Furnivals' Jerry provided.

'Let's deal with Jerry first, for I'm inclined to think that he may provide us with our key. He's the common or garden poltergeist, a mischievous, childish, inconsequent force that seems capable of expressing itself through ordinary physical channels. There are any number of such things on record. Wesley's is the classic example, because, I suppose the evidence of such a sober and reasonable man as Wesley must be accepted. Then there's a furniture-moving poltergeist, first cousin to Jerry, at Magdalen College, Cambridge; and I know of another who occupies the attic of a man of letters who lives near Salisbury.

'Now, the Furnivals' Jerry is a very versatile member of his species. The trick that he played on Mr Lowe was extremely ingenious: it almost suggests a rudimentary sense of humour, as does the incident of the governess' watch. The furniture-moving business is merely silly and irritating, though actually more typical; while the incident of Miss Harrow and her torn cheek implies a very unusual maliciousness. There remains the incident of the broken chalice. That, of course, is very remarkable, and religious-minded people must be excused if they regard it with horror, for although it's possible that this freakish force may have stumbled on the most obvious way of teasing the Abbot of St Chad's, it really does look as if its choice had been directed by a malignant intelligence. Purposely or accidentally, the gesture was remarkably effective, and when Mrs Furnival found it "perfectly dreadful" I quite agree with her.

'Very well. Now let's consider poltergeists in general. So far as I know, there is just one thing that has been established about them, and that is that their power of expression seems always to depend on the presence of one particular person. Note that the person concerned may be totally unaware of his or her connection with the phenomena. You may remember a case recently recorded in the eastern counties. It took place in the house of a clergyman – curious, Padre, how the members of your calling seem to be pestered! – and the person round whom the manifestations centred was a small and not very intelligent servant girl. As soon as she was removed from the parsonage, the phenomena ceased.

'That's my significant point. It seems to me remarkable that, though Cold Harbour had what we've agreed to call a "bad reputation" for years before the Furnivals took it, there's no local record of poltergeist phenomena having occurred before they entered it. Supposing that some member of the Furnival household is responsible, unconsciously, maybe, for the whole business?

'Let's argue along those lines. First of all,

we can dismiss the children. At the present time they've all gone out into the world, yet, as Mrs Furnival told you, "Jerry's as bad as ever". At present, also, there's only one maid in the house, the creature with the mediaeval face whom you saw through the kitchen window. She happens to be just the right sort of person, and seemed to fit the case until I realized that Jerry had begun his tricks before she came, in the days of Rose. That leaves us with nobody but Mr and Mrs Furnival; and here, unfortunately, we can't argue by exclusion; for Mrs Furnival never leaves the house, and nothing ever happens to her husband. So there we are, in a blind alley, as far as Jerry's concerned, but so near to a solution that a series of simple experiments might decide. Mr Furnival doesn't like experiments. Perhaps he knows.

'But still we're only on the outer edge of your mysteries. I haven't mentioned, so far, the series of apparitions. On the surface, they're not very extraordinary. I mean that you could find a dozen of the same kind in the proceedings of the SPR. However, we'll try to deal with them as we dealt with Jerry; in the light, I mean, of the theory generally accepted.

'Roughly speaking, it's this. The thing that we've labelled "aether", although nobody has the faintest idea what the aether is, is supposed to be capable of receiving and retaining impressions of light and sound at certain times when the events from which these impressions arise are intensified by some extremity of emotion in a human soul. It's only in such an emotional extremity as is reached, say, at the moment of death, that the soul is able to implant these impressions on that everlasting and unchanging medium. Probably other physical conditions of which we are ignorant are involved. For instance, the shape of rooms: even acoustics, as every one knows, is a mystery rather than a science. At any rate, the aether, under these conditions, is more or less comparable to a gramophone record, which is nothing more than a sheet of wax with lines of varying depth until it is attached to some mechanism of transmission. We'll think of the aether, then, as an indestructible record holding these impressions eternally and secretly until the moment when it makes contact with a suitable instrument of transmission in the soul of one of those people whom the spiritualists call "sensitives" and Mrs Furnival calls "unlucky".

'Now comes our first difficulty. The typical ghost story is this: in certain places, at certain hours, with certain people, certain things are imagined, heard, or seen. If our gramophone theory is valid, it couldn't be otherwise; for the impression on the wax doesn't change, and a disc can only play one tune. But at

Cold Harbour, according to what you have told us, apart from certain apparitions which are true to type and so familiar that Mrs Furnival, by her own account, takes no heed of them, the ghostly phenomena are all different and never repeated; so varied, in fact, that they give one the effect of improvisations or new inventions.

'Of course, it's possible that the aether at Cold Harbour has an inexhaustible repertory of ancient horrors; but with the same instruments of transmission available over a long period it seems strange that each tune should not have been repeated. It looks as though the accepted theory will have to be abandoned in this case. Nobody regrets that more than I do, because I'd like to comfort myself with a quasi-scientific explanation, and this forces me into the region of the supernatural, where, frankly, I'm not at home.

'It's this element of improvisation that bothers me. I wonder if it wasn't some difficulty of the same kind that made Mrs Furnival's medium friend declare that the phenomena were under "active control". "Control" is a word out of the spiritualistic vocabulary, and therefore I'm suspicious of it, but it does seem, somehow, to describe the thing that I can't explain. I've adopted it because it's enabled me to improvise a theory just about as plausible as that which Mr Harley evolved from his medical metaphor.

'We've already decided that Jerry is only able to act by virtue of the presence of some human individual. In this case you have to toss up between Mr and Mrs Furnival. The presence of this individual liberates Jerry's powers in a series of physical phenomena. Suppose, then, that we imagine the existence of other forces, incapable of Jerry's powers of physical expression, but capable of influencing the mental processes – vision, hearing, and so on – of living people through the presence of an agent in the same manner as the poltergeist. If we are willing to swallow the camel, we can't strain the gnat, though, personally, I'd much rather do neither.

'You remember Mrs Furnival's medium, who said that all the horrors of Cold Harbour were directed at Mr Furnival? "At him" is not the phrase I want. Why not "through him"? or "through her"? It doesn't matter which, for either offers us a possible explanation for the variety of the Cold Harbour apparitions.

'But even if we accept that, we're not at the end of our puzzle. We can't pick and choose the things we want to explain; and after we've dealt with Jerry and the apparitions, we're left face to face with something much less tangible: the influence of evil, the corruption of character, the impulse to do Mrs Furnival's cryptic "evil things".

'Whatever that may be, the influence that can make a mitred Abbot unable to pray must be a pretty powerful one. Mr Lowe, too. And Cousin Muriel. That, I confess, beats me. I can't offer any plausible explanation. My imagination carries me no further. Only people with religious experience are competent to discuss a matter of that kind. So I leave it alone. All I'll say is this: that these parsons seem to have thrown up the sponge pretty quickly. What do you think, Harley?'

'Honestly, I don't blame them,' he replied. 'It seems to me that they did what they could. Beyond that point, the Church – particularly the Roman Church – discourages investigation.'

'Very well, then,' I said, 'we'll leave it at that. There's only one other point. The blood. On that, at least, Wake and I have a right to speak. When Evelyn first told us of that incident, she cut short all my theorising. There was something tangible and material that one could take away with one and analyse. Evelyn's sharp mind realized this as quickly as I did. And now comes a curious point. When Furnival, an engineer, another man with a scientific mind, hears for the first time of this material piece of evidence, he reacts in a totally different way. He flies into a rage – "Jane, you've been ferreting in my spook books!" – and threatens her, instead of admitting at once that here was something worth investigating! His whole attitude seemed to me so unnatural that I became suspicious, and the fact that he explained his sudden loss of control by solicitude for Mrs Furnival's nerves didn't reassure me when I considered the gross spiritual cruelties he'd been inflicting on her all afternoon.'

During the last moments, Harley, who had sat listening to me with his head in his hands, began to show a sudden restlessness, leaning forward in his chair as though he'd like to launch his body into the middle of the argument. At this point he broke in with an interruption. 'Excuse me,' he said. 'I know that this is against the rules of the game, but, honestly, I can't help it. This blood, you know—'

'Fire away,' I said.

'This blood, that you people insist on regarding in a scientific light... Hasn't it struck you that the whole hagiology of the Church is saturated with the idea of materialisations of that kind? The stigmata of the saints; the yearly liquefaction of the blood of St Januarius? Why, daily, hourly, the miracle of the Eucharist is taking place in Christian churches all over the globe. You see my point?' he added eagerly.

'Perfectly,' I told him. 'It's a good one. Curious that it hadn't occurred to me before. But it doesn't affect my argument, which is just this: the appearance of blood in that house was a phenomenon for which Mr Furnival might easily be responsible if one could think the man capable of such devilry. According to Alma Higgins, the country people did, and so did you two, after a couple of hours in his company. Certainly there was something extremely ugly in his callousness towards his wife and the other "unlucky ones" at Cold Harbour. That thick curtain slung between his bed and Mrs Furnival's is a sinister piece of furniture.

'And yet, before one looks for a motive in this persecution, it's one's duty to establish the possibility of his being responsible. You can't. Apart from that one incident of the blood, there's nothing in the whole story with which you can connect him, unless it be the relatively unimportant furniture-moving pranks that we've already ascribed to Jerry. In the case of the broken chalice, the body on the floor, and Miss Harrow's torn face, Mrs Furnival herself gives us his "alibi"; and in all the phenomena which Mr Harley thinks most serious, the atmospheric influence that urges Mrs Furnival's mind to evil and prevents her parson friends from praying, it seems quite impossible that he should have been concerned. The evidence forces me to acquit him; and so I have to fall back on my expansion of the poltergeist theory, which, I admit, only covers part of the field. Mr Harley's theory, in point of fact, is the only one that will explain everything. Unluckily, I'm constitutionally unable to accept it. So I may as well confess myself beaten – unless, of course, you have any other evidence to offer us.'

'As a matter of fact,' said Ronald Wake quietly, 'there is other evidence, but as it came into our hands considerably later, I don't propose, for the moment, to make you acquainted with it. What I wanted to do, and what I've done, was to put you in the same position as ourselves at the time when we left Cold Harbour, and to compare your conclusions with our own.

'I can assure you that we've been through it all. There's practically nothing that you and Mr Harley have said that hasn't, at some time or other, passed through our minds, with just the one difference that all our conjectures were coloured by our dislike of Furnival, and that, for this reason, we weren't inclined to accept anything that came from his lips. Evelyn more positively than myself. From the moment when she met Furnival's eyes in the library, and shouted to herself: "*You* are the devil in this house!" she was completely satisfied that he was at the bottom of the whole business. She believes that instincts of that kind are infallible, and I'm not sure that she isn't right. I wish I had them myself.

'Well, there we were, in the same position as yourselves. We started off in the same way, and, one by one, we found ourselves up against the same obstacles. The thing that struck us most of all was exactly what troubled you: the element of "improvisation", as you've called it, which puts the good old gramophone theory out of court, and drives one back to Mrs Furnival's "active control". Now Evelyn was convinced, and I was inclined to agree with her, that this control emanated from Mr Furnival. The first snag we had to deal with was Furnival's series of alibis. They had always seemed to me too carefully established to be healthy: that underlining, for instance, of the fact that he was taking off his boots in the hall when Miss Harrow's face was torn, seemed so triumphantly deliberate. It was all very well distrusting Furnival's alibis; but there they were, quite definite and unshakeable; and the fact remained that nearly every incident of importance had occurred while he was at a distance.

'Still we couldn't be satisfied. By day and night we thought and talked the matter over, and whatever line of conjecture we followed we always came back to Furnival as the fount and origin. His face and figure seemed to dominate the whole problem, almost as if he were present, in the spirit, at our deliberations. And so, gradually, we found ourselves being drawn back, into a conception of the affair which evidently hasn't occurred to either of you, though I must confess it's been enormously strengthened by what you've told us tonight of your early encounter with the man at Dulston.

'That, thanks to you, is where my story begins. I want you to picture him just as you saw him on the day when he arrived unexpectedly at Moorhouse's cottage. A figure of terrific force, bodily and spiritual. A commanding personality. The most remarkable man in the Midlands, your friend called him. And such a restless, vigorous mind! Not only a towering figure in his profession, which is a life's work for anyone, but a keen archaeologist, full of historical erudition; artistic; imaginative; and, at the same time, exceptionally skilled and far-seeing in affairs.

'So much for his capabilities. Now consider his domestic character. The first thing that strikes one is his attitude to his unfortunate wife, who must have been, in those days, a reasonably attractive woman. At that curious Sunday dinner party he entirely neglected her; he only introduced her to Moorhouse as an afterthought, and never addressed a word to her during the whole meal. More than that. He openly humiliated her in the most scandalous way by his attentions to the governess. And that isn't the only way in which his strain of cruelty shows itself. In the same open, ruthless fashion, he embarrasses the poor girl with whom he's flirting by whispering indecencies to her. I can still see your picture of the children, those wretched, cowed little animals, sitting at the table without daring to open their mouths, and, even more, that of the unfortunate infant being dragged in to be made drunk with port. All these things, to my mind, are cruel and devilish, though Mr Furnival, as it seems, thought them merely amusing.

'Very well. Here you have an intellectual superman, a monster of intellect I should almost call him, sensual, cruel, enormous in all his appetites, a religious bigot, an artist, perilously sensitive to beauty and greedily seeking ugliness, prepotent, insatiable, at the very zenith of his power. And then comes the crash. The most precious of all his schemes, the one in which he's proved himself to be in advance of his time and moulded the wills of his most important contemporaries to his own, fails suddenly, dramatically, with the catastrophe of a Greek tragedy. And down goes Furnival like a log on the boardroom floor!

'When he recovers himself, according to Mrs Furnival, he's a changed man. But not a broken one. He declares to her that he will never work again, but that in itself is evidence that his will has survived. He acts ruthlessly, without hesitation. He cuts his losses; gets rid of the house at Dulston which has been one of his masterpieces, and whirls the whole family away into Devonshire to vegetate for twelve months among his books.

'Vegetation, in this case, is only a relative term. The man's mind and body are equally incapable of inactivity. He spends his strength in immense walks; he scours the whole length of the country on a bicycle looking for a place in which to store his library and settle down again. He finds it in Cold Harbour, within sight of the headgear of Fatherless Bairn, an eternal, irritating reminder of his great failure.

'The family, poor things, are whirled back again into the Midlands. Mr Furnival throws himself into the job of restoring Cold Harbour with all his old passion and erudition and taste. He falls in love with the place. The fact that his wife dislikes it from the first doesn't count with him. He's infatuated with it, and determined to make it satisfy his desire. The household is kept short of servants on the plea of expense, and Mrs Furnival works herself to a shadow, while thousands of pounds worth of beautiful things contribute to his ideal of beauty in the house. He sweeps into it like a tornado – like himself. It becomes a new and dominating factor in his life.

'At last they are established. Cold Harbour approximates itself to his vision. In a short time he reaches a point when there is nothing more to be done with it. And he has finished with work. Up there on the skyline the headgear of Fatherless Bairn stands to remind him of that decision, and Furnival isn't the kind of man who can change his mind. He's too proud for that.

'But he can't be idle. He's still in possession of immense reserves of energy without any medium for expressing them; he's still full of the lust of power without any material on which to exert it. He's made himself king of a desert island. Napoleon on Elba. For a man of Furnival's temperament, the situation is impossible. Somehow or other he must assert himself.

'He does so, by quarrelling with his neighbours; but that's a poor sport. Everyone in the Midlands knows all about the failure of Fatherless Bairn and can throw that in his face. He falls back on his books, and increases his already enormous store of erudition, making himself master of strange new provinces of learning.

'Now wait a moment. It was at this point in my imagination that I began to see light ... darkness, if you prefer the word. I was thinking myself backward into Furnival's study, and became consciously aware, for the first time since I'd left it, of his particular

250

concentration on the old religions and the psychic problems involved in them. I've already called him a Mediaevalist. When I did that I had nothing in my mind but the spurious mediaevalism of the pre-Raphaelite era in art – but now I began to see that his mediaevalism was deeper than that; that he'd managed, in fact, to identify himself with the life of the period of which Mr Harley was talking just now, a period when men were acutely aware and afraid of the surviving powers of paganism, whatever they may have been.

'Don't imagine for a moment that I myself take these powers seriously, or that Furnival treated them from anything but an academic point of view. All I want you to do is to picture Furnival led by the traditions of Cold Harbour to saturate himself in the most curious records of those dark ages, among which the literature of Black Magic takes an important place.

'It's possible that this new interest was only one expression of his passionate interest in Cold Harbour; the very stones of the place were soaked in associations of that kind; but you mustn't forget that the man's nature, as shown by his incongruous religious convictions, had a bias in that mystical direction. And then, to the delight of his inquiring spirit, he finds that the house is infested with memories that take a positive shape in ghostly apparitions, and in poltergeist tricks. This, in a certain way, is only an extension of his subject; it opens a field beyond that which he's already explored. His restless, energetic mind embraces it with the same fury of concentration, and he makes himself master of that as well.

'Now, for one moment, consider again those two radical characteristics of the man: his lust of power and his strange strain of cruelty. I don't think, as a matter of fact, that the first ever exists without the second. And imagine, again, the savage joy that he must have taken in finding that his wife, the object against which most of his cruelty had been directed, was suffering from these spiritual torments. I don't think that any one who hasn't seen them together can quite appreciate the fervour of his hatred for that small creature, a hatred that probably gained in refinement from her devotion to himself, and was aggravated by jealousy of anything that tended to diminish her complete subjection to him, such as her children, her spiritual advisers, and her friends. These, you will notice, apart from Mrs Furnival herself, became the principal objects of the ghostly terrors that followed. To me, that is significant.

'I don't mean – let me make this quite clear – that Cold Harbour, apart from Furnival, was an innocent place. I'm not sure that I don't agree with Mr Harley's verdict that it should be destroyed. What I do mean is this: that Furnival, consciously and deliberately, set about magnifying the horrors that existed, with the combined purpose of gratifying his lust of power and venting his natural cruelty.

'How did he do it? Well, that's a difficult question. At first, no doubt, in a clumsy and elementary way. That curtain in the bedroom is a device comparable with a medium's "cabinet". Furnival, you may be quite sure, knew all about the mechanics of the medium's stock-in-trade. In this category of early experiments, I should put most of his augmentations of the Jerry phenomena, which are only protected by Mrs Furnival's "alibis", evidence carefully planted by Furnival in a subject and credulous brain.

'It's only when we come to the incident of the torn cheek, the children's apparitions, and the alarming spiritual frustrations of Mrs Furnival's niece and her advisers, that we have to look farther afield for our explanation. In all these persecutions, at any rate, a motive is easily found. With the children the motive is jealousy, and a knowledge that it was through them that Mrs Furnival's soft heart could be most deeply wounded. With Mr Lowe, the confidant, jealousy again. With the Abbot of St Chad's, something more: the hatred of a bigot for a religion other than his own, and the fear that through this religion his ascendancy was threatened. With Miss Harrow, another motive appears. This unfortunate young woman had been foolish enough to challenge Furnival's power. "You needn't think you can frighten me!" she says; and Furnival picks up her gage.

'But how did he carry it off in all these cases? By this time, you may take it for granted that he'd mastered his subject; but, even so, I'm not going to ask you to believe that his textbooks of Black Magic enabled him to prevent a mitred Abbot from praying. The effective part of Black Magic, as far as it ever achieved anything, was, in my opinion, the power of hypnotic suggestion. And that was the science in which Mr Furnival became an adept. That was the channel into which, I believe, he diverted his torrential energy and will. As a basis, he found, ready to hand, the traditions and the admitted ghostly phenomena of Cold Harbour which produced an atmosphere of uncertainty, if not of fear, in all that entered the house. I've had some experience of that, and can vouch for it myself. And on this basis, little by little, he erected the superstructure of horror under which poor Mrs Furnival's reason was tottering when we met her.

'Possibly, in the early stages, he didn't realize the potentialities of his talent; but when once hypnotic subjection is established there are no limits to the powers of suggestions once implanted, even though the subject be at a distance from the hypnotist. Furnival's telepathic power, I admit, was no ordinary power; but Furnival, as his whole history shows us, is no ordinary man. I doubt if a more extraordinary man exists.

'Now let me anticipate an objection. Science holds, and probably rightly, that no hypnotist can establish his influence without intimate contact with his subject. In the case of Mrs Furnival and her children, this fact presents no difficulty. In the case of Mrs Furnival's niece, Muriel, it seems to me profoundly significant that during the two hours that preceded her religious perversion she was sitting next to Furnival in church. She even begged him to let her go; but he wouldn't. And equally significant, to my mind, are the long evenings which Mr Lowe and the Abbot of St Chad's spent in religious discussions with Mr Furnival in his study. You may be certain that Furnival didn't insist on the Abbot's company because he loved him. Not a bit of it. By that time Furnival knew exactly the conditions that were necessary to the exhibition of his power, and made certain that they should be fulfilled. No doubt, also, he was lucky in his human material: "A pack of neurotic women", he called them. But Evelyn isn't neurotic. I can answer for that. And yet, by some means or other, he was able to divine her interest in Martock. Remember that.

'And so, having once discovered his unique power, he goes from strength to strength, from audacity to audacity, until he knows that the minds of sixty per cent of the people who enter the doors of Cold Harbour are potentially in his power. Evelyn and myself happened to be bad subjects. That day he drew a blank, and possibly worse than a blank; but that was because of our good fortune, not because of any lapse of power; and, as it was, in my own case I can assure you it was touch and go. Within another hour or two God only knows what phantoms he might have grafted on to my brain. As luck would have it, he failed, and sent me away with nothing more serious than goose-flesh; but nobody need try to persuade me, in future, that the devil doesn't exist. I've seen him and spoken with him.'

He stopped speaking suddenly. His silence invited our discussion, but to me, at any rate, it seemed as if his case was more convincing than my own. It was true that it carried the theory of suggestion beyond any limits that I had ever imagined and yet it gave my materialistic mind an intense relief to find itself near to the bounds of science. It was curiously sweet to feel the solid earth beneath my feet again; and something of the same relief, I think, must have come to Harley; for he, in his dark corner, made no comment. For the moment it seemed as if the darkness of another world was lifted from us, and the story, which had carried us into regions where our imaginations shuddered and were lost, returned to the familiar plane of human reason. But, as Wake had forewarned us, we knew that it was not yet finished. Harley was the first to break silence.

'So much for our theories,' he said. 'Between the three of them there seems to me very little to choose. For the sake of our poor human faith, it is to be hoped that yours is the right one. And in any case, explanations are unimportant. The thing that remains with me and leaves me full of horror is your picture of that sad little woman, as you left her standing on the steps of the porch, with the night falling, and you two, the only links she had with normal humanity, turning the corner, leaving her alone ... or rather worse than alone. If you had ended on that note... It's difficult to imagine how such things are permitted. And yet one feels that, sooner or later, Providence...'

He stopped, as though he couldn't find words to continue.

Chapter Eight

Providence

Ronald Wake laughed softly. 'That, Padre, was more or less what we felt about it ourselves. It happens that we aren't exactly what you'd call religious people, so that the idea of a benignant and avenging Providence didn't present itself to our minds quite as it does to yours. What we did feel to begin with was this: that chance had thrust us without any warning into a bypath where human life took on monstrous, incredible appearances which made us doubt our reason. When once we'd escaped from it, it seemed more fantastic than ever. Even after a day or two, when we'd got back into the ordinary routine of living, it coloured our whole existence. At the hospital, in the operating theatre, in the street, the silence of Cold Harbour seemed to be waiting for me; very near – so near that I don't think I should have felt surprised if I'd suddenly found myself transported into the middle of it.

'And Evelyn was just the same. Whenever we were together the imminence of Cold

Harbour seemed to gather strength from our two minds; its nearness became so actual that when a bell tingled downstairs I had a vision of Mrs Furnival waiting on the doorstep or of some pathetic letter from her imploring our help. Night after night we talked of nothing else, and in a little while we had come to a sort of quiet conviction – a superstition, if you prefer to call it so – that our visit to Cold Harbour wasn't altogether a matter of chance; that some mysterious power had sidetracked us for a definite purpose, and that we, whether we liked it or no, were its chosen instruments. The fact that Cold Harbour refused to leave us alone, that the thought of it and its inhabitants continued to dominate our minds however we tried to subdue it, convinced us that our help was needed. It seemed as if the knowledge we'd acquired had been given us for that reason. We were responsible; no argument could lessen our responsibility; it was up to us to act.

'Of course that was all very well. We had to remember that Mrs Furnival was a married woman, and that interference in the domestic relations of one's intimates, let alone of strangers, was a dangerous and a thankless task. Our knowledge of the Furnivals' situation was limited by an experience of less than three hours; it was presumptuous to imagine that there weren't other people in the world who knew far more about it than we did and were aware of other aspects of the case that might make our own precipitate conclusions look silly. Again, we had to consider that there was such a thing as Law. Our allegations against Mr Furnival were based on the most flimsy theories. In law, we could prove nothing against him. Even if our accusations were accepted, there was no law in existence that could prevent a man from driving his wife mad by suggestion. The conditions of modern life, as Mr Harley has said, are different from those of the Middle Ages. In mediaeval times our evidence would certainly have brought Mr Furnival to the stake and a slow fire; in these he would have the laugh on us.

'And even if we set out to rescue her, on what public opinion would call fantastic grounds, Mrs Furnival herself remained an unknown quantity. The only reasonable solution of the difficulty from our point of view was that she should leave her husband and Cold Harbour at once. But would she ever dream of consenting to do this? From every word that she'd spoken it was clear that she had complete confidence in Mr Furnival. More than this: she regarded Mr Furnival as the persecuted person, and herself as his only protector. The situation had its ludicrous side. "I will never desert Mr Micawber", we said to each other.

'Sometimes it seemed to me as if the only reasonable way of tackling the case was to let Mr Furnival know that his machinations were discovered. That, at least, might give him a shock, if he didn't already suspect something of the kind from our attitude – and particularly Evelyn's – on parting. Supposing I wrote to him at length and told him my own conclusions, what would happen? It was just possible that he might be frightened into holding his hand; but all my whole knowledge of the man's strength and determination suggested that he might do exactly the opposite and push his schemes to their logical conclusion: the destruction of Mrs Furnival's body and mind. A man of that kind was not likely to take risks. We might be perfectly sure that he knew his own legal position; and this, combined with his assurance of Mrs Furnival's confidence, would enable him to defy us to do our worst.

'One result of any interference of this kind was certain. It would turn Mr Furnival into our determined and ruthless enemy, and allow him to frustrate any attempt on our part to help his wife by destroying the confidence that we'd established. He might even be moved to attack us. How it was difficult to imagine, and yet his armoury was so full of secret and deadly weapons that we could never be certain from what angle the attack might come. That, I must confess, didn't worry us when we came to think of it seriously. We'd decided that if, as we now believed, there were such a thing in the world as positive evil, there must also be such a thing as positive good; and we, at any rate, were on the side of the angels.

'But that, after all, was neither here nor there. By this time we'd convinced ourselves that nothing could be done through Mr Furnival. He couldn't be persuaded or intimidated, and nothing short of murder, which wasn't practical policy, could put a stop to his performances. The man was self-contained, safely entrenched behind the modern legal system, and independent of public opinion. The only way in which we could approach the problem was through his unfortunate victim, and her poor mind was so completely beneath his dominance that it seemed sheer futile waste of time to try to influence it.

'We began to examine the mind of Mrs Furnival from every angle, like the spies of a besieging army. And at last it seemed to us that we had found a weakness in Furnival's chain of fortifications: there was one part of her life on which he hadn't enforced complete subjection, and that was her religion. Before this he stood defeated. He'd tried by every conceivable device of scorn and persecution to take it; and he had failed. Behind the doors of her oratory she had found refuge in the very centre of his sphere of influence. Mr Lowe and the Abbot of St Chad's had been driven away from her; but even in that isolation her faith had remained so inviolate that Furnival could do nothing but scoff. There lay her only chance of escape, and our only chance of helping her.

'At first it looked as if we'd hit on an easy method of shifting our responsibility; but when we came down to practical details we were baffled. All the powers of hell seemed to have ranged themselves on Mr Furnival's side. Mr Lowe had been driven out of England to die in some African jungle. The Abbot of St Chad's was in Australia. So Mr Furnival had told us. Of course, I wasn't bound to believe him, but a wire to the Abbey soon settled the question. He had spoken the truth.

'We are not Catholics ourselves, and so it happens that we haven't many Catholic friends; but one name which Mrs Furnival had mentioned was familiar to me: that of the priest who had been entrusted with her initiation, or whatever the process is called. Most people in London have heard of Father Westinghouse: I suppose he's been responsible for more conversions in society than any other fashionable priest. Perhaps you know his books. Quite apart from an extremely subtle propaganda, he is a graceful writer of fiction. A little too graceful, to tell you the truth, for my more robust taste; but, all the same, his writings did give me the impression that he was a man of unusual sensibility: the kind of man, in fact, to whom a story of this kind would make an emotional appeal quite apart from the fact that it was intimately concerned with one of his own converts. Without any doubt, Father Westinghouse was the ticket. I can't tell you how pleased we felt with ourselves!

'Everything began to work out splendidly. I found his name in the telephone directory and rang him up. It was in the evening, after I'd got back from hospital. Evelyn was standing palpitating at my elbow. At first there was no reply. I made them ring again. Eventually I managed to get an answer from some kind of idiotic caretaker. The London house, it appeared, was nothing but a pied à terre: Father Westinghouse spent most of his time at Oxford, and the woman couldn't tell me when he was likely to return to town. She gave me an address in Long Wall Street, Oxford, that would find him. Then I rang off.

'"You must go to Oxford tomorrow," said Evelyn. It just happened that I couldn't; an important operation. But time, as you'll realize, was now running short. We'd booked our berths in the wagon-lits for Rome. Evelyn proposed that she should go herself. I agreed. We sent off a telegram to Oxford asking for an appointment on the most urgent grounds. Just after breakfast next morning came a reply, saying that Father Westinghouse would be in town that evening, and could see me for a short time at a house in Grosvenor Square. Somehow the magnificence of Grosvenor Square seemed a little unpromising. I began to feel sorry that poor Mrs Furnival wasn't a duchess. But then, I had to make the best of it.

'At seven o'clock next evening I went to our appointment. The hall was stiff with footmen. They showed me upstairs to a magnificent mirrored drawing-room that looked as if it had been deserted for years. There was a dead Steinway grand with a shroud over it, and, on the top, a charcoal drawing by Sargent of the lady of the house – unmounted, covered with a film of dust, just left about as if it had been given away with a Christmas number. The room was all empty magnificence, and cold as ice. Then in came Father Westinghouse, looking at his watch.

'He wasn't in the least what I'd imagined from his reputation. His books, when I came to think of it, came nearer to the truth. Every writer gives himself away sooner or later, and here was the literary soul of Father Westinghouse in the flesh: a pale, cold, excessively refined young man of forty, with dark, shy eyes, and hands that were firm and white; pretty hands, you might call them, and carefully manicured too. On second thoughts, his sleekness made him rather charming. He was like a slim black cat, with all that nice, feline disdain that makes you feel flattered when the selfish brutes condescend to rub up against you, as this one did. He had a charming smile that showed long, white teeth, and his voice, when he spoke, completed a conquest that, I'll confess, I rather grudged him. I've heard him called a saint. Perhaps he is one. At any rate, I'll swear to it that he's also a man of the world.

'"Good evening, Dr Wake," he said. "I think I know your name. I believe you operated last summer on dear Lady Lutley?"

'I told him that he was mistaken. He blinked his eyes as if he were trying to remember which of his exalted converts had been my victim. He went on talking, quite charmingly, and not in the least to the point, persuading me that, even if I hadn't this intimate privilege, my social qualifications entitled me to it. And all the time he played with his watch-chain, partly to display his fingers, and partly to suggest that time hung on the end of it. I realized now that his voice was the cause of his success; but as I hadn't embarked on a spiritual flirtation, this didn't move me. I plunged into the beginning of my mission.

"'I want two things from you, Father West-inghouse," I said, "your advice and your help. The case is one that concerns you, and interests me, professionally. As a matter of fact, it relates to a lady, one of your converts. A certain Mrs Furnival."

'The name brought a shadow of disappointment into his face. He shook his head daintily. "Furnival," he said, "I can't say that I remember the name. Of course, I'm a very busy man. Unfortunately, I can't keep in touch with all my converts. I know it's my duty to do so; and yet, I think you'll understand..."

"'Perfectly," I said. And so, with the memory of that watch in my mind, I told him, within the shortest possible space, the history of our visit to Cold Harbour, laying stress, of course, on its religious aspects. He listened uneasily. His dark eyes gave me no hint of what he was thinking until I came to the name of the Abbot of St Chad's. Then he interrupted me.

"'Unfortunate; yes, that's unfortunate," he said. "I'm sorry that the Abbot is mixed up in this. I'm afraid the Abbot has not been a credit to his community. In confidence, I may tell you that there have been scandals. He's in Australia, as you say; but I don't think I'm disclosing any secret when I tell you that he's unlikely to return. England, at the present moment, is a little too hot for him. I won't go into details."

'"Another instance," I suggested, "of the evil influence of Cold Harbour?"

'I tried him with the story of the broken chalice. He shrugged his shoulders. "My dear Dr Wake," he said, "do you seriously tell me that you believe all this?"

'"My dear sir," I said, "it's not for me to pronounce a judgement on the causes. All I pretend to do is to describe the effects, and that I do from a scientific standpoint. This woman is being murdered. Body and soul. In a way I imagine that you consider yourself responsible for the latter. That is why I came to you."

'He shook his head. "Don't you see," he said, "that if one believed that such a state of things could exist, one's life would become impossible?"

'"This woman's life has become so impossible," I told him, "that it's up to you and me to help her."

'"You are a distinguished surgeon, Dr Wake," he said. "I don't want to belittle you when I suggest that this is a case for an alienist, not for a surgeon or a priest. You've allowed the matter to get on your nerves, you and your wife between you. I want to ask you a question: has it never struck either of you that all these horrors which you relate to me are really nothing but the images of delusional insanity? I've no doubt whatever but that Cold Harbour is a bad house, and Mr Furnival a most unpleasant type of proprietor; but also I'm convinced, from what you've told me, that Mrs Furnival is insane. That makes your story, in one way, very horrible; but in another, as far as I'm concerned, it takes all horror away from it."

'He spoke so coldly, so serenely, so remotely, that I had the greatest difficulty in keeping my temper.

'"You can't suggest," I said, "that all the people whom Mrs Furnival calls 'unlucky' suffer from delusions. Insanity isn't infectious in such a degree as that. Even if I am a surgeon, I think you might give me credit for some medical common sense. And don't forget that among those who have suffered at Cold Harbour are two members of your own profession."

'"Both of whom," he reminded me, "are unavailable as witnesses. In any case, I should not consider seriously the evidence of the Abbot of St Chad's. For excellent reasons, which I know you won't press me to give you. Isn't it possible," he went on, "that the unfortunate husband has realized by this time that it's useless to combat these delusions, and that this accounts for his reticence and apparent consent?"

'"You don't know the unfortunate husband as I do," I told him. "But even if we admit that Mrs Furnival is insane, the fact remains that this wretched woman, your spiritual daughter, is suffering at this moment the torments of the damned. I expected you to feel some sense of responsibility. Apparently you don't."

'He smiled gently. "At this point," he said, "we are entering the sphere of theology. If once we grant the premises that this woman is insane, we find that we are no longer dealing with the woman whom I am supposed to have converted. That woman no longer exists; and you yourself must admit it. As for the psychical aspects of the case, those, to you, are a matter of vital interest, and I am tempted, I must admit, to become as interested as yourself. But the Church, in the wisdom of its two thousand years of experience, has decreed that the investigation of such matters is not only dangerous, but impious; and for that reason the problem is one in which I'm not permitted to engage myself. I have no right to dictate to you, Dr Wake; but, if you value my advice, your attitude will be the same as mine.'

'His hand wavered significantly in the direction of his watch.

'"In other words," I said, "you'd advise me to stand by, uninterested, while a devout member of your own church is slowly done to death? Well, I can't do it! What's more, I can't understand your attitude. All questions of theology apart" – he shook his head gently

– "there is only one side of this woman's life that is susceptible to outside influence, and that is the particular side with which you're concerned, her religion. Now you are the only person connected with that part of her life with whom I've been able to establish communication; and I look to you for help on pure grounds of humanity." You can't imagine how empty that word sounded when I addressed it to Father Westinghouse. And yet I suppose that by his own fixed standards he was right.

"'I don't think you do me justice," he said. "The woman in whom you expect me to interest myself is unknown to me. I tell you frankly that I have no remembrance of her, in spite of the mention she made of my name. Isn't it possible that this may be another of her delusions?"

"'At any rate," I said, "she is a devout member of your church."

"'In that case," he replied, "isn't it quite obvious that she must be in touch with some other priest? If she hears Mass regularly and makes her confessions, surely she must be within reach of spiritual guidance? What is more, her own spiritual adviser must be far more intimate with all these circumstances than I, a stranger, could ever be."

"'That's all very well," I said, "but who is he?"

'Father Westinghouse smiled as he rose to his feet. "There, my dear doctor, I'm as ignorant as you are. But you can easily find out."

'"How?" I asked him.

'"By writing to the Oratory at North Bromwich. If you like, I will give you the name of a friend with whom you can communicate."

'He took a slip of paper from his pocket and wrote down a name and an address, beautifully, precisely; it would be impossible to conceive a hand more delicate or inhuman. He gave it to me, and then, without any pretence of politeness, took out his watch.

'"I'm afraid," he began.

'"Oh, not at all," I said, though in reality I felt considerably aggrieved.

'"I hope you haven't felt that I'm unsympathetic," he murmured as we passed to the door. "It just happens that you've come to the wrong person. In a church such as ours – I know it's difficult for a layman and a Protestant to understand – all matters of conduct are standardised down to the last detail. It sounds as if it were inelastic; and yet, in practice, I can assure you that it works. And, in any case," he went on, "I am glad that this business has given me the pleasure of making your acquaintance. Some other day I should be immensely interested in hearing how the matter ends."

'By this time I had no more to say. We left it at that. On the landing he shook hands again, and a moment later I found myself on the pavement of Grosvenor Square.

'Evelyn was anxiously awaiting me at home. "No go," I said, when she met me on the stairs. We sat down to dinner – we were both of us quite incapable of eating – and I told her all that had happened. "Well, at least you have the address," she said, trying to comfort me; but that, as we both knew, was not reassuring. In any case, it looked as if we should find ourselves up against the attitude that Father Westinghouse had made so plain. Besides which, if Mrs Furnival's spiritual adviser had been worth twopence, surely he'd have made some attempt to help her already. Probably he'd come to the same conclusion as the other, and treated her complaints as delusions bordering on a forbidden province. Of course, it was quite possible that the Oratorian's diagnosis was right. If Mrs Furnival wasn't mad already, the odds were that she soon would be. But that made no difference to the human aspects of the case, so we wrote our letter, a dangerous and libellous document.

'Another night passed. Time was growing short. It's curious, in a way, how this sense of urgency, of a definite fight against time, was growing on us both. We'd booked our tickets, as I've told you, and that fact seemed to set a term on our activities. We began to hate the thought of going to Italy. The idea of turning our backs on Cold Harbour without anything accomplished began to seem like a betrayal. We even thought of changing our plans, and that will show you how awfully intense we felt about it. Now, of course, we could do nothing but wait for a reply to the letter that we'd sent to North Bromwich. We calculated the exact time it would take to get an answer, and watched the posts like guilty debtors.

'On the third morning our reply came. A bare acknowledgment. The dignitary whose name and address Father Westinghouse had given me was in Rome. His secretary acknowledged our letter and said that he would lay it before him on his return.

'We began to grow desperate. It seemed to us as if all the powers of evil were frustrating us at Furnival's command. That, of course, is an extravagant way of putting it, and yet it's what we felt. Constantly, during that time, Mr Furnival's face would intrude itself on our minds. I could almost hear his laugh as his mouth twitched up. And then, at other times, we became conscious of Mrs Furnival, pale and pathetic in her black satin, with her sad, piteous smile: a vision not active and malicious like that of her husband, but tormenting in its sheer passivity. I wondered sometimes – and that'll show you how fantastic and unstable was the state of my mind – whether Furnival himself wasn't responsible for this devastating image, if he wasn't taking a delight in taunting us with our own impotence. Of course, that sounds ridiculous. And yet ... those visions which he had succeeded in imposing on the minds of his children! It was better to overrate than underrate his powers.

'Two more days passed. By this time we had only thirty-six hours left. All through that day I found it quite impossible to concentrate on my work. In the morning, at hospital, I performed six operations, but how I did it God only knows! I suppose in a mechanical task of that kind, one's fingers are so well taught that they can act without the help of a conscious mind. When the table was wheeled back into the anaesthetist's room and I was left in the theatre to prepare myself for the next operation, with the nurses bustling round me and the house-surgeon talking shop, I kept scheming to myself, wondering if I could take an evening train to North Bromwich, force an interview with some one at the Oratory, and return to London in the night. Something of that kind must be done if we were to set out for Italy with a clear conscience.

'I told Evelyn of this plan when I came home, fagged out, in the late afternoon. She agreed with me that it was the only thing to do; and, as a matter of fact, it worked in tolerably well with our plans. It so happened that we had arranged to dine with friends at seven o'clock that evening in a small restaurant in the West End: a place that is famous for the proprietor's cooking, but also runs a small hotel. We studied an ABC, and found that if I hurried through dinner, and made the usual surgeon's excuses, I could reach North Bromwich a little after ten. In the meantime, Eve could telephone to the people at the Oratory and tell them I was coming. An hour should see me through my business, and another train at one a.m. would take me back to London in time for the last day at hospital.

'Of course, in spite of all our staff work, this meant cutting it rather fine. We set off early, and reached the hotel in Dover Street at half past six. It was a filthy evening, but a big fire blazing in the lounge cheered us up, and the thought of an adventure planned so carefully against time made me feel like a student waiting for an exam. You know what I mean: the elation that takes one out of oneself on the edge of rapid, critical events, when all is going to be lost or won in the space of a few moments. I wanted to make sure of everything as far as I could, so I went to the office – Madame knows me as an old client – and found that our hosts, the Antrims, had booked a table for eight. That was bad luck in one way: it meant that the other guests might hang us up by coming in late. In another, it was cheering: they wouldn't miss me so much when I made my excuses.

'Then I had a brilliant idea. Why on earth shouldn't Evelyn get the telephone message through while I held the fort, so to speak, until the Antrims arrived? A trunk call would take some time in any case. So off she went to the telephone box, while I strolled up and down before the fire, as conscious of my watch as poor Father Westinghouse.

'Ten minutes passed. Evelyn was still struggling with the exchange, and still the Antrims didn't arrive. Other people came in by twos and threes, shedding their coats and passing through into the restaurant. I amused myself by watching them, and wondering who they were. Each time the swing-doors opened I expected to see dear old Jimmy Antrim's face – he told me to say *"Jambo"* to you, by the way, whatever that may mean – but he still keeps to his soldierly habit of arriving in the nick of time, and I might have known better than to expect him.

'Suddenly the porter appeared, throwing the doors wide open. He burst in, smiling all over his face, with a suitcase smothered in steamer labels in either hand, and behind him came a youngish couple. The man was a big, jolly looking fellow of forty, with a wide Saxon face, a well-clipped beard, and clothes a size too small for him that made him look like an overgrown schoolboy. He went straight up to the office window and shook hands violently with Madame. An old customer, I thought, hence the porter's excitement.

'But neither the porter nor Madame were half as excited as the couple themselves. The woman particularly. I don't think I've ever seen a face or eyes so brilliantly happy. She was like a flame of joy, all tremulous smiles and pride; so bright, and so dazzlingly pretty, that I couldn't help being infected with her emotion. It seemed so innocent and human, such a terrific contrast to the black business that I had in front of me that I was positively grateful for it.

'Evidently a reunion of lovers, so passionately happy that it had no wistfulness in it. The porter stood by grinning, and the wife pulled her husband away from the office window to talk with Madame about rooms. I could imagine it all. She wanted, for sentimental reasons, to get the suite they'd occupied on their honeymoon. She leaned there, whispering eagerly, and the man, who couldn't resist the joy of touching her as he passed, walked over to the fire and warmed himself. I sympathized with him. I'd spotted his Union Castle labels. I guessed that he'd come from some part of tropical Africa, and hadn't seen a fire for months, perhaps years. So I made a place for him to get as much as he wanted of it, and he thanked me with the most radiant, companionable smile.

Then a curious thing happened. You mustn't think that Evelyn has the monopoly of instinctive feelings. In any case, don't you know, the tension of that evening, the sense of momentous uncertainty, had put my mind into a state of – I don't know – call it fluidity, in which even real things, like this arrival, seemed a trifle airy and fantastic. I didn't attempt to explain it then, and I won't now, but this is how it was: I felt suddenly, in a flash of the most uncanny comprehension, that this ecstatic husband, who'd been flung in at me out of the Atlantic like a spar, was definitely connected with me in some way. I couldn't explain this sudden significance in him. His face wasn't even particularly familiar; he was just like dozens of other fellows I'd met in the war, an ordinary, beefy Englishman. And I'd never been in Africa. It struck me, for a moment, that he might be in some way connected with Jimmy Antrim, who had. But that was hardly good enough. What was more, I could swear that the connection, whatever it might be, was personal and intimate.

'I stared at him, then gave it up, and at that moment his wife hurried up to him, palpitating, flaming with happiness. "Charlie,'" she said, "do you know you've forgotten to register?" And off he went, flushed and obedient, to write his name in the book which stands on a table behind a little glass screen, while she waited for him, babbling to their friend the porter, in the lift. I heard the words: "The Congo ... *hasn't* he?... Yes, fifteen months!" And then he joined them, with his look of dazed exaltation, and the lift slid upward and left me gaping.

'"This is damned queer," I thought to myself. "When Eve comes I'll tell her: perhaps she can help me." And then I found myself examining the words he'd written in the register in a painful, schoolboyish hand, all smudged with excitement:

"Mr and Mrs Charles Strefford, Cold Harbour, Halesby, Worcs."

'Then, if you like, I thought I'd gone off my head. It was staggering. They can't live there, I told myself. It's all nonsense. Mr Furnival lives there. Unless all the Furnival household are phantasmal and have no existence outside our imaginations. Unless all the Furnival family are dead and buried. Years ago. My brain swam. No, no, that couldn't be true. Father Westinghouse couldn't remember. But Alma ... Alma! I clung to Alma and Mrs Higgins as the only stable things in a reeling world.

'Then came another ghastly thought. Was this the first of Mr Furnival's counterblows? Had he made me see the words "Cold Harbour" written in that book in the same way as he had forced the vision of the body on the floor into the mind of the unfortunate Guen? Was this his latest triumph in that unimaginable domain of his? The bright hotel lounge became ghastly, unsubstantial. I pushed rudely through a party who had just entered and stood joking between me and the telephone box. I forced my way in on poor Evelyn. She turned and smiled at me. She, thank God! was real enough. "These *trunks* are too exasperating," she said. "I thought I'd managed to get through, and now they've put me on to the wrong number. My arm's aching: I wish you'd hold on a moment. Why Ronald, what's the matter?"

'"Never mind," I said. "Come along with me."

'"But the call?" she said. "I've nearly got them. You can't leave it like this!"

'"Come along," I said. "The call be damned! Come and look at this."

'I took her over to the register. "Look at that," I said. "Look at it!"

'If she had seen nothing but some ordinary address I shouldn't have been surprised. I was quite convinced that the whole thing was my own delusion. Good Lord! The joy, the elation, the blessed sense of returning sanity I felt when I heard her murmur the word! "Cold Harbour!" she said. "But it's ridiculous. It's impossible."

'I burst out laughing. "It's true, then. They've just come in. Not horrors: just ordinary people. They've been talking in the office. Evidently they're well-known here. She was talking to Madame. Look here, you'd better go and make inquiries. I can't: my brain's in a pulp. Hurry up, for God's sake. I want to get it over."

'In a moment she came back to me. "Yes, it's perfectly true," she said. "They're number thirty-five. He's an engineer or something in Katanga ... been away there for fifteen months. Madame knows them quite well: they were here on their honeymoon, and she always stays here when she's in town. Madame's never heard of Cold Harbour. She showed me the letter ordering rooms. Enid Strefford. You remember: Enid, the step-sister, the lucky one!"

'I began to think that we were the lucky ones. Providence ... certainly it looked like it. Positive evil implies positive good. Oh, but I was too silly to think!

'"We must see them; we must get hold of them at once," I said. "Don't you realize that we've got to do that? It's played into our hands. Now it's our turn. I'm so glad

282

that *trunks* made a mess of it. They must be in it too."

'"But, my dear boy," said Eve, "what about the Antrims?"

'"Oh, damn the Antrims," I said. "They'll have to understand. We'll tell them all about it later. Janet's a wise woman; she's all right. Did you say number thirty-five?"

'"Yes, thirty-five," she said. You should have seen the social distress in her face! "Mystical numbers," I said. "A multiple of seven. We're on the side of the golden candlesticks. Come along. Don't let's waste a moment."

'Then the clock struck seven, and Jimmy Antrim came smiling into the lounge with Janet beside him. Eve looked at me pathetically. "No good, Ronald; we're done," she said.

'But we weren't. Not a bit of it. Of course, the Antrims must have thought I was crazy; and so I was, pretty nearly. I went right up to him. "Look here, Jimmy," I said, "you've got to excuse me. Something very special. I'm most awfully sorry, but it can't be helped." I could see he was disappointed, but he took it like a gentleman. "You old butcher," he said. "Never happy unless you've got your knife into some poor devil! Never mind. We'll look after Evelyn." "No you won't." I said. "Eve's coming with me. Explanations and apologies later."

'I took hold of Eve by the arm and dragged her over to the lift. '"Thirty-five," I said. "That's the wrong number, sir," said the liftman. "Not this time!" I said. And up we went, with the Antrims staring at our disappearing feet.

'We stepped out on to the handing. Evelyn hung on my arm. "Really we'd better think it over for a moment," she said. "You must make some sort of plan as to what you're going to say. It's not fair, you know. You've barely given him time to kiss her. Honestly, under the circumstances, I think it's rather brutal, just when they're so happy. Besides, you really can't go bursting into a strange man's bedroom and say to him: 'Excuse me, I don't know you from Adam, but I feel I have a duty, and that is to tell you that your brother-in-law's a criminal lunatic and is murdering his wife by Black Magic.'"

'It was just her sense of humour that saved me. We stood on the landing together, laughing at the fantastic way in which she'd put it. It was the first moment for over a week in which we'd felt that we could laugh. I can't tell you how this discovery had disburdened our spirits, how curiously light and irresponsible we felt. And yet that, in effect, was what I did tell him. I can assure you that it took some doing.

'I knocked at the bedroom door. It wasn't like that of an ordinary hotel bedroom. So quiet. We might almost have been side-tracked into one of the corridors of Cold Harbour. Then Strefford came pounding across the room in his shirtsleeves and opened it. He wasn't irritable, as you'd imagine, and as he'd a right to be. He just stared at us with a good-humoured grin. "Got the wrong number, I'm afraid," he said. "This is... I say, Enid, what's our number? Of course. It's on the door. Thirty-five."

"'You are Mr Strefford?" I said.

"'Yes, my name's Strefford all right. But I don't think I've the pleasure–"

"'No," I said. "You don't know who we are. My name's Wake. That doesn't matter. I want to speak to you urgently if you can spare me a few minutes."

"'Well, you know, as a matter of fact–" he said. It was a miracle that he didn't lose his temper, but as he began to blunder on to telling us that he was just unpacking, a fact that we could see for ourselves, his wife came up behind him to find out what was happening. So radiantly pretty. Evidently she wasn't going to have her husband bullied by strangers. "What is it?"' she said. "I think there must be some mistake."

"'No, there's no mistake," I told her. "I happened to see your husband's name in the register. My wife and I have just come from Cold Harbour."

'"Oh, that's it, is it?" said Strefford. "By jove, it's a small world. Come in, sir, come in! If it isn't too late for a sundowner–" He moved to the bell. I stopped him. "No, don't do that," I said. He looked at me curiously. Evidently the strangeness of our invasion was putting a heavy strain on his good humour and hospitality. The poor fellow hadn't the faintest idea what it was about. But his wife had.

'"You've been staying there?" she said.

'"No. We were only there for a couple of hours, but–"

'"Yes?" she said.

'Strefford looked from one of us to the other, utterly mystified. "Well, you'd better take a pew in any case," he said, and Evelyn, out of the kindness of her heart, obliged him.

'"Mrs Strefford," I said, "I think you'll understand me. Those two hours were quite enough. I want to speak to you about your sister. I'm a doctor, by the way. From what I saw at Cold Harbour, I think she's in grave danger – her reason, I mean. Danger of body and mind. I've been trying to see what we could do for her, unsuccessfully, until, by the merest accident, I saw your address in the register downstairs. It seemed as if Providence were giving me my chance; and, at the risk of appearing grossly ill-mannered, I've taken it. I want you to help me. To help her."

'All this time poor Strefford's eyes grew more bulgy with amazement. Standing there in his shirtsleeves, the big man looked so helpless that one couldn't help being sorry for him. As for Mrs Strefford, her face went paler and paler. The flush of happiness and excitement disappeared. Still she gave nothing away. "Well?" she said.

'Sooner or later I had to get it off my chest. "I must warn you," I began, "that I shall have to say some pretty strong things about your brother-in-law."

'The blood rushed back into her face. "Please go on," she said.

'"Well, thank heaven for that!" I thought. And so I went on. I told them, in as few words as possible, what had happened to us at Cold Harbour, an abridgment of the story as I've told it you tonight, and she listened to it without a tremor, without a sound.

'With her I could be sure enough. Her husband was another question. I watched him out of the corner of my eye. You could see the waves of anger and consternation swelling up inside his solid and placid frame, and all the time he watched like a devoted dog, doubtful of what was demanded of him, but eager, at the least hint of need, to spring up in her defence. If for one moment he'd suspected that I was hurting her, he'd have flown at me; and pretty unpleasant it'd have been, for he was a hard customer, and could have given me four stone. It was almost comical to see his bewilderment as I went on with enormity after enormity; for she never looked at him for one instant; all the time her eyes were set on mine. Never for one instant did she show the least trace of emotion until I'd finished. Then she said, quite calmly, "You are quite right. There's not a word that you've spoken that isn't the absolute truth."

'This seemed to stir him. "But, my dear child," he said, "this is a nightmare. It's monstrous. Why on earth haven't you told me all this before?"

'She put her arm round his neck. "Charlie, you know it was impossible," she said. "Five thousand miles away... I knew you could never have been happy."

'"My God!" he said, "this is an eye-opener to me, I can tell you. Of course, I knew that my wife's childhood had been miserable. But this! I'd never dreamed of anything of this kind..."

'"It's all true," she said. "There's not a word in it that isn't true. On the surface, I mean..."

'I waited for her to go on, but Strefford interrupted her. "Well, look here, sir," he said, "you're a doctor; you've taken the trouble to go into this business; I'll be obliged if you'll tell me straight out what you make of it."

"'This is what I make of it," I said. "Your brother-in-law is a criminal of the most dangerous type I've ever met. I don't know what his motives are, but his object's clear enough; and that's murder. Of course, he's had something to build on. I've no doubt but that Cold Harbour is 'haunted', as the saying is."

"'By Gad, that's a tall order!" said Strefford. "That's the sort of thing that makes my head spin round. And to think that Enid–"

"'Oh, Charlie, don't worry about *me*," she cried. She turned to me. "Well, Dr Wake, you're a clever man, I'll give you credit for that, but he's been too clever for you all the same. Ghosts and hauntings! That's all rubbish. Cold Harbour's a beastly place anyway, but the only ghost that was ever in it is Humphrey. Don't I know it!"

"'You were one of the lucky ones," I reminded her.

"'The lucky ones! Poor, dear Jane, you've got her to the life! Oh, I know all about their stories; but you've only been about two hours in the house and I've spent eight years in it. I know all that is to be known, and I know Humphrey. There's no end to his tricks. I was his favourite; and I suppose that's why he never tried any of them on me. Why, even when I was quite a little child, I knew what he was up to, but I never let him know that I knew, and I never have done."

"'My dear Enid, I say, you know–" Strefford began.

"'It's true, Charlie, it's true," she cried. "Oh, if you knew! This Jerry business... Don't I know his whole bag of tricks? That snoring curtain in Jane's bedroom. Poor little darling! And then this blood... Do you know, she never told me a word about it when I was there in the summer; she kept it all to herself, because, she knew, of course, that I should tell her the truth, and the truth always hurts her."

"'Then you *have* told her?" I said.

"'Told her? My dear man, of course I've told her. But that makes no difference. She's so loyal. She's such a fool. She goes on talking about Humphrey being blind: *she's* blind, if you like. You spoke just now about motives. If you want any motives I can give you them by the dozen. You'd better understand, from the first, that he's a real bad hat. And as for women... Well, it's almost too disgusting to talk about. He can't see a woman without wanting to run after her. You ask the people in the district. He's a passion, I may tell you, for fair women. He's never been faithful to poor Jane from the day he married her.

"'The things I could tell you! Things I saw when I was quite a kid. Well, it speaks for itself: they were never able to keep a servant or a governess in the house for that reason. From the first moment, he'd start glaring at them with those beastly eyes of his. Then he'd get to work, and if it didn't turn out as he wanted he'd start his Jerry tricks. It makes me sick to think of them."

"'But surely,' I suggested, 'some of these people must have spoken to your sister?'

"'Of course they did,' she said, 'and they might as well have spoken to a block of stone. She just wouldn't believe them. Not a word. You see, he wouldn't let her. He had her under his thumb. She simply thought that they were telling lies to her and slandering her poor, darling husband. Or else she'd put it down to the house, and think how dreadful it was that its influences had put such terrible ideas into their heads. That's one of the bees in her bonnet; and, of course, he encourages her. Oh, he's disgusting. I suppose you didn't hear of Alma Higgins?'

"'We put up at the Fox,' I said. 'Alma seemed to us a decent girl.'

"'She was decent enough when we knew her first, before Humphrey got hold of her. Now... Well, I won't tell you what Alma is now. But you ask any one in Halesby, and they'll tell you soon enough. Why, he used to take her into North Bromwich and give her lunch at the Grand Midland. It was barefaced: I've seen them there myself. He used to buy her clothes, too, and tell Jane that he was educating her. Educating her, indeed!

'"But didn't you guess that was why all the decent people in the neighbourhood will have nothing to do with him? Didn't she tell you that he was misunderstood, and that people never called on her for that reason? Of course, he's jolly glad of it: the less she hears about his reputation, the better for him. If you could only realize the way he hates her!" She gave a shudder of disgust.

'"I'm still puzzled," I said. "It seems to me that if he's been going on like this for so many years, your sister must, at some time or other, have had it brought to her notice in such a way that she couldn't deceive herself."

'"You're quite right," she told us. "That did happen once. You remember the medium that a friend of Jane's sent down to Cold Harbour to investigate? She was another. I could see that myself by the way she looked at him on the first day she came into the house. Medium! That's not what I should have called her. In twenty-four hours she and Humphrey were hand in glove. I shouldn't mind betting that it was she who put him up to some of his conjuring tricks. I knew what was going on, although I was only a kid of fifteen. I'd had a nice education, of the Alma

292

kind, already.

'"Well, this woman was a bit of a black-mailer as well, and when Humphrey got tired of her she wrote and asked Jane to go and meet her in London. Jane, poor innocent, thought that she'd found out something new about the house in one of her séances, and didn't tell Humphrey. She went up to town and met the medium in the tearoom at Harrods. Of course, I didn't know at the time what happened: that all came out later, but Jane, poor dear, must have had a pretty heavy let-down. This woman told her all about her affair with him at Cold Harbour and afterwards, and it just happened that she was one of the few persons in the world that Jane would have believed. She must have given her chapter and verse. I suppose she thought the poor dear would divorce him and that she'd get him, which shows how jolly little she knew about either of them!

'"Jane told me about it afterwards when we were married. 'Well, there you are,' I said. 'Why on earth *don't* you divorce him: there's nothing he'd like better.' But then, of course, the whole idea of a scandal's terrible to her; she thinks they've had such a happy married life. Besides, she's a Catholic, and I suppose Catholics don't recognise it. Anyhow, she forgave him, and put it all down to the wickedness of the medium. I told her what I thought of it; you can be certain of that; but you know what she is. Poor little thing! Honestly, I believe she's still in love with him. She still thinks of him as the brilliant young man she married, so much her superior in every way, and she can't, she simply can't see, what he really is. Why, even you, an absolute stranger, were able to size him up for yourself in a couple of hours."

"'This is amazing,' I said. "I'd no idea there was so much behind it. Of course, we'd made our own theories; very sound ones we thought them, too, and now you tell us that all the supernatural events at Cold Harbour are engineered by this man—"

"'Of course they are, every one of them,' she said.

"'The stories of your nieces... There was one about a dead body lying on the floor in Guen's room. Your sister told us—"

"'Oh, that old yarn!' she broke in. "Dr Wake, you don't understand, you can't understand the kind of tyranny and persecution that Guen and Elaine underwent when they were small children. Poor Gareth, too, though he was only at home in the holidays. Humphrey never left them alone; he was always at them in one way or another, until they almost ceased to be reasonable creatures. Jane didn't see that. Mothers don't. But I did. And if the poor dears made a tragic mess of their lives, as I'm afraid they did, it wasn't their fault. He was responsible."

'"But these visions," I persisted. "I don't see how Mr Furnival could be responsible for those?"

'"Because he *willed* them to see things," she said. "Mesmerism, hypnotism, or whatever it's called. You needn't say it's impossible. I can believe my own eyes. You see, I was odd man out. Guen and Elaine always used to hunt in couples, leaving me and Gawain pretty much alone. So I never really *knew* Guen and Elaine, if you understand. I didn't even sleep in the same room with them. Well, one day – I seem to be going a long way round to get to the point – one day I happened to be sitting in an upstairs window playing with one of my dolls. It was a summer afternoon, and I'd been sent there to rest after lunch. Guen and Elaine were lying out in hammocks on the lawn, and had gone to sleep in them.

"Well, while I was there, just playing quietly by myself, I looked down and saw him creeping out of the shrubbery. He went right up to the hammock in which Guen was lying, and began to make funny movements with his hands, passes, I suppose, over her face. It woke her. I heard her cry out, and him swearing at her – his language was always too dreadful – but I didn't wait to see any more. I scrambled off the window-seat and on to Jane's bed, where I pretended to be asleep. And of course I never told her or let Guen know what I'd seen. Even though I didn't understand it, I knew there was something wrong, and I should have been scolded for playing in the window when I ought to have been resting.

'"That's the thing that sticks in my memory; but I'm quite certain that he often tried experiments of that kind. I remember the time when I had whooping cough. It used to keep me awake, and time after time in the middle of the night I used to hear his footsteps passing along the corridor to Guen's room. He always used to ramble about the house at night, and I'm sure that's what he was up to. Oh, he's a devil. There's no other word for him. You can never guess where his tricks begin or end."

'"And you think," I said, "that he still keeps up this practice of hypnotism?"

'"Think?" she said. "Why, I know he does. Even this summer. Did poor Jane tell you that I went to stay there for a month and took Babs with me?"

'"Yes," said Evelyn, "she showed me your room. She said what a joy it had been to her."

'"Poor darling!" said Mrs Strefford, "it wasn't much of a joy to me, I can tell you. You see, Babs is getting on for two, and just beginning to talk – such a lovely kiddy – and when we went down to Cold Harbour I said to myself: 'If he begins to play any of his tricks on her, there's going to be trouble.'"

"'I should damned well think so," growled Strefford. It was the first sentence that had issued from his bewildered face. "By Gad, if I thought he'd–"

'She put her hand on his shoulder. He subsided, and she went on:

"Well, at first he behaved himself quite decently. He always has done so with me. Of course, Halesby was buzzing with stories about him and Alma Higgins: I suppose that affair kept him busy. Then I began to get anxious. Babs lost her appetite. It was so unlike her; generally she can't be satisfied. And I could see that she was losing flesh, with little black rings round her eyes."

"'Look here, Enid," Strefford began ominously, "you never–"

"'Now *do* be good, Charlie," she said. "Please don't interrupt me. Then I began to see why it was that she wouldn't eat. All through mealtimes he used to sit and stare at her with that queer, concentrated look of his. And when I took her up to bed after tea, he used to insist on picking her up in his arms and kissing her and talking to her. I hated it, but you couldn't very well stop it. So I used to say, 'Now come along, Babs, darling, Uncle's busy.' Babs always used to call him 'Uncle'. And he'd glare back at me so savagely! But I got my way, as I generally do with him, and managed to rescue Babs from his arms and smuggle her up to my room safely. The wonderful thing is that I don't believe he ever guessed that I was doing it deliberately.

"'I changed our seats at table, too, so that I came in between them, and he couldn't look straight at her, it was a regular battle between us, and I was determined to win. It seemed as if I was going to, too; for Babs began to get her appetite back, although she never seemed as fit at Cold Harbour as she'd been at Lapton.

"'And then, one evening, I got the shock of my life. I'd bathed Babs and put her to bed at half past six as usual. But when I went up to bed myself at about ten o'clock I found her awake and sobbing her little heart out. She was so frightened I couldn't stop her crying, though I kissed her and kissed her, and held her close to me. 'What is it, my sweetheart?' I said. And then she told me. Something about a strange 'daddy' that used to come in and wake her in the night. She's very indiscriminate with her 'daddies'."

'Mrs Strefford laughed nervously. Then came the earthquake. All through the early part of the story, Strefford had sat with a look of sheer bewilderment on his bearded face. You could see that he was angry that any of these things should have touched his wife; but as soon as the baby came into the story he had grown restless, clasping and unclasping his hands, as though they were anxious of themselves to get at Furnival's throat. Once or twice she'd managed to quieten him, but at this point she could do so no more. He jumped up to his feet. He'd been a big man to begin with, but this anger made him seem monstrous.

'"By God, Enid," he cried, "you've never breathed a word of this to me! Why didn't you let me know? I'd have thrashed the life out of him. If that devil dares–" He almost choked with passion. "Why didn't you? My God, if I'd known..."

'She clung to his arms. "Charlie, dearest," she said, "how could I? You must be reasonable. I could trust myself that nothing should happen to Babs. And you so far away! What good would it have done?"

'But Strefford was too angry to reason. "You could have cabled," he said.

'"Cabled?" she said. "But, dearest, don't be silly. *What* could I have cabled?"

'"You could have cabled," he persisted.

'"And five or six weeks later you could have come. When it was all over. Of course, I didn't stay another night at Cold Harbour after that. I took Babs straight back into Devonshire. And now she's splendid; she's lovely. You wait till you see her tomorrow!"

"'I'm damned if I shall take her to Cold Harbour," he said. "You'd better send them a wire at once and say our plans are changed."

"'I hope to goodness you *are* going to Cold Harbour," I said. "I can assure you you're needed there."

"'Needed? That's all very well," he said more calmly. "I've got to think of my wife and child first."

"'Unless you go soon," I told them, "you may be too late. As things are, something is bound to happen, and pretty soon in my opinion."

"'Something?" said Enid Strefford eagerly. "What do you mean?"

"'I leave that to your imagination," I said. "I came only tell you, as a doctor, that I think your sister has come to the end of her strength. She's reached the breaking-point. She can't go on."

"'By Gad, it's terrible!" Strefford muttered. "After what Enid's said about the kid, I doubt if I should be able to keep my hands off him. You haven't half opened my eyes. It's – it's like a nightmare. I'm an ordinary fellow. I've seen a bit of what they call witchcraft in Africa, but this, by Gad, this beats everything. Look here, doctor, do you really mean to say you *believe* in it?"

"'I shouldn't have taken the risk of tackling you," I told him, "if I hadn't."

"'But are such things possible?" he asked.

'"A fortnight ago," I said, "I should have answered, 'No'. Now I can't."

'"But there must be some way," he protested. "What about the law?"

'"The law," I said, "is made for ordinary human beings, not for devils. It doesn't recognise their existence. Neither did I, a fortnight ago."

'"So you can't do anything in that way?" he said. "In this case, the law's a washout?"

'"Absolutely," I said. "You've got to take the law into your own hands."

'"And, by Gad, I would," he muttered, "if it wasn't that I'd leave a widow behind. Is there no way of doing it quietly? You're a doctor – you ought to know."

'I laughed. This figure of the conscientious murderer was new to me; certainly I shouldn't have expected to find him in Strefford. "No," I said, "I can't put you up to any short cuts."

'"I'd do it," he said gravely, "I'd do it like a shot if it were possible."

'"It isn't," said Mrs Strefford, "Dr Wake's quite right. It isn't. The only thing that I can think of–"

'"I'll tell you the only thing that's possible," I said. "Tomorrow they're expecting you at Cold Harbour. Very well. Even though your husband hates the idea, you've got to go down there. If he objects to taking the child, you can easily make some excuse."

301

'"Yes, Charlie, we can easily do that," she said, "though I *did* so want you to see her. I left her with Charlie's sister at Rugby," she explained to us.

'"Well, that seems simple," I went on. "Anyhow, you go to Cold Harbour, and I hope to goodness it won't be too late. Then, by some means or other, you've got to persuade your sister to return with you to Devonshire. Surely that's a possibility?"

'"One moment, doctor," said Strefford, awkwardly. "I know it sounds mean and all that on my part, but I can't help it. I want you to tell me straight out. Can the presence of my sister-in-law at Lapton in the same house, you know, have any effect on my child? Infection, I mean. Like consumption or that kind of thing."

'I assured him that it couldn't.

'"Well, then, in that case, we'll carry on," he said.

'Mrs Strefford shook her head. "I know that you're right," she said. "I know that there's no other way. But I'm quite certain that I shall never be able to persuade her to leave."

'"You've *got* to persuade her," I said. "Remember it's literally a matter of life and death."

'"I believe she'd be happier dead," said Enid Strefford. "She's told me that she longs for death. The only thing that's made her go on fighting is the thought of leaving him behind."

"'But we can't consider the matter on those lines,' I told her. "It's our duty, as far as it's humanly possible, to save her.'

"'You're right, doctor,' said Strefford suddenly. "And what's more, if it's humanly possible, we'll do it. Perhaps I'm not quite such a fool as you'd think. Anyway, even if it is impossible, I'm going to have a damned good shot at it. What's more, I'm grateful to you and your wife for having given me the chance. After all, I'm an old hunter. I've been up against more than one kind of devil in my time." He laughed to himself. "But what beats me," he said, "is the fact of your having struck us in this place.'

"'It beats us, too,' I said.

"'A million to one chance,' he said. "I suppose that's what you've got to call it?'

"'I'm not so sure of that,' I said. He stared at me, not quite sure if I were laughing.

"'Providence?' he said. "Well, well. I'm not so sure either. If you seriously thought that, it'd give you a tremendous amount of confidence in yourself.'

"'That's what I want you to have,' I said. "Personally I think you're justified, that we're all justified in having it. What's more, I believe that you're going to bring it off. The stars in their courses fought against Sisera.'

'I didn't want to be theatrical, and yet, somehow, I couldn't help holding out my hand to him. He took it. I don't know that I've ever felt so much satisfaction in a handgrip. A topping good fellow, this Strefford, as stout as they make 'em. I don't know... His strength, and the fair loveliness of his wife that seemed to me like some miraculous flower pushing itself out of the carnage of Cold Harbour... Eve and I both felt curiously affected by this combination of things, young and strong and bravely hopeful.

'"You can trust me, doctor," Strefford said, as he took my hand.

'And I did, you know. This bearded, bull-necked Englishman was the first spiritually stable thing that I'd met in all my searching since we'd left Cold Harbour. I didn't suppose, for one instant, that we should ever touch hands again, and I don't suppose we shall; but in that moment I – and Evelyn with me – felt the weight under which we'd been struggling suddenly released and lifted from us. Like Christian, in the story, when his burden fell from his back. And suddenly the imminence of Cold Harbour, which had blackened all our lives from the day of our visit, dissolved like a cloud in summer, shattered by thunder. That gigantic phantom ... all blown away to nothing! A clear sky. And hope. So dazzling a hope.

'As we left them, Strefford thanked us again. It was ridiculous, we felt; for he was our benefactor, and we'd done nothing but transfer our burden to his enormous shoulders. We went downstairs, hand in hand, like a couple of children. Evelyn's conscience compelled her to inquire for Mrs Antrim, but she and her party had disappeared. We wandered out into Dover Street, intoxicated by our own irresponsibility; that was the only word for it. We suddenly realized that we hadn't dined. We didn't care a damn for that. It was over. We were free. Ten minutes later, God knows how, we found ourselves in Piccadilly Circus. It thrilled us. Because – I wonder if you can understand this? – because during the last ten days all the swarming human activities of London had seemed to us unreal, automatic, phantasmal, against the background of the Cold Harbour façade and its bleak beeches.

'I think people must have stared at us, if anyone takes any notice of people in Coventry Street. Two lovers from the country. Lord knows what they thought! A moment later we found ourselves inside Scott's, eating oysters, and drinking Roederer to Mr Furnival's damnation, and Strefford's victory. It was like a new lease of life to us. Somehow or other, in our bones, we felt absolutely certain that he'd bring it off.'

Chapter Nine

Cold Harbour

He stopped. We waited for him to continue. Not a word was spoken. For a moment time stood still; life was suspended. It was as quiet as death. Not a shiver in the olives; no whisper from the sea; the mountain loomed behind us like a cloud becalmed; only, in the void above it, out of which the moon had passed without our knowledge, the burning blue of Sirius throbbed through moonlit mist. Remote in space, remote in time by the measure of its eight light years, that heart of fire seemed powerless to penetrate with its spent vibrations the immortal oppression in which our bodies and souls lay sealed within their ghost hedge of dark imaginings. For, behind the elation, the forced, fey gaiety of Wake's conclusion, we knew – I knew, at any rate – that the shattered phantom of Cold Harbour gathered itself together, imminent, undefeated, monstrous in its will to survive. We knew that there was more to come; we didn't dare to ask for it. And yet it was impossible to measure the thankfulness with which, at last, I heard the sound of Harley's voice:

'And did he bring it off?'

'No, he didn't,' Wake answered quietly. 'I think we might have known that he wouldn't. That triumphant interlude, when Evelyn and I went strolling like lunatics through Piccadilly, was too high-pitched to be true. Of course, we were fools not to guess it. I suppose we'd hypnotised ourselves and each other into thinking that because our own responsibility was at an end the problem no longer existed. It's curious how this quite fallacious ecstasy sustained us during the rest of our time in London. Of course, the holiday spirit was on us; we hadn't time to think of anything but our journey south; it's an extraordinary commentary on the fallibility of human reason to confess that when the truth reached us we were quite unprepared for it.' He paused again.

'The truth...' I said at last. 'Probably I'm stupid; but for the moment I can't get my bearings. Thirty-six hours after you left your burden in the Dover Street Hotel, you set out from London. On the second evening you were in Paris–'

'That evening and all next day. It was on the fourth morning, an hour after we'd left Paris in the train-de-luxe, that the news came. I won't mystify you any longer. It was a paragraph in the Continental *Daily Mail*. I saw the headline: "Country House Tragedy", and in a second I knew. I'm as ignorant as you of what really happened. There weren't many details, and I don't propose to tell you what there were. I haven't even told Evelyn. She'd had enough of it already, and I didn't want our holiday mood contaminated by this business. All that matters to me is that the story's finished. The problem has reached its logical, horrible conclusion. I'm not an imaginative man; I can't fill in the picture. I don't think I want to. All the same, now that it's all over and we can think of it without any personal anxiety, I should like to hear what your imagination makes of it.'

'The paragraph,' I said: 'I think you had better let us see that first.'

Wake shook his head. 'No, no, I want you to treat it as a piece of creative deduction. That is your job. Imaginative reasoning. You've heard all that we can tell you. Now finish the story.'

Once more we were silent. Then Harley moved uneasily in his chair.

'Personally,' he began, 'I make no claims to an imaginative mind. Let us get this clear first. We may take it that Mr and Mrs Strefford were too late?'

'Too late,' Wake nodded.

'Which means,' he went on, 'that Mr Furnival succeeded in his object. Those powers of divination – I'm thinking backward to the infallible instinct with which he pitched on Mrs Wake's soft spot for Martock's poems on that evening at the Fox. Is it possible, in the same way, that he knew of Dr Wake's activities in London: the interview with Father Westinghouse, and even the encounter with the Streffords? Supposing he were aware of all this? In that case, without any doubt, he'd realize that his schemes were in danger, and try his very worst to bring them to a conclusion. Some new terrors. God knows what a man of that kind might not have up his sleeve! He'd say to himself, "This cat and mouse game has gone on long enough. Now I'm going to strike." And so he struck, with every power that the devil had given him.'

Harley shuddered at the suggestion of his own words.

'We can't guess how,' he went on, 'but I think we can imagine what the result would be: that poor, strained mind, bending beneath the weight of the blow, bending beneath its ruthlessness, and then breaking...' His own voice broke on the word.

'The rest is easy,' he went on, 'easy and forgivable. After that blow, Mrs Furnival ceased to exist. Nothing left of her but a poor, mad, distorted shadow of a mind. What could life mean to her then? Nothing, nothing! Religion? A gabble of words! Ah, better end it! Let the broken body follow the broken mind. There are many ways of suicide. One was as good as another in the eyes of her murderer. And so, I suppose, it ended. God rest her!'

I sat there, moved by the anguished tenderness of his last words. From the shadow in which Evelyn Wake's chair was concealed I heard the sound of a sob. Ronald's hand went out to meet hers in the darkness. It seemed as if the last word had been spoken.

And then a light leapt up in my mind. It was as though that stifled sob of Evelyn Wake's had worked some spell in me, admitting me, for one moment, to the visions of her own anguished and clairvoyant brain. Behind my closed eyelids I seemed to see the site of Cold Harbour, lonely beneath the hills that I knew, those twin domes that dominated all my childhood: Cold Harbour, a black clot in the wintry darkness. And then, suddenly, the sky grew red, as with the gleam of molten iron gushing from the Black Country's apocalyptic furnace mouths. The beeches stood blackly transfigured, their bare twigs tremulous with flame; and, behind them, the house – the house, gaunt, huge and black as doom.

I couldn't tell what it meant. I didn't ask what it meant. Only, in my brain there was a clanging of iron and the smell of fire and the beating of titanic hammers; my mind a red malleable metal that rang beneath monstrous forging; my soul a buried furnace, like the bowels of Etna. And then the flame died away, and what was left of me found itself, ghostly and dazzled, in a low chamber, stone-flagged and oak-panelled. I was not alone. There, with a brass candlestick in her hand and a lighted candle, stood a little woman in a dress of black satin with a white muslin apron. Her back was toward me, so that I could not see her face, but I knew that she was Mrs Furnival. And I watched her as she moved about the hall, shaking the tapestries into shape, rearranging the row of candles on the settle, carefully, unreasonably, with a tense, unworldly preoccupation. She sighed and patted down the front of her dress. She turned her face: I saw the fixed, pale smile on her lips. I found myself staring into her innocent, puzzled eyes. She vanished; and then, as from the distance of a thousand miles, I heard Ronald's wife speaking:

'It isn't nearly as horrible as you'd imagine,' she said. 'Of course she *is* mad. If you could see her eyes you'd know it. They look beyond you, beyond the things she touches, beyond everything. And yet she's happy. I've never seen any eyes so serenely happy before. She touches everything. It's like a ritual. The chairs, the row of boots on the floor, the clock. Three minutes past twelve. It's just as if she were taking an inventory, or coming back to things to which she's attached herself after a long absence. Greeting or farewell. And it's so automatic. No hesitation: as if her course were all mapped out beforehand and she had to follow it, while I follow her. No, that's not right. Follow's the wrong word; I'm part of her. I'm seeing everything through those dreadfully calm eyes of hers, and when she sighs it's exactly as if I were sighing. I mustn't lose my identity. I won't.

'She's going upstairs; the steps creak beneath us. She's heard that too. We stop, as if we were afraid of waking somebody. For fear of waking Mr Furnival. That's a habit. Ghosts are creatures of habit; that's all they have left.

'Somnambulism, of course. Why didn't I guess that before? And this is the dining-room. I never realized before that the pictures were alive. That leering little thing in the three-cornered hat; how I hate her! He's a passion for fair women, you know. What does she want to put that picture straight for? Much better leave the wretched thing alone.

'Off we go again down the long passages. Gareth's room. The football cap with the tarnished tassel hanging limp over the bed. She touches it. Dear Gareth! The sky is like brass, a brazen salamander. Why don't they find an ice-bag that doesn't leak? The

312

water's trickling out of it and matting the hair where they haven't shaved him. And why don't they let me know in time? Oh, Gareth, Gareth! The room wants dusting. You can write your name with your finger in the dust on the mantelpiece, like this: "Jane Furnival". But it's difficult in a house of this size with only one servant. Electric light would make all the difference. Danger of fire. Of course he knows best.

'She closes the door softly. Mr Furnival is such a light sleeper. Room after room ... so many rooms one after another that I can't keep count of them. And yet she goes slowly, methodically: a chair out of place here, a curtain hanging unevenly there. Stop! Blood on the mirror! But she's not afraid of it now. She wipes it off with her handkerchief, carefully, methodically. The handkerchief is mottled with stains of blood and dust. Habit, again. She'll go on wiping up blood-stains till the end of the world, poor thing!

'The moon looks in through the library window: the panes of the bookcases reflect it like cold, glazed eyes. Those books used to be companionable, but they aren't companionable now. They're dead; or else we're dead. Different worlds... I wonder why she stays here; it isn't here that she'll find it. Nothing here but dead books and stale incense. I mustn't stay near her too long or identify myself with her too closely. Never forget that the woman's mad...

'Upstairs again. That's better. The door of Mr Furnival's study. Now she can go in without knocking. Did you say it was definitely evil? "It's evil, I can't say more". Those spook books all in a row; they aren't evil. There's nothing in them but ignorance and superstition. She touches them and smiles. Fancy having allowed oneself to be frightened by printed words! The real evil is more powerful than that, too powerful for her to go on fighting against it for ever. And oh, the luxury, the relief, the serenity of this surrender after fifteen years of struggling! This is the peace of heaven or the peace of hell; but peace ... peace! Those words come back to me. "I feel that some day I may do something really dreadful." I'm losing her.'

Quite near to me I heard Ronald's voice: 'No, no, you mustn't. Go on! Go on!'

'I've lost her. But I think it's all right. I think she's gone into the alcove, where the altar of Astarte is. I don't want to follow her. I shouldn't be frightened of a dead thing like that – funerary junk, ha? – but I can't help it. No; it's all right: here she is again. Don't tell me that those eyes are evil: mad, they may be, but so tender, so peaceful. She's brought something with her; she's hiding it under her white apron as if she were afraid that I should see it. Fire! I smell fire, just as I smelt it before.'

314

'Fire! Tell us more. You must look!' somebody whispered.

'I can't. You're disturbing me. There's no time, and I don't want to lose her. For God's sake leave me alone. Upstairs again. This is the way to the oratory in the angle of the roof. No; I told you before I'm frightened of it: the two things won't mix. Still, you can't help seeing over her shoulder. My God! This is worse than snapped chalices; the plaster Christ on His Cross broken and blackened as though someone had smashed it with a coal hammer. And she's laughing, laughing! Furnival never laughed like that at his most devilish.

'I can't keep pace with her. Really, I don't want to, but I suppose I must. Downstairs again. I know this room as well as if I'd slept in it. There's a chest outside the door on which she puts down her candle. No need for candles. The garden's full of moonlight: the hunter's moon, isn't it? And there's that curtain. Furnival hasn't drawn it tonight. There's no need for curtains now; he's won, and he knows it.

'Two chaste little beds, side by side. Chaste! Furnival's lying on his back like a man under an anaesthetic. A very heavy sleeper; you see, he has nothing on his mind. Now I know what she carried away from the altar alcove: a knife with a thin blade. "My sacrificial knife I call it: it's still up to its job." A sacrifice to the powers of evil! Still she's smiling. This is his victory, his crowning victory, I must stop her: I've no hands to stop her with: it happened a week ago. My God!' Her voice rose in an appeal of agony:

'Victory? It's his eternal defeat. She makes no mistake; an anatomist couldn't do it better. She bends over him; on the left side, just above the heart. The point sinks in – all her weight behind it. Right through to the hilt; not a struggle, not a groan! That's how he goes to his eternal damnation.

'Ah, it's too terrible! And she so mild and smiling ... you'd think she was a saint. That's how I'd paint religious ecstasy if I were a painter. Judith. No, Judith was sane. Judith could never have known such beatific calm as this. And she just sighs again, as if her work were finished. She lies down like a child beside him and kisses his lips. Poor thing ... poor thing! This must be the end. What's that?'

Suddenly Wake's hand had clutched her arm.

'Eve, my darling, it isn't the end. Tell me quickly. The fire ... the fire!'

'The fire?' she answered slowly. Her voice was dazed and resentful, like that of a sleeper violently awakened. 'I've told you already. Is that you, Ronald? The place smelt of fire. The sky was red with it. The beeches stood up black against it. It was pouring out of the windows, out of the stones of the house; forked flames, not blood. Burn it! Burn it! It should go up in flame of its own hellishness!'

'It's burnt already,' said Wake's steady voice, 'burnt and gutted a week ago, with those two in it. That is what happened.'

I drew a deep breath. How strangely sweet it tasted, this air of earth! Slowly I recovered myself. But over Evelyn's mind the horror still held sway.

'I knew, I knew,' she cried. 'Why didn't I tell you? Pray for her soul, Padre, pray for her sad soul!'

Rowberrow: Mendip, 1923.

The publishers hope that this book has given you enjoyable reading. Large Print Books are especially designed to be as easy to see and hold as possible. If you wish a complete list of our books please ask at your local library or write directly to:

Dales Large Print Books
Magna House, Long Preston,
Skipton, North Yorkshire.
BD23 4ND

This Large Print Book, for people
who cannot read normal print,
is published under the auspices of

THE ULVERSCROFT FOUNDATION

... we hope you have enjoyed this book.
Please think for a moment about those
who have worse eyesight than you ...
and are unable to even read or enjoy
Large Print without great difficulty.

You can help them by sending a
donation, large or small, to:

**The Ulverscroft Foundation,
1, The Green, Bradgate Road,
Anstey, Leicestershire, LE7 7FU,
England.**
or request a copy of our brochure for
more details.

The Foundation will use all donations
to assist those people who are visually
impaired and need special attention
with medical research, diagnosis
and treatment.

Thank you very much for your help.